CASCADE HUNGER

A DUPAGE PARISH MYSTERY

GREGORY ASHE

H&B

Cascade Hunger
Copyright © 2021 Gregory Ashe

Published by Hodgkin & Blount
https://www.hodgkinandblount.com/
contact@hodgkinandblount.com

Published 2021
Printed in the United States of America

Trade Paperback ISBN: 978-1-63621-027-8
eBook ISBN: 978-1-63621-026-1

I

A basic principle in the study of folklore and anthropology is that in order to understand a cultural feature, one must understand the context in which it exists.

- *Swapping Stories: Folktales from Louisiana*, Maida Owens

ELI (1)

At first, they were nothing more than a light bobbing in front of me, leading me through the dark.

The golden arches took shape slowly as they called me back—the dietary equivalent of a toxic guy I couldn't give up. I studied the menu. The girl behind the counter tugged on her plaits and kept looking over my shoulder. Nobody was waiting; it was after eleven on a Thursday night, and she and I were alone in the restaurant's dining room. She played with her hair some more. She sighed. I kept my gaze on the menu; this part was half the fun. I could have gone to a dive or a local place, somewhere they weren't required to post the calories, but that would have been like playing Russian roulette and knowing all the chambers were loaded—where's the joy in that?

Double Quarter Pounder with cheese – 770 calories.

Big Mac – 540 calories.

McChicken – 400 calories.

We were headed in the wrong direction.

"Sir?"

"The easy thing would be to buy McFlurries," I told her. "Four of them."

"M&M or Oreo?"

"No, you're missing the point."

She shifted her weight and looked at the spray bottle and cloth waiting for her. She needed to wipe down the tables. Or maybe she was going to clean the windows. My reflection smeared the glass; outside, the amber glow of streetlights, the neon haze of a Moulinbas night, the air textured with late October humidity.

"Spritz, spritz, a little elbow grease. Is that right?"

She gave me another sigh. She had to be fifteen, and she was already used to dealing with drunks.

"That's almost three thousand calories," I said. "Four of them."

"Tell you what: I think you'd like the M&Ms better."

I shook my head. "Never mind. I'll have the Double Quarter Pounder with cheese. The combo meal. Supersized, or whatever it's called now. Sprite. Light ice. Oh, and an M&M McFlurry." I smiled. "Just the one."

She didn't smile back. A year ago, I would have wondered if she played for the other team. "You don't look so good," she said. "You need hope."

"How many calories are in that?"

Rolling her eyes, she pulled her purse out from under the counter. She dug through it, produced a business card, and handed it to me. It had a Moulinbas address and the words: HOPE LEVINE – PSYCHIC, MEDIUM, SPIRIT GUIDE – BACHELORETTE PARTIES, FAMILY REUNIONS, AND CORPORATE EVENTS.

When my food came, I carried it outside on the plastic tray, ignoring the way the girl rolled her eyes at me. I sat on the curb. I stared at the food. At nine years old, I'd ridden the Ladybug at City Park, the year before Katrina. After that, the Ladybug had been out of commission for almost ten years, and then I'd been too old for roller coasters. But I remembered Gard, twelve then, complaining to Mom that I was going to wuss out. And I remembered the knot in my stomach as the chain towed us away from the platform and up the lift hill. I remembered gritting my teeth, my hands wrapped around the lap bar, the smell of steel and sweat and the popcorn shrimp someone had spilled in the footwell. As we crested the hill and gravity began to drag us down, I looked over at Gard. He was staring out at the park, jaw still tight with irritation. Then we fell.

This part, unwrapping the Double Quarter Pounder, was the click of the chain. My stomach was the same tangle that made it uncomfortable to breathe. I told myself that I was only going to eat a little. Just a taste. A bite of the hamburger. A few fries. Maybe I'd indulge myself and have the McFlurry, the whole thing. You can get anything right if you try enough times. Practice makes perfect. Eli Martins, everyone. Master of swallowing his own bullshit.

Headlights swept over me, and an engine purred as a BMW rolled past. Up the street, a bar called Escape had its operable walls open to the warm autumn night, and even though it was a Thursday, the place was hopping. Bragg was a city on the north side of Lake Pontchartrain, the small seat of a small parish, and Moulinbas was Bragg's seedy answer to New Orleans's French Quarter—which was really saying something. Outdoor speakers played The Chainsmokers. They'd found the cigarettes; now they were asking the tough questions, and it wasn't going to end well. Judging by the number of white guys in polos and khaki shorts and expensive tennis shoes, I figured I was looking at either the preamble to a fraternity brothers' reunion jerkoff session, or a Yankee bachelor party. One of the white boys was bending over the gutter, hands on knees as he puked. That seemed like my cue, so I picked up the burger and started.

I finished the Double Quarter Pounder. With cheese.

I finished the supersized fries.

I finished the McFlurry. I used the end of the spoon to scrape out the broken M&Ms that had gotten stuck at the bottom of the plastic cup. Then I sat there, the spoon hanging from my mouth, my stomach heavy, the greasy food already churning. I closed my eyes. I remembered the rush of wind when the roller coaster fell, the sense of flying that was really just another way of falling. Falling in disguise, I guess. Gard had run ahead, after we'd pulled back up to the platform, and I'd seen him say something to Mom. She'd nodded, and he'd run off. He hadn't even looked back.

I was starting to sweat, so I picked up the tray and carried it inside to the trash can. I shook the tray to get the oil-spotted paper free, and then I left it on top of the can. The girl was wiping tables; she had ear buds in, and she moved her head in time to a song. If she noticed me, she didn't give any sign of it.

Outside, The Chainsmokers had given up trying to figure things out, and now Joan Jett was asking his name—doesn't matter cause it's all the same. Sure it is, Joan. Sure they are. The air was stagnant with the end-of-day smells of sun-warmed garbage, piss, and puke. Drunk-dog-city smells. We made New Orleans look like a real classy lady when she gave us the chance.

I wandered for a while, dipping into pools of neon reds and blues and pinks and purples— XXX and BARELY LEGAL and LIVE LIVE LIVE. Sometimes I'd stand in dark spots, and the words would be painted on the inside of my eyelids. I hadn't grown up in Bragg, and I hadn't come to Moulinbas as a child. All my memories from that time were from the other side of the lake. But I'd spent time here with Richard. We'd had coffee and beignets at Le Cocon. We'd walked Asturias one April day, and he'd bought me a silver necklace and fastened it for me when I fumbled with the clasp. One afternoon, he'd packed a picnic basket with all sorts of good things—I remembered a fig jam and crusty French bread—and we'd eaten it at Bonne Heure City Park, on a swell of ground near blooming jessamine. I came here because I'd loved him and I'd trusted him and because, like pretty much every other man in my life, there'd been a monster hiding inside him, and I didn't know how to handle that.

When I stopped at the mouth of an alley, perfecting my frat-boy posture, hands on knees as my gut cramped, I heard something moving in the thick shadows. I told myself it was a rat, but then I saw the strung-out guy. His eyes were open and met mine. My stomach clenched again. A strand of saliva hung from my mouth, but nothing came out, and I was embarrassed and aware of the dangling, glistening thread. His mouth was open too, and his teeth were very good. He'd had braces.

Nothing came up, and I wiped away spit with the back of my hand. Hello, almost rock bottom. I thought about Dag seeing me like this. I tried to trace my own thoughts back, to find the why. Why was I here? Why was I like this? What kept drawing me back? Somebody else probably had a better chance of figuring me out, outsider's perspective and all that. That sounded plausible, anyway, so I dug out the business card the girl had given me, checked the address, and stumbled away from the alley.

The address was on Duke Street, another section of Creole townhouses with painted brick, cast-iron scrollwork, and dark balconies that looked down through the neon flood. The bell on a door jingled, and two white girls stumbled out, laughing as they held on to each other—and, in the process, managed to keep themselves upright. One of them did a double-take of me—it's all real, ladies; looking is free, but touching is going to cost you—and then the other one said, "Oh my God, I can't believe she said twins," and then they were both laughing the raucous, croaking laugh of white girls who had found the bottom of a tequila bottle.

As I was passing the door, the bell jingled again. I looked up. A sign in the door said PSYCHIC, with the Eye of Horus in India ink below it. It spun on a current of air as the door opened, and then I was looking at a woman. She crouched to lower the door stop, even though it was the kick-down kind, and my first impression of her was of something incomplete—a painting half-finished, a photograph only partially developed. Dark hair swung in front of her face. She wore a beaded tunic. Her legs were bare, and her varicose veins looked painful. The Birkenstocks had obviously clocked a few hundred miles. The bell gave another soft rattle, and she stood.

Then it all locked into place. She had the look down perfectly: the red head scarf with gold coins clinking as they swung and brushed each other; the straight, dark hair; the huge eyes and full lips. Gypsy fortune teller costume, Amazon, $54.99. She grinned as though she was in on the joke too.

"Too much?"

"Not enough," I said. "You need at least six more shawls."

She laughed. She was younger than I'd realized, and she had a voice like the bourbon Dag kept, darkly sweet. "It brings the tourists in." Then she cocked her head, frowned, and laughed again. "And now I feel like a horse's behind."

"Come on; I've got resting bitch face, but not that bad."

"No, I mean—well, it's embarrassing, you know. Because you're—you know..."

"Mixed? Queer? Chunky?"

Her laugh was slightly scandalized. "No. Because you've got the gift too."

The McFlurry was giving another cramp-inducing spin in my gut.

"It's one thing," she continued, "when it's Yankees and thirty-something moms who just want a night out, but—God, I am so embarrassed."

Down the street, someone let out a whooping war cry, and I glanced over. Two kids, barely into their twenties—which meant that, biologically at least, they were my age—were shirtless, and one of them was trying to give the other a piggyback ride. White boy homoeroticism at its finest; three years ago, it would have given me an aneurysm-inducing boner.

"It's just a shtick," the psychic said, and I turned to look at her again.

It was the light, I decided: the only light came from buzzing neon fixtures, and it ruddled everything, giving her the look of something still being finished in a darkroom.

"Never mind," she said. "Have a good night."

"It's a nice try," I said, "and I bet it works on the right people, but I'm not one of them."

Her smile was odd. Strangely tight. "They forgive you."

I fixed my collar and looked up at the piggyback bros, who were staggering away. I looked back at her. "I bet that one works pretty well too."

"All these men. The ghosts you're dragging around. They forgive you. They want you to know that."

"It's cruel," I said. "Everybody wants something, and sometimes it's nice for them to hear it, but this is cruel."

"And they want you to know that you're in danger."

"As someone who specializes in it," I said, turning away, "you ought to be ashamed of yourself."

"Goodnight, Eli. When you're ready, come find me. My name's Hope." She raised her voice to call after me, "And be careful."

I walked faster. I was halfway down the block before I figured she'd seen it on the care tag on the back of my shirt. Dag had written my name there in Rub-a-Dub on all my clothes, presumably in case I was accidentally shipped off to an orphanage or left on someone's doorstep. That's how she'd known my name. Simple as that.

Two blocks later, I was back at Escape. The party was still going strong. Dolly, poor thing, was working nine to five. I didn't call an Uber this time; instead, I called Dag and told him where I was.

He didn't sound like he'd been asleep, even though I always waited for his breathing to change before I snuck out. "I'll be there in a few minutes."

It was less than five, which told me what he'd been doing all this time. When he pulled up, the faint ambient light cut out his silhouette: big shoulders, big arms, everything locked into hard lines around the curve of the steering wheel.

"I'm sorry," I whispered as I slid into the passenger seat.

Whale songs were playing. He pushed the volume dial, and the sound cut off.

"I couldn't sleep, and—"

"I can't talk to you about this right now."

I nodded and sank lower into my seat.

We were near the end of the bridge, the salt grass a stop-motion flicker in the headlights, when he said, "I have class at eight."

"I know."

"I have a midterm next week."

"I know, Dag. I'm sorry. Oh. Oh shit, Dag, pull over. Pull over!"

We were still on I-10, but we'd reached land, and he pulled into an emergency turn lane in the median. I threw open the door and puked.

I was still heaving when I felt his hand on my back, rubbing lightly. His voice was almost inaudible as he asked, "E, what is going on?"

DAG (2)

"—ecological phenomenon initiated by the addition or removal of top predators," Dr. Delanuville was saying as I slunk into the classroom. Zoology 1000 had thirty students enrolled, but the classroom was fairly large, which meant everyone had room to spread out. It also meant it was impossible to sneak into class late without being noticed. Dr. Delanuville was a large woman with graying hair worn in a no-nonsense braid. She paused and looked at me just long enough to communicate a message I'd been getting since high school: *You. Are. Screwed.*

I tried not to groan as I dropped into a seat near the door. The door was near the front of the classroom. And Dr. Delanuville was, of course, at the front of the classroom. Another very simple A + B type scenario, which meant Dr. Delanuville kept looking over at me as I pulled out my spiral notebook and flipped to the next blank page.

"Top predators, also known as apex predators, have a substantial influence not only on prey but also on other predators and, therefore, on prey species that might not otherwise be part of their food chain."

No pencils. No pens. The pouch Eli had given me when I started school was gone. And then I remembered: I had taken it out in the car last night when I'd been following Eli. I'd decided to pass the time making notecards while I waited for him to call me, confess, and ask to be picked up. The pouch was probably still there.

"While the effect of trophic cascade may be seen most easily in prey populations—"

I glanced around. Sal sat behind me. He was one of those straight boys with perfect hair and perfect teeth and a perfect tan. He was some kind of big deal, which I'd picked up on when half the girls in class started swooning the first time he walked in. Apparently he'd been in a TV show with vampires. About vampires. You know what I mean. One episode. And he'd been killed. And his character had been a recidivist drug user. But sure, yeah, let's not pay attention to any of that. I was eight years older (Eli had spent an afternoon reading Sal's

IMDB page), and the two times I'd talked to him, he'd looked at me like I was a dinosaur.

"Sal," I whispered.

He pretended not to hear me. This was the kind of acting that had gotten him four minutes of screen time in a fictional world where, just like the real one, everybody with a brain wanted him dead.

"Nutrient cycling—" Dr. Delanuville was saying.

"Sal," I whispered again, more loudly.

This time, his eye twitched, and after a moment he gave up the act and glanced at me.

"Can I borrow a pencil?"

He didn't even shake his head no. His whole expression tightened, and I realized what I was seeing. I'd spent enough years as a sheriff's deputy, enough years rounding up juiceheads and hobos, witnessing the mixture of shock and disgust and kneejerk pity on the faces of the sober matrons of DuPage Parish, not to recognize it.

"Dag, is there a problem?" Dr. Delanuville asked.

I shook my head.

"He wants to borrow a pencil," Sal called up to her.

"Can somebody please lend Dag a pencil so we can move forward with the lecture? Yes, Lannette, thank you."

The girl who approached wore secondhand embarrassment and a really good weave. She passed me the pencil and scurried back to her seat. Dr. Delanuville waited a few seconds, probably on the off chance that somebody else would suddenly be caught up in a pencil-related emergency. Then she continued her lecture, and I scribbled notes and tried to keep up.

The headache I was carrying didn't help. Neither did the exhaustion. Both were results of the fight that had started when Eli and I were getting ready for bed. Not a fight about the lying. Not a fight about the sneaking around, the nights he ran away and I had to make sure he didn't get knifed or shot. No, the fight was because I had stopped brushing my teeth long enough to tell him that the marine biology program was having a happy hour, and Tristan had asked if I was bringing my boyfriend. Eli had gone ballistic.

That was the best word for it. He went off like a rocket. Hit the stratosphere in 0.1 seconds. I knew it was going to happen, of course. We'd had the fight plenty of times before. He didn't like to label things. He was too young for that kind of thing. Why couldn't we just enjoy being together? It wasn't even the monogamy—Eli was about as monogamous as a bullet to the back of the head, and scarily jealous, which I completely did not understand. But mention the b word, and it was the domestic equivalent of splashing gasoline everywhere.

I knew what the word was going to do. And I said it anyway. And I slept on the couch as a result, spending most of the night waking and tossing and having a conversation in my head with Mason Comeaux. Mason was dead, and he hadn't exactly been eloquent even in life. But he'd been my best friend since elementary school, and he'd been my first straight-boy crush and my first love, and he'd been killed by a monster that had ruined every good thing before taking Mason's life, and if there was a way to uproot someone like that from my heart, I didn't know it, and I wasn't sure I wanted to. I asked him what I was supposed to do. And Mason, in typical Mason fashion, boiled it down to the basics: *Get laid. Get your shit together. Rinse and repeat.* As I said, not exactly eloquent, but thinking about him saying dumb, straight-boy shit like that made me feel weirdly better, at least a little, and it made me miss him a million times more and a little bit less.

Sleeping on the couch meant I woke up late because my phone died during the middle of the night. No shower. No clean clothes because I'd left the load in the washer the night before. I'd had to settle for what I'd slept in, a tee and mesh shorts, and now, sitting at the tablet-arm chair, I was painfully aware of Sal's boutique cologne and my own eau de hamper funk.

"I'll pass back your energy pyramid analyses now," Dr. Delanuville said at the end of class. "I'm happy to answer any questions about my written comments during office hours. Don't forget the midterm is next Friday."

She moved around the room, scanning names on the assignment and then handing back the stapled pages. When she reached me, she said, "I'd like to talk to you after class."

I sank back into my seat, nodded, and turned my analysis faceup.

69.5. D+.

The room blurred. I folded the analysis in half so nobody else would see. I took deep breaths.

This was why I hadn't done college when I was younger. One of the reasons, anyway.

Behind me, Sal and his harem were taking their time leaving, and Sal was speaking in an aggrieved undertone.

"I don't know why she took off two points for the formatting. I had the formatting just the way she told us."

I didn't know the name of the girl who spoke next: "A ninety-six is really good, though. I bet it's the highest score in the class."

"Maybe for some people," Sal said. The way the volume of his voice shifted suggested that he was facing in my direction, and the breathy giggles from the girls confirmed it. "They'll let anyone in here.

I have higher standards for myself. I should have gone to Duke, but my parents wanted me to focus on college and my career at the same time, so I needed more of a support system. What I don't need is this lard-ass nobody marking off two points because she thinks I didn't indent far enough."

"She's such a bitch," a different girl said.

"I don't say bitch because it's sexist," Sal announced airily. I stared at the linoleum as he and his swarm of girls passed me. His voice rose just enough to be risky as he added, "I'd say she's a cunt."

The girls burst into nervous laughter, and then the swarm had moved out into the hallway, voices fading into the hub and bustle of the stampede between classes. The door swung shut on its pneumatic closer, and silence settled over the classroom. I hoisted my backpack over one shoulder, still clutching the analysis in my other hand, and trudged to the lectern.

"Hello, Dag," Dr. Delanuville said. "How are you?"

"I'm sorry I was late, ma'am."

She nodded. "How are things? How's school going?"

"Fine, ma'am."

Her next breath had a trace of vexation. "Really? Is there anything you want to talk about?"

I shook my head and added a belated "No, ma'am."

"Dag, nontraditional students often struggle, especially at the beginning of their transition back to school. Finding time to work and study, dealing with self-esteem issues, using modern technology, balancing family commitments, especially small children—"

"I don't have children."

Her eyes went to a spot high on my shirt, and I pulled on the collar to see what she was staring at: a Smartie was stuck to the cotton, right next to a surprisingly large stain—from what, I had no idea.

She must have been at a total loss for what to say next because she dusted off the age-old line of every teacher everywhere. "Dag, you have a great deal of potential, and I think you could succeed in this class if you applied yourself."

"Thank you, ma'am."

"You could come to office hours."

"Yes, ma'am."

"And the department keeps a list of tutors."

"Yes, ma'am."

"But nobody can do this for you. You're the only one who can do the work and commit to getting the most out of your education."

I thought of the hours with textbooks and highlighters and notecards. The hours I could have been spending with Eli, or with my parents, or with my friends. "Yes, Dr. Delanuville."

She sighed, and it sounded eerily reminiscent of my mother. "Is there anything you'd like to talk about?"

"No, ma'am."

"All right. I need to get to my next class, and I suppose you do too. I'll see you Monday, Dag." She smiled, and I knew it was half a joke, but it still stung when she added, "On time."

By the time I got out of the building, my tee was sticking to my back, and the smell of hamper funk and my need for a shower was overpowering. The day was beautiful, mild, the sky a deep blue that lightened on the horizon. A Rasta girl skateboarded past me, trailing the smell of weed. The campus was already emptying again; with only ten minutes between most of the scheduled classes, sometimes you had to rush to get to the next building. I had Introduction to English Literature Part 1, which I enjoyed about as much as having my foot run over, and I decided to skip. It was too nice a day, and I could get in an extra hour of studying for Zoology before the midterm next week.

I hadn't gone more than ten feet, though, when a voice called out, "Dag?"

I recognized that voice. My hands balled into fists. My brain short-circuited. Walk away? Break his nose?

Footsteps quickened on the brick sidewalk. I spun around.

Lanny Fontenot was a couple of inches shorter than me, and where I was built big—as my mom liked to say, solid—Lanny was all lean, golden muscle and this mane of thick, blond curls. He ate whatever he wanted, never worked out, and basically had a country mile's worth of abs. He'd been my boyfriend who lasted the longest— and perhaps my most serious one in light of Eli, my not-boyfriend. He'd made me wear my badge and gun once when we fucked. When he'd left, he'd stolen my life savings, and I'd been so humiliated that I hadn't told anyone; I'd just moved in with my parents and tried to pretend life could go on.

"Doggo," he said, smiling as he jogged up to me. "God, you have no idea how good it is to—"

"Go away, Lanny," I said, starting off at a quick walk. "Before I call the cops."

"Hold on, hold on." He circled around me and jogged backward; he'd always been graceful. His eyes were blue like periwinkle petals.

I sped up and tried to cut past him, but he laughed and got in my way again.

"Come on, Doggo. You're really not going to say anything?" His voice tentative, he added, "It's good to see you again. I missed you."

"Yeah? Looking for another ATM? Sorry, Lanny; I left my debit card at home."

"I deserve that."

"You deserve a lot worse. Get out of my way."

We were halfway across Johnston Quad when I stopped, and I felt like I was in one of those dreams where no matter how fast you run, you're always in the same place. The St. Augustine grass glittered like glass in the late morning light. The branches of a mimosa tree stirred in the breeze, and shadows rolled over me and ebbed again. He smelled like Lanny, just Lanny, the way he did after sex. His eyes wrinkled up at the corners, and he held his hands out, palms up.

"I know you're mad at me. I really fucked up."

"Move, Lanny."

"I got scared because of how quickly things were moving. What I was feeling for you, it scared me."

"Move."

"I want to make things right."

I shook my head, unable to stop the laugh that slipped out, and turned around. I was just getting going when Lanny caught my arm.

"Doggo, please—"

"Please? You stole all my money!" The shout echoed across the quad, and I drew in a deep breath. At a lower volume, I continued, "You took everything, Lanny. Not just my money. My self-respect. My—" I wanted to say, my chance at a healthy relationship. Instead, I swallowed. "Go away. I don't know how you found me, but—"

"Your mom," Lanny said with a lazy grin. He reached into a pocket. "I want to make things right between us. I've had some good scores, and I've got a really big one coming up—" He caught himself, blushed, and grinned. "I mean, this really good job. Bartending. At the Cabildo Cabaret. I'm going to get you the money, Doggo. Every penny."

He drew out a roll of bills.

I shook my head. It was like somebody ringing all the bells in the cathedral, only they were inside my skull. I took another step.

Lanny grabbed me. Again.

I spun back, and the punch caught him on the jaw. He went down on his butt, the bills fluttering down around him, staring at me. I stared back. Then I left.

ELI (3)

I was in the kitchen when the front door opened. Dag's phone started ringing as he walked into the house—the song of a humpback whale. I lit the burner under the battered aluminum pot we'd gotten at the Salvation Army Family Store for thirty-five cents, and I started grating the block of cheddar. The curtain was going up on Act 2, 'After the Fight.' I knew my part—Dutiful Boyfriend, or whatever we were calling it—and I wasn't going to fuck it up.

Boards creaked under Dag's steps as he moved around the living room. The house we'd bought was old, desperately in need of renovations but within our price range. I'd had some money—when my parents and brother had died, I'd inherited everything. We'd settled on this place: shotgun-style, which meant that you could stand in the front door and fire a shotgun down the length of the house, and in theory, the shot would pass through the back door without hitting anything. It wasn't exactly a practice we encouraged guests to try.

The layout was simple. The living room was at the front, then the bathroom, then the bedroom, then the kitchen, everything connected by a single, narrow hallway. Outside, the siding was turquoise, the door and shutters red, and the trim yellow. Dag still grumbled about living in a funhouse or a clown college, but it was Dag, so it was about the softest, gentlest grumbling you can imagine. We'd redone the living room, but that was as far as we'd gotten before Dag had needed to start catch-up classes before beginning at Tulane in the fall, and the rest of the house dated back to approximately the Louisiana Purchase.

The kitchen was no exception. It didn't have anything built in— no cabinets, no real fixtures except the sink, only a single overhead light that was yellow and always had dead moths in it, no matter how many times I asked Dag to empty it. The stove was freestanding. The fridge was an ancient, ivory-colored Amana that rattled and growled and occasionally, when it thought I wasn't listening, made terrible wheezing noises. Instead of countertops, I had two tables—one pushed up against the wall—my improvised counter—with a skirt to cover where I stored pots, pans, and pantry staples underneath—my improvised storage area. Dag had bought me a countertop (well, ok, tabletop) dishwasher for my birthday, and I'm embarrassed to admit I cried when I unwrapped it. The other table was a drop-leaf, and it was currently open and taking up every remaining inch of the kitchen. I'd set two places, with the blue fringe placemats and the copper napkin rings and the heavy farmhouse-style plates. Two candles were burning—we'd learned the hard way that two was the limit before the smoke detector started wailing and shrieking and gnashing its teeth.

The house was a far cry from the multi-million-dollar mansion I'd lived in with Richard. I didn't mind; I hadn't grown up with money, although not quite at this level. Here, I'd wake up next to Dag, his arm over me, or I'd walk in the door with the groceries and see where he'd left his textbook bristling with sticky notes, or I'd turn around, and the sunlight would be coming in at exactly the right angle, and I'd see the magnolia tree in the backyard blooming, and I'd be so happy that I thought something was wrong. A leaky valve. More than my body could hold.

But most of the time, I was dear old Eli Martins, which meant I was constitutionally incapable of happiness and wired for fucking up every good thing that came into my life.

"Dinner's almost ready," I called. "Do you want me to wait on the grits?"

No answer, only the creak of the floorboards.

Cheese grated, I checked the water—about to boil. I started the butter in the frying pan with the wobbly handle—fifteen cents, Salvation Army Family Store—and crumbled the goat cheese into the salad. The apples were local, Dorset Gold, and they were sweet, crunchy, and firm.

"Dag?" I called. "Should I cut the apples?" Silence. "They're going to brown, so maybe I should wait."

Nothing, not even the creak of the floorboards.

I set down the apple and the knife. I wiped my hands on the towel—a miniature pride flag, which wasn't really my style, but which Dag had gotten as a housewarming gift and which, therefore, was part of the regular rotation—and slung it over my shoulder. I found him in the living room, still wearing the shirt and shorts he'd slept in, a textbook on his lap.

"I'm doing homework," he said without looking up. He paused, probably what he considered a believable length of time, and turned the page.

His socks were gray from too many washings; I'd bought him new ones, but he kept going back to these. The tee was from Braxton Bragg Memorial High School, the 2009 basketball season, and the stitches had come out in part of the shoulder seam. I'd fix it the next time I saw it in the hamper. His jaw was set as he studied the page. He was my height, but much more muscular, although his movements were still surprisingly childlike sometimes. His hair had gone gray early; he'd turned twenty-eight in May, and it was this perfect color, like steel, that he refused to believe (no matter how many times I told him) was gorgeous. When I'd met him, he'd had it buzzed short because he was a deputy, but now he'd grown it out just long enough to wear in a severe part. I'd heard people talk about their hearts stopping, and it wasn't like that. Or maybe it was; I don't know. I didn't even think about my heart when I was looking at him.

I sat down on the few inches of sofa cushion available. I put my hand on his arm. He shifted, nominally to turn the page, but enough to pull away from the touch. I sighed and tried to kiss the top of his head, and that turned out to be the exact moment he needed to sit up to reach for a highlighter, putting himself just out of reach.

The role of Dutiful Boyfriend—or whatever we were calling it— for history of theater buffs, is a direct descendant of the role of Dutiful Son and Dutiful Brother. I had a lifetime's worth of experience with pissing off the most important men in my life and then trying to figure out how to fix things. My older brother Gard had gotten pissed off with just about everything I did—with my mere existence, I think. With Gard, it had been brownies, and listening to him talk about computer games, and talking to him about high scores and rare drops and whatever else made him forget it was me he was talking to because he was so excited. My dad had been a quiet man, but he got tired of the fights with Gard, or he got tired of the bad grades from school, or he got tired of me giving him and my mother lip. With Dad, it had been taking him a Miller Lite while he worked on the porch, the brown glass slick with condensation in the Louisiana humidity, the edge of the white-gold paper the safe spot for my thumb. With Richard, it had been a Sazerac ready for him when he got home.

With Dag?

An apology. Food. Cuddling—not even sex, just time together.

"I'm sorry about last night," I said, tracing the curve of his ear.

He pulled his head away again. "It's all right."

"I know that's not fair to you, leaving like that, calling you, expecting you to come pick me up. Especially on a school night."

He laughed and shook his head, turning another page.

"What?" I asked.

"On a school night."

I decided to leave that one. "I'm really sorry, Dag. I'm not going to do that again. It's—I'm still trying to figure some stuff out, and sometimes it helps to—to do it somewhere else. But I recognize that it's affecting you, and I'm going to stop. I'm going to find healthier ways to deal with what I'm feeling."

"Ok."

I traced the inside of his arm. He had huge biceps. Massive shoulders. Once, he had picked me up, just as a joke, until he'd seen how freaked out I was. I don't even know why it happened. Or I did, but I didn't want to chain the thoughts together. Being held down and fucked. Being held down and cut. Being held down, breath on my ear, words.

"I'm trying to work, Eli," he said, pulling my arm away.

"I rewashed the clothes, and I dried them and folded them."

It sounded like it cost him to say, "Thank you."

"And I cleaned."

He made a noise of acknowledgment.

"I looked for a job."

His hand hovered over the page. He marked something with a highlighter, a short, sharp slash. "We talked about this."

"I know. But I want a job. I want to do something, even if we don't need the money yet. And I don't want you taking out loans."

Jamming the cap back on the highlighter, he said, "I need to do this."

"Can you do your homework after we eat?"

"No, actually. I can't. I got a terrible grade on my zoo paper, and I've got a midterm next week, and I'd like to actually get some studying done."

From the kitchen came the sound of water boiling. I stood and made my way back there. I turned off the burner, and the blue flame flickered and went out. I shouldn't have been surprised; the Dutiful Boyfriend—or whatever we were calling it—routine didn't always work. Gard had stopped talking to me at the end, no matter how many pans of brownies I baked. After I came out to my parents, while Mom was still crying in her room, I had taken a Miller Lite out to the porch. Dad had been working on a section of screen, tacking it back into place. My pinkie found the dimple in the base of the bottle, sliding along the slick glass. Dad had lifted his head, eyes hard, face closed off, and walked across the yard and into the shed. And, after all, Richard had tried to kill me.

A hand at the small of my back startled me. I bumped the stove, and the whole unit rocked with a hollow, clanging noise. Dag chuckled, but the laugh died quickly. When his touch landed again, it was light, one finger brushing my back through the tee.

"Can we start over?"

"Yeah." My voice was thick, and I cleared my throat. "Welcome home, honey."

"Bad day?"

"Awful. I'm sorry about last night, and I'm sorry I ruined your day too."

"You didn't ruin my day. I'm sorry about last night too. I know I got things started."

I rolled my eyes—for my benefit only, since my back was to Dag—and reached behind me to find his hand. Only Dagobert LeBlanc would blame himself for starting a fight after his boyfriend—or whatever we were calling it—snuck out of the house, Ubered over an hour away, binged on junk food, wandered a semi-bad neighborhood, called for an emergency ride, and puked on the way home. He had big hands, and I squeezed lightly.

He let out an involuntary noise, and I turned around.

"It's nothing," he said.

"Show me."

After a moment, he rolled those huge shoulders and held up his hand. The knuckles were swollen and, in one place, freshly split. I hadn't broken the torn skin open again, but that was only by chance.

"Did you break anything?"

"His jaw, maybe," Dag said with a crooked smile that didn't look right on his face. "Ow, E."

"Owie?" I raised my eyebrows. "I know your parents baby you, but..."

"You baby me too," he said with another shrug. "Apparently I bring it out in people."

What he brought out, I wanted to tell him, was sleepless nights, the hours I'd lost thinking about new ways to style his hair (if he'd let me), my heart galloping toward a panic attack on lazy Sunday afternoons, when we napped on the couch together and it felt like the weight of his arm across my chest was the only thing that kept me from floating away. I probed his hand, and he grunted.

"Butch it up," I said.

"Says the guy in the five-inch linen shorts." But he really smiled this time, and a moment later, his hand was snaking up the leg of said shorts. The effect, now that I'd had months to get the Prozac out of my system, was instantaneous. I was twenty-three; sue me. "You didn't tell me you were making sausage."

"Oh my God."

"I should probably make sure it's edible."

"Is this food porn? A chef fetish? Oh Jesus, Dag." When he reached for my waistband, though, I stopped him. "Uh uh. Tell me about this."

"This is how I show you how sorry I am and how much I love you."

"Very sweet," I said, extracting his hand.

"And very big, especially for a guy who works so hard to look like a twink."

I rolled my eyes again, this time for Dag's benefit. "If marine biologist doesn't work out, you can always go write for PornHub. Now focus up, buttercup, and tell me what happened."

His eyes moved down to my chest. I had on a gray tee, washed so many times that it was see-through in places. He tugged on it. He blew out a breath and looked away.

I caught his chin and pulled his head back. His eyes were wet.

"Christ, Dag, what happened?"

"Lanny."

I knew all about Lanny. Or enough, anyway. And I had my theories about the rest. "You found him?"

"More like he found me." Dag dipped his head, wiping his eyes on his shoulder. Then he told me.

"Ok," I said. "I'm going to take care of this."

"Eli."

"Sit down while I finish dinner. Then I want you to tell me about your paper. And then I want you to tell me about your midterm." I lit the burner again. "We'll make flashcards tonight, and every time you get an answer right, I'll take off a piece of clothing."

"You're wearing a shirt and shorts. You don't even have on underwear."

"Are you complaining?"

A grin flashed. In his Serious Voice, he said, "Eli, I don't want you getting involved with Lanny."

"Because he's dangerous?"

"Well, no. I mean, he's Lanny. But that's not the point. I don't want you doing anything."

"Ok."

"What does that mean, ok?"

I pointed to a seat at the table.

He sat and asked again, "What does that mean, ok?"

"It means ok." The water had boiled again quickly, and I measured out the grits. I whisked them into the pot and lowered the heat. "You told me what you want. I heard you."

He was too smart and, worse, too intuitive to let that pass. "Promise me you won't do anything about Lanny."

Before I could think of a way around that, his phone rang with the song of a humpback whale. Dag pulled it from his shorts and frowned at it.

"You can take it."

"It's Amrey."

That was his old sergeant or chief deputy or whatever his title had been, back when Dag had been a deputy with the DuPage Parish Sheriff's Department. "You can take it," I said again.

"It's the second time."

"Dag, answer it."

He put the phone to his ear. "Amrey? Yes, hello." Pain ratcheted down his expression as he said, "Oh, God, that's awful. Yes. Ok. Yes, just a minute, let me check."

When he set the phone down on the table, I whispered, "What?"

He shook his head and hurried into the bedroom. He came back a minute later carrying a small notebook with a kraft-paper cover. After touching something on the phone's screen, he said, "Amrey?"

"Find it?" came Amrey's low, even voice on speaker.

"It was my first one," Dag said, folding open the notebook to the first page. "I didn't even know what I was supposed to take down."

"That's all right. Whatever you've got."

"Name, Ivy Honsord, white female, age forty-one. Address, 13 Windsor Street—is this what you want?"

"Dag, I don't know what I want, which is why I'm asking."

Dag skimmed the page, and I moved to stand behind him, my hand on his shoulder. The micro-blocks of text were very familiar. This was my boyfriend—or whatever we were calling it—ladies and gentlemen. Relentlessly thorough, which was all right until he decided to tease you.

"The boyfriend's name was Roger Shaver. He denied everything. Ivy had locked herself in the bedroom, and Roger had broken just about everything he could lay a hand on. When we got her out of there, she had a scrape on her back, bruises on her face and arms, and what I thought was the beginning of a black eye. We took Shaver in, but it just gave him time to cool down. She didn't want to press charges. In the end, all we could do was issue a warning about the noise because she wouldn't give us anything else."

But that wasn't the story, not really. Dag had told me about it. Only twice, actually. His first callout, a domestic, and him eighteen, a gentle boy who wanted to help people, who loved whales, who rolled clean socks into balls rather than folding them. He told me about how he had bawled in the men's room after hauling in Roger Shaver. For him, it was the first time he had realized he wasn't going to be a good cop, no matter how many times I tried to tell him it was exactly the opposite.

"Is it really her?" Dag asked. His voice was rough, and he was curling the corner of the notebook's page with his index finger. "You're sure?"

"It's her," Amrey said. "And it sounds like it was Shaver." Another voice spoke, the words indistinct, and Amrey said, "If all she's going to talk about is the fireflies, then tell her I don't have time to speak with her personally." He listened and said, "I don't care about the damn fireflies, Jacobs." His voice grew stronger as he spoke to Dag again: "If you think of anything else, please call." Then he disconnected.

Dag stared at the phone. I was aware of my fingers, painfully tight on his shoulder. It had to have hurt, but he didn't react. Then he stood, the notebook flapping from one hand, and headed into the bedroom.

I got the shrimp going. I checked the grits.

The light was off under the bedroom door.

The sound of the gas hissing through the burners was like a kind of scream at the back of my head.

We had faced a monster the year before. Two monsters. A kind of vampire, which sounded crazy now that we were a year out. Things that fed on pain and suffering, things that propelled people into spirals of violence. I still had the dreams, and I knew Dag did too. Dreams of blue fireflies.

I turned off both burners and walked into the darkness of the bedroom, and the smell of the clean sheets, and Dag's woodsy aftershave. He sat on the bed, a banker's box between his feet, the notebook still open-winged in one hand.

"We have to at least check," I said, proud that my voice didn't crack.

He didn't look up.

"We're going to check," I said.

He closed the notebook carefully and returned it to the banker's box.

I put my hand on the side of his head and pulled him against me until he rested against my hip. I smoothed his stiffly parted hair. It was silver in the weak light.

"What if it's my fault—" he began.

"No," I said, and my hand stopped on his hair. "We're not doing that. Do you hear me?"

He nodded, but his face was hot and wet through my thin tee.

"We're going to make sure it's not—" I tried again. "It's not one of those things again. That's all. It's probably nothing. It's probably a weird coincidence."

He nodded again. His voice was thick when, after a moment, he added, "Thank you."

I bent. I kissed the crown of his head. Then, just to be an ass, I mussed his hair and said, "Come on. We'll get dinner on the way."

DAG (4)

It took more than an hour to get to the trailer park where Ivy Honsord had lived and died. Traffic on the I-10 was bad—there'd been an accident on top of the regular rush hour glut—and we crept across the twin-span. It was dusk by the time we got off the causeway, and the water we left behind us was the color of cement. It had started to rain—just cat spit, as my grandfather would have said—and there was only just enough light to see the drops dimpling the surface of the lake. Then we were passing strip malls and suburbs, and then fields of corn stubble, sorghum waiting for harvest with heavy red heads, a canebrake where men cut sugar cane under halogen lights and tossed the stalks into a waiting wagon. We passed an ancient saltbox house, the wood shingles on the roof rotten and sunken in where the headlights glanced off them. We were headed home, and going home was like going back in time.

Balmoral Castles was a trailer park just outside Bragg's city limits. That had been a fight, a big one, between the county and the city. The county didn't want it on unincorporated land, and they insisted—it had something to do with utilities—that the park was technically part of the city. The city didn't want it under any conditions, and the city must have had better lawyers, or, in true Louisiana fashion, someone had gotten rich off the dilemma, because the trailer park stayed in the county, and that meant the Sheriff's Department handled the callouts. They could have kept us busy all year if we'd let them.

It was one of those places that middle-class people wanted to forget as soon as they blinked past it: mobile and prefabbed homes, many of them from the 1970s, before a lot of the safety codes about manufactured home materials and design had been thought up (not that there were a ton as it was). Eldredge Dupont had been on the brink of retirement when I started, and the old-timer deputy had trained me. The first time we'd gotten a callout to the park—the time I'd met Ivy Honsord and Roger Shaver—he'd been chewing a cold cigar, and he'd pulled it out of his mouth, looked around, and told me it would only take one match for the place to go up faster than a fag in hell.

I was driving. Eli had gotten his license revoked after having an accident while he was taking a strong anti-psychotic, and he still hadn't gotten it back, and there were only so many times I could ask and have him tell me, "Oh, yeah, I'll do that next week," before even a dummy like me realized I should stop asking. As we took one turn and then another, we passed the highlights of Balmoral Castles: a rose-colored trailer whose cinderblock piers on one end were lower than the piers at the other, so that the whole structure was slightly slanted (Sleeping Beauty); a leprously white prefabbed home with a black aluminum skirt, four rusted-out Edsels on the lawn (Snow White and the Four Dwarves); a red trailer, the handrail spray-painted with flaking bronze glitter, and a rice-paper scroll with what I thought were Hanzi, and what Eldredge had called gook writing (Mulan). The deputies had a hell of a sense of humor.

Slowing the Escort, I passed the final turn and took a long, assessing look. There it was: Ivy Honsord's trailer, where she'd lived all those years with Roger beating on her, where I'd—as Eldredge put it—had my cherry popped, where a woman who hadn't known how to escape had eventually been murdered. It looked worse than most of the trailers, but it didn't look that much worse. Whatever the original color had been, it was now a pastel green, with yellow trim that had faded until it was almost white. Two of the treads on the steps up to the front door were gone, but they'd been gone all those years ago, when I'd come the first time. The skirting was latticework, the wood untreated and now rotten after too many years exposed to rain and humidity. As we drove up, something moved under the trailer, and the lattice parted as something brown and furry shot off down the sloping hill, toward the cypresses and water where solid ground dissolved into this side of Bayou Pere Rigaud.

Police tape marked the trailer's door, but the lights inside the trailer were off. A DuPage Parish Sheriff's Department cruiser was parked in front. The car was dark too, but in the last light of day, I could make out the silhouette of a campaign hat pulled low over a face.

"I guess that's a little bit of luck," I said as I followed the street another hundred yards, the gravel crunching under our tires.

"What?" Eli asked.

"They put Maxwell on the trailer."

"They did?" He craned his head. "Why?"

"They're not finished with the scene. It's a small department; they might have gotten another call, or they might be trying to track down Roger, or they might have called it a night because they were tired and hungry."

"Aren't they supposed to finish, um, processing the scene, or whatever it's called?"

"Sure," I said as I parked under a flickering streetlight. "But it's DuPage Parish. When does anything work the way it's supposed to?"

Eli was looking back again. "Why's that lucky? Maxwell, I mean. He's your buddy? He'll let us take a look?"

I snorted. "He's a coonass drunk. He's already passed out. And I can say that because I'm a coonass."

Eli laughed softly as we unbuckled ourselves and got out of the car. Thunder boomed. South, over the lake, lightning flickered, and it cut out the trees in clear black lines. The bayou's water flared green for an instant. The cat-spit drizzle pebbled the surface as we moved through calf-high weeds, cutting between a pair of trailers and across the strip of common ground that separated the last row of trailers from the bayou. Darkness was eating up everything now, and the ground was uneven, giving underfoot sometimes and making me stumble. Pocket gophers, I guessed. Once, my tennis shoe caught a can of Keystone Light. It didn't make any noise—it was tangled in the weeds, and the occasional peals of thunder covered up everything else—but it still made my heart skip.

The back of the trailer was sadder, in its own way, than the front. A riding lawn mower sagged on rotten tires. Faded plastic flamingos froze in mid-search for their next snack. A little 200cc minibike, a Coleman with a fake gas tank hand-painted in olive camo, spilled foam padding from the split vinyl of its seat. The stairs to the back door were even worse, the wood soggy and giving slightly when I tested them. I motioned for Eli to keep his feet near the outside of the steps, and he nodded. I looked back at the trailer. I tried to get myself to move.

Eli's hand rested on the small of my back. I looked over my shoulder. His hair looked a little less windswept and perfect thanks to the drizzle, and microdroplets hung in his eyelashes. "We're just going to take a look."

I nodded and started up the steps. I was ready to loid the latch if I needed to—on trailers this ancient, you didn't need anything more—but the handle turned. Once I had the door open, I paused, swore, and wiped down the handle.

"Don't touch anything," I whispered.

Eli grinned.

I rolled my eyes and headed inside. Darkness met us, thicker than the night outside, and I turned on the flashlight on my phone. That was on the off chance that Maxwell's coonass-self decided to actually do his job. Eli copied me, and we panned the lights side to side.

We stood in the living room. The TV was obviously new, a thin LED style, the kind Eli had bought me on my birthday so I could enjoy the Saints games without getting a headache from watching them on my phone. Everything else was ancient. The sectional sofa was swaybacked in places, the brown fabric upholstery looking stiff where different liquids had obviously stained and dried on it. The carpet looked like it had once been a peacock blue—where the sectional had been moved, I could see some of the original color—but was now matted and grey-brown. I took a breath and regretted it—body odor, old cooking smells, and a musty fabric odor that made me think of an abundance of soiled clothes.

"God," Eli said, pulling his shirt up over his nose.

"It's going to get worse," I said. "You might want to wait outside."

For an instant, Eli's expression contracted—fight mode. Then he let out a breath, kissed my cheek, and shook his head as he moved deeper into the trouble.

I stared after him, trying to figure out what had just happened, and then followed.

I had been right—more right than I had expected, actually. The rest of the trailer was worse. Much worse. In many places, the wall panels were broken, the vinyl top layer torn and the gypsum core crumbling, leaving a layer of white dust at the base of the walls. In the cramped bathroom, the shower/tub combo had a ring of black grime, and the toilet was gone, a rag plugging the pipe. A five-gallon bucket with a toilet seat was clearly the replacement. Eli looked inside; I didn't. And everywhere, in every room, flyswatters. Some of them were the cheap kind with the wire handle. Others were plastic. Heavy duty.

"They must have been crazy about flies," Eli said, shining the light in the disaster-zone bedroom—a stained mattress overturned, the slats of the box spring staved in. "I haven't seen one, but I guess that's why they had all these flyswatters."

I thought about not telling him. In a lot of ways, Eli was tougher than I was. He was smarter in just about every way. And he'd been through things, hard things, and come out more or less whole. But in some ways, he hadn't seen anything—he was young, and he'd lived most of his life sheltered.

When I thought about it again, though, I decided I needed to tell him. Because it might matter for what we were trying to figure out. "They weren't for flies," I said.

It took him a moment. Then he paled. He crouched, inspecting one of the swatters, bringing his light as close as he dared. When he stood, he wiped his hand on his shirt, even though he hadn't touched anything. "There's dried blood on that thing. And hair. Long, dark hair."

I nodded.

"Dag!"

"I said maybe you should wait outside."

"He was hitting her with those fucking things. Hard. He must have been beating the shit out of her."

I nodded again.

"Why the fuck didn't you do anything? I mean, that's evidence, right?"

Rain pattered against the trailer's aluminum skin. As a kid— heck, still—I liked falling asleep to the sound of raindrops.

"That's not what I meant," Eli said, running a knuckle under his lip. "Dag, you know that's not what I meant. I just..."

"She'd have said she cut herself. She'd have said that's the curse of long hair, it's always ending up where you least expect it, or she was cleaning her hairbrush, or something."

"Dag, I'm really sorry. I didn't mean—it hit me hard, that's all."

"And he wasn't using flyswatters when I got the callouts, so I couldn't have done anything with them even if I wanted to."

"Dag."

I turned and headed toward the back door. Eli caught up with me in the hall and seized my elbow. When I pulled free, he didn't try again. He had hazel eyes. In the weak light from the flashlight, they shimmered.

"I know this—" He gestured around us. "I know how much this hurt you. I know you wanted to fix it. What I said, it just came out."

"All right," I said.

"All right," he echoed, and he pinched the bridge of his nose and stared at the filthy carpet.

"I know you didn't mean anything by it." I shrugged. "Still hurts. That's all right; I'll get over it."

He took a few deep breaths. He closed his eyes and nodded.

I thought about holding his hand. He liked that. Instead, I said, "We didn't find anything that tells us one way or another, did we? I mean, if this is the hashok again, then we're looking for a creature that feeds on suffering. Eli?"

He nodded, cleared his throat, and looked up. It might have been the light, but now his hazel eyes looked red rimmed. "Plenty of human suffering here."

"But nothing that confirms it was a hashok. I mean, I met Roger Shaver. I looked him in the eyes, and he's the kind of man who would keep a flyswatter in every room to hurt and humiliate a woman who was too frightened to get away from him. There doesn't have to be anything supernatural about that."

"The cycle," Eli said.

I nodded. "With the hashok, there was a cycle of violence, one person connected to another. It went through the PTSD support group in a matter of weeks once it was ready to feed."

"Just because we haven't seen a cycle doesn't mean there isn't one. And there's the neighbor. She was trying to tell your friend something about fireflies."

"She might be nuts," I said. When Eli's expression didn't change, I let out a sigh. "Or she might not. Let's go talk to her."

When we stepped outside, I caught a whiff of decay, and now my brain made me question if that wasn't what I'd smelled when I'd first stepped inside the trailer. An alligator gar on the banks of the bayou, maybe. A nutria. A coon that had dragged itself into the trees to die. Then the wind threw drops of rain against my cheek, and all I could smell was the water and the clouds.

We tried the mobile home to the north of Ivy's trailer, but the windows remained dark and no one answered. Then we tried the one to the south. It was the same color as the storm, with a sagging trellis of morning glory trying to cover a dent in one of the aluminum panels. A duckboard path led from the front door to a barbeque pit made out of an old oil drum, and now I tasted old char and gasoline on every breath.

The woman who answered the door was big. She wore short shorts and a tank top that exposed rolls of flesh on her arms and thighs. Her dishwater hair was up in curlers, and in one hand, she had a thumb marking her place in a dogeared copy of David Foster Wallace's *Infinite Jest*, which I only recognized because years ago a Tulane boy I'd gone on a few dates with had been writing his thesis on that book. He made references to a lot of TV shows that I'd never heard of, and he said things in German sometimes and then nodded to himself like he'd made a very good point. At the end of our third night out, he'd told me that he was looking for someone *at the same place in life.*

"May I help you?"

"Evening, ma'am," I said. "We're doing some follow-up into Miss Honsord's death."

Her eyes didn't give away anything, but her thumb slid fractionally in the book, and she shifted her weight toward the door.

"We're not police," Eli said. "But we—well, Dag knew her, and we wanted to get some answers."

She looked at me. She looked past me. When the rain hit the tin roof of the porch, it sounded like falling quarters. Deeper in the trailer, the floor creaked, and a TV came on with sitcom yammering. "I can't invite you in, if that's what you're thinking."

"That's all right."

"I would if I could."

"No," I said, "that's really fine. We wanted to ask you a few questions."

This time, Eli scowled at me, the expression darkening his perfect features only for a moment before he smiled at the woman. "I'm Eli."

She hesitated. "Jeannette."

"Did you plant this morning glory?"

"Kevin put up the trellis. I wanted something to grow on it."

"My grandmother would have chased you down with her slipper in one hand," Eli said with a grin. "She said she'd spent most of her life trying to keep morning glory out of her flower beds."

Jeannette laughed softly. "Nobody cares about that kind of thing. Not around here."

"About Miss Honsord—" I said.

Eli threw me another of those looks, and I cut off.

It was too late; Jeannette's laughter died, and she whacked her leg with the paperback. "I don't really know anything."

"Jeannette," a man shouted from deeper in the trailer. "Are we eating dinner tonight, or am I gonna starve to death?"

"That's Kevin," she told them. She shouted over her shoulder, "It's in the oven, so keep your pants on."

"What are you doing?" Kevin bellowed, but the question sounded automatic, and the TV's babbling filled the silence that followed.

Eli leaned a little closer. "We heard that you saw—well, could you tell us what you saw?"

Jeannette shook her head. Her expression was distant. "We've lived here five years, and Ivy was here before us. The first year, every other night when Roger would start beating on her, I thought he was going to kill her. I called the police, but they'd been out here a million times, and all they'd do was take Roger off, dry him out, and send him home in the morning."

My face was hot, and I had to look down at the muddy steel sill.

"Then, after a year of telling Kevin to go check on them, a year of that woman at the sheriff's with that tone every time I called, I figured that was just their way, and I didn't think anything was going to come of it. Honest to God, I didn't. Then it got worse."

"Worse?" Eli asked.

I brought my head up. "When?"

"A few months ago. Something was different about Roger. Meaner. He'd always been mean, always liked the dogfights at the Stoplight, sick stuff that men think passes for tough. But this wasn't the same. He'd look at me like he wanted to cut me up and string me on a trotline. I heard he was going to Angola, only they never came and took him, and Ivy told me that was a mistake—it was some other man, not Roger. One time, I watched him chase her around the trailer with a broom."

My mouth felt dry.

"He broke it across her back," Jeannette said, her eyes welling. "The broom, I mean. Made her pick up the pieces and crawl inside on her hands on knees. I watched the whole thing and didn't know what to do. Kevin told me to stay out of their mess; he didn't want me getting hurt." She turned her head, displaying a bruise on the side of her face that Dag hadn't been able to see before. "That man will be saying, 'I told you so,' for the next year."

"Jeannie, can you get me a beer?" Kevin shouted.

"You can get it yourself," she called back, wiping her eyes.

"What happened?" Eli asked.

"I tried to get her away from him." She let out a shockingly nasty laugh, although most of the bitterness seemed directed at herself. "You can see how well that went. Kevin was fit to be tied."

"That bruise is too old to be from tonight," I said.

"Last week," she said.

"And tonight?" Eli asked.

For a moment, the terror in her face was bright and white like bone laid bare. "I know what I saw."

"What'd you see?"

She pressed the fingers of her free hand to one doughy cheek, the digits sinking into the flesh and leaving pale marks when she pulled them away. She seemed to struggle for words. "There's an evil spirit in this place. I know there is. I felt it. And I seen the lights out on the water." The grammatical slip came as her voice thickened. "They look like fireflies, but I know they ain't."

"How do you know that?" Eli asked.

"How long have you been seeing these things?" I asked.

"A long time. Months." She took a shivering breath and seemed to make an effort of will. Her voice was steadier when she said, "He dragged her out of the house. She was dead; I knew as soon as I saw her. I shouldn't have even been outside; we never go in the back, only I've been trying to exercise—" A blush pinkened her cheeks. "—and Kevin put the railroad ties out back. They're good for stretching. I saw him. And he saw me. I screamed." She swallowed. "I swear to God, he turned into one of them lights that aren't fireflies, and he flew down into the bayou."

A heavy step broke the silence that followed her words. The man who appeared behind her was rail thin, with stringy hair cut at his jaw and something in his appearance that suggested grime although I couldn't have put my finger on anything specific. He was wearing ripped jeans and a t-shirt that said I PREFER DOES, which featured an anatomically incorrect female deer standing on her rear legs to display enormous human breasts. Mason, the dumbshit, would have loved it, and if he'd still been alive, I would have bought it for him for Christmas.

"Who the hell are you?" he asked.

"We're following up—" I began.

"Is she going on about all that bull again?"

"Kevin," she said in a weary voice.

"It's bull, that's what it is. And it's Satanism. And I won't have it in this house. We're at Bragg First Baptist, and I'm telling you, we're a Christian family and we aren't having anything to do with this. The whole world can go to hell in a ham basket, but not this family."

After blinking at that choice of words, I began, "Sir—"

Eli spoke over me, a trace of irritation in his voice that I suspected was aimed at me. "I'm not sure what you're talking about, Mr.—"

"Witches, that's what I'm talking about. Don't let the innocent act fool you." He jerked a thumb at Jeannette, who was blushing splotchily. "This one will get her head turned all around if I'm not there to keep it on straight. What did I tell you about staying out of the neighbors' business?"

"You said I'd get hurt," Jeannette said with a tinge of exasperation.

"Darn right. And you just about got your block knocked off. That's assault, do you realize that?" The question was directed at me and Eli. "That's not a mister meaner. That's felony-ass assault."

It took me another second to catch up, and again, Eli was quicker. "You're talking about—"

"Yep, them two. And then this one—" Another thumb at Jeannette. "—decides to bring that witch around, and I'm telling you,

I knew she was evil from the minute I saw her. I called on the Lord, and if I hadn't been recovering from my quarter zone injection, and that's on account of the doctor's orders, I'd have thrown that witch right out of here."

"For the last time, Kevin Knox, she wasn't a witch—"

"I seen her tonight. As soon as the police left, she was poking around. And did that deputy do anything? You bet your fanny he didn't. I could smell the drink on him even with the windows rolled up. If I wasn't taking it easy, on account of the doctor's orders, I'd have gone out there and hauled her out by her drawers."

"There is no way—" Jeannette began.

"You gentlemen have a good day," Kevin said as he reached past Jeannette to close the door.

The last thing I saw was her face still etched with the fear of what she had seen.

"Fuck," Eli whispered as we made our way down the steps. The rain was falling harder now—this wasn't cat-spit stuff anymore. The fat drops darkened Eli's tee in patches, and then the whole thing was soaked and clinging to him. His eyes found mine.

"We don't know—" I tried, but the words crumbled under the intensity of his look. Then I remembered the smell, and I said, "I need to check something."

I led him back to Ivy's trailer; he was shivering, and he was breathing too fast, but when I touched his arm, he pulled away. We went around the back, past the minibike, past the riding lawnmower and the smell of the rubber tires breaking down. Then I caught the stench of corruption again. I bent at the waist, grabbed the lattice skirting where it had already pulled loose from its staples, and pulled. The rotten wood was soggy in my hand, and when one of the slats tore wetly, I shifted my grip. This time when I pulled, a section of the skirting came away, and something red rolled into the grass.

I let the section of lattice fall into the high weeds and knelt. The red thing was a small bag made of what looked like flannel. It had been tied with a string, and on the string hung a dime, with Roosevelt staring off into the distance and the year 1961 stamped on it.

Eli frowned, chafing his arms. The storm was coming in cold, and his breath steamed. Out on the bayou, mist was also gathering above the relatively warmer water, glowing hazily whenever lightning flashed. "Open it."

My Puma hunting knife parted the string. The staghorn grip was slick, heightening the ribbed texture against my palm. When I shook out the bag, metal jingled. Nails came out first, fat and rusting—old iron, not steel. Then a few dry, heart-shaped leaves fluttered out of the bag.

"What the hell?" I whispered.

"I bet there are more," Eli said, and he turned and jogged toward the end of the trailer.

"Eli, wait!" I called after him, but a peal of thunder swallowed the words.

I considered going after him. Then another whiff of decay reached me, and my stomach turned. Alternating chills and heat ran through me. An all-over prickling sensation made me steady myself against the remaining lattice. I dropped the flannel bag and drew out my phone and turned on the flashlight.

Blackened, bloated skin.

Broken bones jutting through torn flesh.

A Levi's trucker jacket stained with blood and other bodily fluids.

Faces mostly eaten away by scavengers.

The buzz of flies.

I recoiled, fell back, and ended up sitting on the wet grass, staring at the boneyard under Ivy Honsord's trailer.

"I found another one," Eli called as he came back toward me. "I think we should—what happened?"

I played the light over the bodies. Then I looked away and twisted at the waist to throw up.

Eli's hand was warm and solid against the back of my neck. "Don't look anymore," he said. "I'll wake up the deputy."

Wiping my mouth, I got to my feet. "He knows me. I'd better do it."

II

Popular Acadian belief included several methods to prevent *lutins* from entering or staying in one's barn. One could place holy water, a medal of Saint Benedict or a blessed palm, or scatter flaxseed on the ground, as it is said that they are unable to count beyond a certain number and will become distracted.

– *Folklore Figures of French and Creole Louisiana,* Nathan Rabalais

ELI (1)

It was a long night. The deputy—Maxwell—was fairly drunk and still partially asleep, and he didn't seem to understand what Dag was saying. Dag ended up calling his old sergeant on his own phone. It gave me enough time to hide the second flannel bag, which I'd found at the other end of the trailer, in the spare tire well of Dag's car. After that, the sheriff's department cruisers started showing up pretty quickly, lights burning blue cones into the night, sirens wailing. And once things started, they didn't slow down for a long time.

Amrey Kimmons was older, probably pushing fifty, his gray hair clipped short. He was quite a bit darker than me, and although it couldn't have been easy being black in a parish and a department that mostly consisted of peckerwoods, he didn't shout, and he didn't swear. He didn't need to. I figured that out pretty quickly.

He separated Dag and me, putting us in the backs of different cars, and after brief interviews about what we'd been doing and what we'd found, we were left alone. At least, I was. I got the feeling Dag wasn't getting off quite as easy. Then we were driven back to the DuPage Parish Sheriff's Department, where I drank old, slightly burned coffee with non-dairy creamer in a room that had corkboard on the walls and a two-way mirror and a cassette recorder chained to a scarred table. When Amrey finally came to talk to me, we went through it all again. And again. And again. I'm not smart like Dag, but after enough rounds, even I figured out that what Amrey really wanted was an explanation for why we'd gone out there that night.

"Dag said he needed to follow up on something" was the only answer I gave.

Finally, Amrey walked me out to what looked like the building's central area, a bullpen full of long tables covered in papers, abandoned coffee mugs, pens, scratched-up staplers. Dag was sitting in a chair at one of the tables, right where an iron ring was bolted to the wood. He wasn't wearing cuffs, but the message wasn't exactly subtle. The woman he was talking to looked almost as young as me, white and petite and bristling with an energy I remembered from every time I'd gone to a gay club—a mixture of aggression and the need for approval.

"All right," Amrey said. "Let me walk you boys outside."

The Escort waited at the curb—a deputy had driven it over for us—and Amrey stopped to fish out the keys. He held them over Dag's outstretched hand and said, "You were a good deputy, Dag, and I was sorry to see you go the way you did. We'll have more questions for you, I'm sure, but I hope I'm making myself clear when I say I don't want to see you again until I call you."

Dag nodded, and after another long moment, Amrey released the keys. They clinked as they landed in Dag's hand.

We drove home. We slept, both of us too tired to rehash the madness of that night. Dreams chased me, and I woke over and over again, sweat-soaked and shaking. At some point, Dag must have gotten fed up with it because he pulled my back to his chest, one big arm looping me against him, and then I slipped into a dark and dreamless place. I woke to the sound of Dag rehearsing his flash cards in between vigorous brushing.

"Kemp's ridley sea turtle. Smallest sea turtle. Rarest. Endangered."

Brushing. Spitting. Water running.

Dag's blue LED plug-in made underwater ripples on the bedroom wall. The door was ajar, and the light from the bath painted a triangle in the hall. I could smell Dag's aftershave, woodsy, and the winter mint (whatever the hell that was) of the toothpaste.

"Grunion. Mate at high tide. Females dig their tails into the sand to lay eggs. Events called grunion runs where people catch grunion on the beach."

"It's Saturday," I said hoarsely.

The water shut off. Dag was a shadow in the bedroom doorway. He was holding the brush with only his teeth as he flipped to the next card, and his words were garbled as he explained, "'tudy grou'."

My response wasn't exactly intelligible, but Dag must have gotten the message because he went back to the bathroom, and I fell asleep again as he mumbled a definition of cavitation.

When I woke again, the sun was coming in through the snarl of ancient aluminum mini blinds. I peed, stripped off my briefs, and dug around in the back of the closet to find the scale—behind a stack of shoeboxes and an unframed watercolor Dag had bought me on a date, a walk on the levee, from a teenage girl who was working at an easel. I weighed myself. I went back to the mirror. I examined my arms today.

"Who the fuck am I kidding?" I asked.

I returned the scale, straightened the watercolor, stacked the shoeboxes neatly, because Dag had been trained as a police officer and he noticed things like that. Then I pulled on a pair of running shorts and shoes, locked the front door, and tied the key in my laces. I set off at a jog. I went south. Our street wasn't much to look at, mostly shotgun-style houses on cinderblock pilings, so I cut a couple streets over. There were a lot of the old Victorian houses, well maintained in spite of their years, with big white columns and freshly painted siding, all turrets and quirky windows and spindles and mossy shingles.

The trail along the levee gave me the city on my right and the muddy ribbon of the Mississippi on my left. Overhead, the sun was high and white, the day cool enough that I was glad when I started to build up enough heat from the run that I wasn't trying to shiver. Every breath brought me the smell of the river—fish, diesel, rotting vegetation. Barges dotted the water. On the banks, as though competing with the stands of oaks that ran to the shore, the skeletal frames of cranes hung out over the river.

Three pounds over, so I ran six miles, two for every pound.

I limped the last half-mile home. I turned on the shower and sat under the lukewarm water. My eyes felt puffy. I'd heard about runner's high, and maybe this was the come-down, when all I could think about was Quarter Pounders, a cardboard sleeve of fries—hell, two cardboard sleeves—the mirror, that thing in the mirror, me. When the water started to get cold, I stood and soaped up, wincing at the pull in my calf. I'd have to remember that, be careful when Dag was around.

After the shower, I dried my hair. I pulled on an extra-long white tee, so thin it was almost see-through. Acid-wash moto jeans and the new Adidas completed the package.

As I boiled eggs, my mind went to the trailer, the flyswatters, the hurt on Dag's face that I'd been responsible for, the neighbor, Jeannette, the fireflies, the flannel bag, the bodies, the pain in Dag's face that I'd been responsible for in another way. I turned off the burner, covered the pot, and went into the bedroom.

The flannel bag was still under the bed where I'd placed it. Still tied with its string and dime. I considered it. I thought about Dag asking questions the way a cop did. I thought about how badly he didn't want to be a cop. I thought about what I was asking of him, even though I hadn't asked yet, and what it meant for him to face the other deputies again after they'd run him out the year before. I thought about all those bodies under the trailer.

I drained the eggs. I ate one and a half and threw the other half away. I brushed my teeth.

We'd been to the Audubon Aquarium God only knew how many times together. It hadn't even been the first time, but it was the time I remembered best, when I'd turned around and seen Dag's face rapt as he studied a white alligator. The expression wasn't happiness or focus or interest. It was a fusion of all three. It was more. It was childlike wonder and avid intelligence and adult fascination. It had been so pure that it had broken me, and I'd had to go into the bathroom and wash my face while two teenage boys stared at me, and one of them asked me if I was ok, mister. The mister part didn't exactly help.

So I'd do it without him because he deserved to be happy, not to be mired in this shit.

I put the flannel bag in a backpack that Dag took when we went hiking. I called an Uber, wincing at the rate to take me across the lake and into DuPage Parish and Bragg. I promised myself that, for the last time, I'd quit being such a coward and get my driver's license. And a car. As I sat on the porch, waiting, I thought of telling Dag I was getting a motorcycle and burst out laughing at the expression I imagined on his face. Mrs. Dominguez, across the street, paused her digging in the flowerbeds to glance up at me, and I waved and shook my head.

The Uber dropped me in front of Escape. It was barely mid-morning, but the bar was already open, a few eager tourists drinking their breakfasts while Jimmy Buffet told them about a mythical place where you had to be careful not to step on pop tops. One of the tourists, red-faced and cornfed in his Hawaiian shirt and Birkenstocks, was slurping a frozen margarita, although the day was on the wrong side of chilly. I wanted to ask him if he knew how many calories were in one of those.

Instead, I followed the cobblestone streets, trying to retrace my steps from a few nights before. The white October sunlight washed out all the romance, exposing the spiderwebbing fissures in the stucco, the rust trails on the brick, the weekend's detritus in the street. Someone had lost an ivory-colored flat with a red sole, and it lay on its side in the gutter. A Styrofoam takeaway cup had cracked and leaked across the sidewalk, the faint smell of rum and pineapple suggesting some dumbfuck from Iowa or Missouri enjoying a vacation drink. A faded circular for Rouses was pasted to a lamppost. Cold cuts $6.99 / LB. Cajun style or Cajun fried turkey. Maybe that sounded good to the dumbfuck from Missouri.

I found her almost by accident. Almost. I remembered the alley where I'd seen the drunk—the bum?—and I remembered some of the turns, but not all of them. So it was accident. Or luck. Or persistence. The door was locked, and the sign was turned to CLOSED. The Eye of Horus stared back at me. Dipshit, I told myself. She doesn't live here. She's not going to be here on a Saturday morning. She's got to do her laundry or get her car washed or pick up that Cajun-style deli meat at Rouses. She'll be here this afternoon and work until late, pulling the tourists off the street and charging them double or triple because they're too deep in their takeaway drinks to know better.

I knocked anyway. The shopkeeper's bell hanging on the other side of the door jingled faintly. Up the street, a dog was barking, and a woman was shouting, "No barking, no barking," and I figured one of them was training the other, but it wasn't clear who. I turned and headed down the street, trying to figure out how to justify the money I'd spent getting here.

The bolt thumped back, and the bell rang out behind me. "Sorry." Her voice was what I remembered: honey dark, bourbon sweet. "I was straightening up and—oh. It's you."

Hope had ditched the gypsy getup, and her straight, dark hair fell to her shoulders. Today, she wore a Champion t-shirt and mesh shorts—I was pretty sure Dag had the same pair, although a few sizes larger. The varicose veins still looked painful.

"It's me," I said.

She shifted her weight. She was barefoot, and she had one hand looped around the door's handle as though she might need to pull it shut quickly. "Did it already happen?"

"What?"

After another moment, she sighed and pushed the door open wider. "I'll take that as a yes. Come on in and lock the door behind you."

I followed her into the store. Office? Den of iniquity? I wasn't sure of the correct term for a psychic's place of business; last year, I'd had occasion to make phone calls to a lot of psychic parlors. The front room was pretty much what I expected: Ikea chairs, lots of veils and battery-powered candles, brass ornaments that seemed designed to up the woo-woo factor, even a crystal ball. At the back of the room, a curtain was tied back, revealing a much more prosaic office space: a desk covered in papers, a filing cabinet with a small oscillating fan on top, a narrow door standing open to reveal a cramped washroom. The smell of incense, even day old, made me sneeze.

"Sorry," she said again, threading her fingers through her hair as she looked around and threw nervous glances at me. "It's part of the shtick."

"That's all right."

I couldn't see a clock anywhere, but my heartbeat ticked out the seconds.

"Ok," she finally said. "Let's hear it."

"You're the psychic. You tell me."

With a disgusted noise, she pulled out a chair and sat. She crossed her legs and massaged her thigh, wincing, and paused to probe a particular spot. "If you're going to be an asshole, you can leave."

"I'm not going to be an asshole. I am an asshole. It's like my cosmic identity; just ask my let's-not-put-a-label-on-it."

She snorted a laugh, but her eyes were softer as she studied me directly this time. "It doesn't work like that, you know. It's not like I'm watching the C-SPAN version of the future."

"Thank God."

Another, more genuine laugh. "It happened." Half question, half statement.

I tugged on the tee, twisting the hem. This was it. Surrender to the reality of the universe. "It happened."

"Tell me about it."

So I sat and told her. All of it. About the hashoks—Richard and Muriel. About Gard. About my parents. About Ivy Honsord and the bodies under her trailer. The woo-woo part was hard. The rest of it was old hat. The nice part about being emotionally dead inside is you can talk about the murder-suicide in your family without getting blotchy.

"Mary, Mother of God," Hope said. She reached across the table and squeezed my hand. I was good at this part too. I was good at pretty much all the parts, although I definitely needed to brush up on Dutiful Boyfriend—or whatever we were calling it. "Sweetheart, I had no idea it was this bad."

"You believe me?"

"Of course I believe you."

"So this whole thing, it's not just a gimmick? You're not just telling people what they want to hear, helping them believe whatever they want to believe?"

She shook her head. "I told you, it's a shtick. I know it's not a good way to make money, but everybody's got to earn a living, and I'm not cut out for retail."

"Can you read my thoughts?"

"You're how old? Eighteen? I don't need to be psychic to read your thoughts."

I grinned, but it faded quickly. "Can you tell me where the hashok is?"

She frowned. "I don't know."

"You don't know?" Her silence was another hesitation. After a moment, I opened the backpack and pulled out the flannel bag. "What can you tell me about this?"

"That's not me." The words were quick and hard.

I blinked. "What does that mean?"

She seemed startled herself, and when she spoke, she said slowly, "I mean, that's hoodoo. Or witchcraft. It's hard to draw a hard line between the two. Me, on the other hand, I'm a psychic."

"Different woo-woo."

"Something like that," she said drily.

"Damn."

She studied me for another moment. Then she stretched her other arm across the table. "Would you like a reading? A real one, I mean?"

"You're not going to tell me that I'm going to meet a dark, mysterious stranger who will ravish me?"

"Do you want to be ravished?"

"It's nice to feel wanted." But I took her other hand, and now our bodies and our clasped hands made a circle around the crystal ball.

"Focus on the crystal."

"You can save it for the moms from Bumfuck."

Irritation flickered in her expression. "I can only work with what you give me, Eli. Relax. Open up. Let me see what's going on."

Relax, I thought. Open up, I thought. Sure, why not? Dag's only been trying for the same thing with a solid year of patience, kindness, and unrelenting teddy-bear love.

But I did my best, focusing on my breathing, staring into the crystal ball. It was just a big chunk of glass, I decided. Reflections from the room around us warped along its surface. But the longer I looked, the more I thought maybe it wasn't only glass. There was something at the center. A flaw. Those were the breaks when you bought in bulk from China or Vietnam or wherever they were outsourcing American woo-woo these days. A flaw that caught the light differently sometimes, milky when the morning sun touched it. A flaw—

"It feeds on human lives," Hope said. "Suffering and pain and fear. It has seen you."

I barely heard her. Sometimes, the whole ball flared up with that white brilliance. Sometimes the flaw, in contrast, actually seemed dark. Like a window to somewhere else. I felt myself drifting. It was like the tide washing me out to sea, out toward that dark chink in the intense white of the crystal. Yes, I thought. Exactly like a window. And if I got close enough, I could see.

The tide carried me up. I rode a swell of that pale light. The chink loomed above me, so much bigger than I had realized. Not a window. No, more like a maw—

But then I was through, and the shop was gone, the crystal was gone, the blinding white light and the dark gap were gone. I was back home. I was in the bedroom I shared with Dag, only the windows were open, and afternoon light made the space sunny and spacious, bigger than it was in reality. I was watching myself.

This other Eli had just gotten out of the shower. He had a towel wrapped around his waist as he padded through the sunlight that dappled the floor. He had better hair—trendier, an asymmetrical cut with a skin fade that looked like way less work. He had better shoulders. A better chest. Better abs—an eight-pack. He dropped the towel. Muscle corded his legs. Pulling a bottle of lube from a drawer, he squirted some into one hand and then reached back to finger himself. When he looked over his shoulder, our eyes met. He took me in, a long up-and-down laced with derision, and smirked. His gaze moved on.

"Dag," he called. "Come fuck me."

"Hell yeah," came Dag's breathless reply from the other room, and then pounding steps as he ran.

I tried to hold on, but the dream slipped away, and I was in the shop again. Hope was still holding my hands; I yanked them free. It was still morning. It was the same room with the veils and the curtains and the faux-bronze ornaments. The crystal ball glinted with sunlight, but there was no white radiance, no dark flaw waiting to swallow me. My vision felt washed out, as though I'd been staring at something too bright for too long. I realized, distantly, that I was exhausted, as though I'd burned through a whole day's worth of energy in the adrenaline rush.

"Oh," Hope said, massaging one hand.

"What was that?"

"Well—"

"What the fuck was that?" I stood up too fast. I could still see him, that other me, the me that hadn't had his body wrecked by Prozac, the me that hadn't had his sex life screwed up with trauma. The erotic charge, part voyeuristic, part jerk-off fantasy, still made me flush, and

I was half hard in my jeans. But I felt queasy, too, remembering that other-me, how he had stared at me and seen—what? The extra pounds, the mummy arms, the skinny calves? "Was that the future? You said you don't see the future."

"Kid, you've got one hell of a grip."

I slapped the table, and the crystal ball wobbled. Hope flinched. "What did I just see?"

"You break my table, and you're paying for it. And I don't know. If I knew, I'd be making a lot more money than forty-five dollars a pop to tell tourists their wives aren't cheating on them."

My heart was still racing, but underneath the excitement, bone-deep fatigue was settling in. I thought about kids who got overstimulated, pushed past the point of exhaustion, and couldn't calm down. I couldn't slow my breathing.

"Eli, it was just one possibility. If it upset you—"

The laugh was wild and slipped free before I could rein it in. "Yeah." I realized I was twisting the tee again, and I forced myself to let go. I straightened the shirt and tried to smooth out the wrinkles. Then I gave it up for a lost cause. "Yeah," I said again. "A possibility. Ok."

"This is why I prefer the shtick. Nobody gets angry because I tell them they've got money coming to them."

"I'm not angry." The laugh burst out of me again. Part of me knew I was acting like a lunatic, and I tried to cover by packing the flannel bag back into the backpack. "Holy God, I've got to go."

"If you want me to try again," Hope said. "To help you identify this thing—"

"Yes. Yeah. I'll be back," I said as I rushed out the door.

DAG (2)

Something was not right.

On the couch, I flipped another page in my zoology textbook and tried to commit the entire page to memory; I was considering a permanent hiatus from flashcards. *Mesopredator release occurs in ecosystems when a higher-tier predator is removed. The rapid growth of mesopredators, previously held in check by the presence of apex predators, can have drastic effects on an ecosystem. In the Midwest, for example, the near-extermination of wolves (Canis lupus) allowed coyotes (Canis latrans) to—*

A sound from the bedroom, a soft click, pulled me out of the book, and the words slipped away. I knew that sound. I thought I knew that sound. We had rules about this.

The day had been hard. I'd left for an early-morning study group while Eli was still sleeping, which meant we hadn't talked about the discovery of the bodies and the growing possibility that another hashok was preying on people in DuPage Parish. Then, at the study group, stupid Sal with his stupid perfect teeth and stupid perfect clothes had taken one look at the flashcard sets I'd made and groaned and told me I'd done them wrong. I'd done them wrong in two ways, actually. And everybody else had stared at the table or their feet or found something important to do on their phones.

And then Lanny had called. Fourteen times. And he'd left fourteen different messages. And because he was Lanny, I had listened to all of them. Multiple times. Hell, I'd only managed to delete them because I had imagined Eli somehow spotting them and asking me about them. Lanny was doing the same old song and dance. He was sorry. He missed me. He wanted to make it up to me. Couldn't we at least talk about this like adults?

I dragged my attention back to the book. *Shrinking populations of large sharks in the ocean permitted smaller-bodied sharks and rays to increase—in one case, as a consequence of the explosion of mesopredator populations and the accompanying rates of predation, decimating North Carolina scallop fisheries.*

But it hadn't just been stupid Sal and his stupid perfect tan and his stupidly perfect flashcard app that everybody else had known about except me. And it hadn't just been Lanny, with that wild tangle of blond hair, or the pics he'd started sending, pics of him fondling himself, pics of him with sex-heavy eyes and precome glistening on his washboard stomach. Pics of today. The little monster had shown himself teasing the slit of his dick with one hand, in the other holding a copy of the *Times-Picayune*, so I'd know this was all for me.

It hadn't even been the discovery the night before, all those bodies, or the possibility that we were dealing with another hashok.

The worm burrowing through my gut was because of Eli.

When I'd gotten home, he'd seemed fine. A little overly energetic. A little too...happy, I guess, considering the sleepless night and the fears we shared. He'd cleaned the whole house, and he'd made a baked fettucine alfredo, the creamy, saucy pasta topped with butter-toasted breadcrumbs. While I'd cut the grass—for what I hoped was the last time this year, although there was enough St. Augustine grass in the lawn that I figured I wasn't going to be that lucky—he'd put together a salad. When we ate, he filled up my plate with pasta and Caesar salad and garlic bread, which I hadn't even known was in the mix. He'd had the salad—no dressing—and a seared chicken breast.

I tapped my highlighter on the page. I took the cap off. I put the cap back on. I looked over my shoulder, trying to see down the hallway, but the angle from the sofa was wrong. I sat up, swinging my legs off the cushions. Then I stopped.

He'd eaten everything on his plate. It was real food, and it was healthy, which was part of the rules. There was nothing I could say. Nothing I could even point to.

But when I'd wanted to talk about the hashok, he'd shaken his head and said I didn't need to worry about that tonight. And when I'd pressed the issue, he'd kissed me and told me to go relax. And when I'd tried to take over the clean-up duties, he'd pushed me into the living room, turned on the TV, and made me a Sugarfield on the rocks. A double, actually. And if I hadn't known better, I would have thought maybe he was trying to get me a little drunk.

A normal Saturday night might have included any of the following: Eli insisting we go for a drive; Eli asking me to go on a walk; Eli squeezing onto the sofa beside me and then nudging me with his foot, over and over again, and pretending he didn't know what I was talking about when I finally told him to knock it off; Eli standing in front of the TV when I was trying to watch a really good *Nova,* one about a ship, and pretending he was looking for something—and then pretending he'd forgotten what he was looking for; Eli pulling my hair when he walked past the sofa; Eli working the waistband of my gym shorts under my balls and licking the head of my dick while I tried to study; Eli fucking me—anywhere, anytime. Once, I'd gone into the kitchen to get a snack, and he'd fucked me while I was half inside the refrigerator, the bottles of pickles and condiments rattling in the open door.

Tonight, though—what? Blessed peace and quiet.

Which meant something was wrong.

I hadn't heard anything in a few minutes. Nothing except that click. Which was against the rules. I laid the highlighter between the pages to mark my spot and closed the textbook. I got to my feet. A board squeaked, and I stopped and listened again. Then I took slow, quiet steps toward the hall. I stopped outside our bedroom door. Nothing. Silence. And then a muffled noise—a grunt.

The first time was right after we'd moved in together. I thought he had food poisoning, and I forced open the door. Too late. He'd already finished, and he'd passed it off with a story about a bad po'boy. The next time, I'd loided the lock with an ancient Blockbuster card. He'd still had his fingers down his throat. That was when we made the rules.

Rule number one: we respect each other's privacy, but no locked doors.

As lightly as I could, I tested the knob on the bedroom door. It didn't turn. That's what I'd heard, the thumb lock clicking when he set it. My first thought was of the food again, the plain chicken and the undressed salad. But he wasn't in the bathroom; he was in the bedroom. So, what? Was he using a bucket this time instead of the toilet? Or was it something else? A needle? A razor blade?

I closed my eyes. My heartbeat felt huge inside that darkness. When I opened them, it was the same hallway, the same incandescent bulb, the same bright, warm home. I went back to the living room and dug through my school supplies until I found a travel-size dispenser of clear tape. Then I went outside. From the shed at the back of the lot, I retrieved the step ladder and a flathead screwdriver, and I placed the ladder under the bedroom window. I popped out the screen with the screwdriver. Then I went back to the front door. It was almost nine, and our block was dark and empty. The air smelled like fall and the river and the spearmint I'd trampled along the side of the house.

I taped down the doorbell, and it began to ring. I sprinted back to the step ladder, wedged the blade of the screwdriver between the sashes, and forced the lock. I shoved the window up and climbed into the room.

Eli was naked except for what my grandfather would have called a T-back—a white thong with a thin strap that disappeared between his butt cheeks. He was standing at the door, facing away from me, probably trying to figure out why I hadn't answered the door and if he should risk going out there. In one hand, he held shorts and a tank, which meant he was on the brink of venturing out.

No razor blades. No needles. No bucket.

Weights. And a thick rubber mat. And a removable pullup bar he'd installed in the closet. His back and shoulders glistened with sweat, and I could smell it now, the slight funk of his body.

"Do you want to talk about this?" I asked.

He spun around. The thong cupped him perfectly, but then, he could have been wearing a tube sock down there and it would have had the same effect. It was his face (I was convinced he had perfect features). It was the hollow of his collarbone. It was the vee of his torso. It was the freckles at the cleft of his thigh, and the relative lightness of his skin there. It was the sparse hair on his legs, the scar on the back of one calf, the long feet and long toes that seemed proportionate to the overall length of his lean build. Hazel eyes widened in shock.

"Did you come through the window?"

"No locked doors."

"Were you spying on me?"

"No locked doors, Eli."

"I can't believe this. I cannot believe you."

The doorbell was still ringing. I jerked a thumb at the open window behind me. "If I go take the tape off the bell, are you going to try to lock me out again? Or can I close this?"

"I thought something was wrong. You scared me out of my goddamn head!"

I shrugged, slid the sash down, and set the lock again. "Ditto."

When I let myself out into the hall, he followed me. "Dagobert LeBlanc—"

"We agreed, Eli."

His voice had reached maximum volume. "I fucking know what we said, but tonight, what you did, you had no fucking right—"

I turned around, and he stopped. I put my hands on my hips. He swallowed. Something must have showed on my face because Eli backed up a step.

"Please don't yell at me," I said, but the hammer of my blood made it hard to hear my own words.

After a moment, Eli said, "I'll yell whenever I want to yell!" But it was at a normal volume. He whirled and ran back into the bedroom and slammed the door behind him. It bounced out of the frame and wobbled open again.

Sighing, I went to the front door. I took the tape off the bell. I returned the screen to the window, and then I returned the ladder and the screwdriver to the shed. I went into the house. He was crying as I locked up and turned off the lights, and then I was swimming through the darkness toward the warm glow of the bedroom.

He lay on the bed, facedown. The smell of sweat and rubber still hung in the air. I closed the curtains. I plugged in the LED. I turned off the overhead light, and then I sat on the bed. We floated in the undulating blue. After a moment, he let out a shaky sob and turned his face into my thigh. I released a breath and stroked his back, fingers gliding lightly over sweat-slick skin.

"I'm sorry," he said, crying harder, the words hitching as he tried to get them out. "This is just so fucking embarrassing."

"It's not embarrassing. I know my way around weights pretty well. I can show you how to use them."

His body tensed. Then all the tension went out, and he laughed, rubbing his face against my shorts. When he raised his head, his hazel eyes were puffy, full of blue-tinged shadows from the light. "Not the weights, dummy."

"So I'm a dummy now," I said, brushing back his hair.

"All of it. The fact that you caught me like I'm a teenager. The fact that I'm not allowed to lock the door. The fact that I'm so messed up."

I had to think for a moment. "It's not that you're not allowed—"

"Oh my God," he groaned. "I know. We agreed. I agree."

"I'm not changing my mind, Eli."

He groaned again and flopped onto his back.

"It's important to me to know that you're not hurting yourself."

Covering his face with both hands, he said, "I know, I know, I know. And I love you for it. I love you for not letting me, I don't know, get away with it. But please stop before I die from humiliation."

I scratched my leg. He lay there, hands over his face. The blue light rippled on the wall. Then I stretched out next to him and laid my hand on his belly, the softness of the extra padding there. I could feel the muscles of his stomach contracting and releasing under my fingers. His nipples had stiffened into peaks.

"You're the most beautiful person I've ever seen," I said, and my fingers trailed down to trace his erection trapped in the white thong.

The noise he let out was soft and needy.

"You haven't been to see Barbie in a couple weeks," I said.

"I'll go." His voice was thick. "I'll make an appointment."

"Exercise can be another way people hurt themselves."

Eyes half closed, he nodded.

I slid his dick out of the side of the pouch and ran my thumb across the head. He whimpered and turned into his arm.

"E," I said.

"Won't," he managed. "I won't. Just—just adding muscle."

"With the door open."

"Uh. Yes, yes, yes. Don't stop."

"And eating."

"I ate. I ate tonight." He drew in a shuddering breath and clutched my wrist. "Oh Dag."

"Come on," I said and gave a tug. "I want you to make love to me."

His eyes opened a little, and he offered a lopsided smile.

"What?" I asked as I stripped. I was hard, my dick bouncing as I climbed onto the bed and lay next to him.

Rolling onto his side, he ran his hand down my chest. His mouth closed around my nipple, and I arched my back. He was there a while, and I made all sorts of ungodly noises as a slick finger pressed into me. When he pulled away, my body felt loose and warm, and a red ring marked my chest from heat and suction and his day's worth of stubble. When two fingers came back, wet and probing, I closed my knees and made a noise.

"I love you," he whispered into my side.

I ran fingers through his hair, curled them, and tugged.

His eyes came up to mine barely long enough to say, "I love you," before he looked away again.

"I love you too," I said and spread my legs again.

He got onto his knees, and for a while he was focused on me, and I was focused on the knot of whiteout pleasure he was pressing against. Then he was touching himself, lubing up. I opened my eyes. He was staring down at himself, his hazel eyes restless. He'd gone down to half-mast.

"Let me," I said.

He shook his head. Then he asked, "Will you ride me?"

"Why?"

"I like it. I like looking up at you."

It might have been true, but it was also a lie. I ran my hand over his knee. I cupped his belly.

"What about missionary? Sometimes I like to look up at you."

His eyes betrayed him, flicking down to his own body again.

I sat up and said, "Stretch out."

It only took him a moment. With his long body splayed against the mattress, gravity pulling on him, he looked even thinner than he already was. He had the smooth, round musculature of someone freshly out of adolescence, but how long would that last when he didn't eat, when he ran for the calorie burn, when what he saw in the mirror wasn't what anyone else could see? I straddled his chest and traced the soft brown of his arm, the slight swell of his biceps. He shivered. Goose bumps broke out across his chest and shoulders.

"You ok?"

He blinked rapidly. "It's just a lot sometimes."

I sat back, taking him inside me slowly, and he whimpered. I rocked. Then I raised myself up and brought myself down hard. Again. Again. He came first, his face tight in a spasm that suddenly opened wide. A revelation. I brought myself off with my hand, a white spray across the brown of his chest and throat.

When my body had relaxed, I slid off him and lay alongside him, one arm scooping him against me. I couldn't see it, but I could feel the roll of his eyes.

"No free rides," I whispered in his ear.

That made him laugh. His hand had an unfamiliar texture when he rested it over mine. Raw from the weights, I guessed. Tonight, he slept first, but I was awake a long time, dragged by the undertow of blue light and dark thoughts.

ELI (3)

"I swear to God, I will not disappear," I said.

It was Sunday. I had spent the day catching up on chores around the house; Dag had spent the day trying to make a set of flashcards on some sort of app on his phone, swearing a blue streak—which was unusual for him—and then making an entirely new set on notecards. The sky was gunmetal, and the air was cold. A stiff breeze off the lake slapped leaves from the black oaks and the tupelo trees and sent them cartwheeling up the street.

We were headed for dinner with Dag's parents, which involved more than just the meal. On a normal Sunday, we'd get there in the afternoon, and Dag and his dad would watch golf, or they'd work on whatever project Hubert needed help with—last week, it had been sanding something in the basement, which meant Dag had smelled like sawdust all night and which, to my surprise, I had found extremely hot. Gloria, his mom, would usually corral me in the kitchen to do girl talk and teach me how to cook Dag's favorite meals. For some reason, Dag seemed to think this was sexist; the first time, he had delivered an impassioned twenty-minute speech about why he should learn how to cook his own meals, and about how I wasn't his housewife or maid, at which point his mother had said, "That's very nice dear, but I still think Eli needs to know how to devein shrimp." Which apparently was the end of that argument.

Right then, from the driver's seat of the brown Ford Escort, Dag was looking at me with a shocking lack of boyfriendly—or whatever we were calling it—trust and good faith.

"I'll just go to the library," I said, "and I'll look for the books I want, and I'll walk over to your parents."

"I'll park. We'll go inside together."

"Dagobert."

"Fine. You call me when you're done, and I'll come pick you up."

"It's half a mile. It's chilly, but it's not freezing. I'm not calling you."

"If you wanted to walk," he said, fingering the strap of my CAFÉ DU MONDE tank, which featured a smiling cartoon beignet, "you should have chosen something that wasn't out of the Redneck Riviera collection."

I kissed him and opened the door. "I'll see you—"

His hand closed around my upper arm. I liked that he was strong, but God damn, sometimes it was a pain.

"I'll call," I said and sighed.

He didn't answer immediately, and I realized he was watching something in the rearview mirror.

"What?" I asked.

After a moment, he shook his head. Kissing my cheek, he released me. Then he said, "If you walk, we're going to have a fight."

"You're no good at fights. I scream and get hysterical and break things, and you sit there like a lump, and eventually I wear myself out, and then it's over."

"Try walking to my parents' house," he said, "and see how good I am at a fight."

I rolled my eyes—because it made him smile—and got out of the sedan. I looked both ways, spotted the little Chevy idling at the end of the block, and wondered at the back of my brain if Dag was back in cop mode and thinking about giving the guy a ticket for some reason. But by then, I was jogging across the street and headed toward the library.

The Bragg branch of the DuPage Parish Library had been built in the '70s, I guessed. It was brick, with skinny floor-to-ceiling windows studding the walls at regular intervals. Inside, beyond the RFID gates, it had the usual library smells: paper, binding glue, hot toner, and the penny-pincher crowd—everybody too cheap to buy their own book or newspaper. Probably not coincidentally, that also seemed to be the Bengay crowd, and the orthopedic shoe crowd, and the medical support hose crowd. Ok, I was being bitchy; I had to get it all out of my system, because it wasn't any fun when Dag was looking at me with those dark, kind eyes.

I walked past shelves with displays of children's books, displays of popular adult titles—reverse harems were in, it seemed—displays of new releases, displays of puzzles, displays of crafts and makerspace projects. On Sunday afternoon, the place was hopping: the line of patrons waiting to check out materials doubled on itself twice, following a route laid out by retractable belt stanchions. The line for the computers, printers, and copiers was almost as long. One skinny white lady was holding a bloody bandage against her face with one hand and, in the other, what looked like her resume.

On my previous visits, I had relied on my animal magnetism, raw sex appeal, perfect body, and unstoppable charisma to find the books I needed, which—with the exception of my initial visit, when I had come to research the hashok—had been pure pleasure reading. I had never needed to use the card catalogue. If libraries still had card catalogues, which might have just been something on old TV shows and movies that Dag sometimes made me watch. I think Indiana Jones might have used a card catalogue once. I had never needed to do any library tasks on my own. But then, I had always come on weekday mornings, walking over from Dag's parents' house while we were still figuring out where to move. I'd never come on the weekends because, well, of all this.

The woman at the front of the circulation line was waving what appeared to be a valued-customer punch card for The Reef, which was a head shop on the edge of Moulinbas. Her voice was rising in outrage as I approached.

"—says right here who I am. Right here. Patricia Carter. See? So I want to check out these books."

The man behind the desk looked like he'd probably grown up with Herbert Hoover and Woodrow Wilson and all those guys. His hair was parted, but long enough to cover his ears, and it was a yellow color that reminded me of scalp creams and unwashed bedding. He was staring fixedly at a point somewhere beyond the woman.

"If you want a library card, you'll need a photo ID with your current address. If your photo ID does not list your current address, you will need to provide additional documentation in the form of utility bills, paycheck stubs, or certified mail to verify your place of residence."

"But it says right here, buy four bongs, get the fifth free, and then my name Patricia—"

"Excuse me," I said with a winning smile, a real knock-their-socks-off charmer. Hands off, ladies, I'm taken. "I just need some help finding a book."

"Help desk," the old man said and pointed.

The line for help looked at least thirty people long. One heavyset man was currently trying to wrangle a pudgy girl who had pulled her skirt over her head and a boy who was obviously an ankle-biter. Literally. The little guy had gotten his teeth in good.

I repressed a shudder. "Really quick, I'm looking for—"

"Excuse me," Patricia Carter said, snapping her fingers in my face. "I was here first."

"Right, but if he could just look something up for me—"

"Help desk," the librarian said.

"It says my name right here," Patricia said. "That's what I don't understand. It says my name—"

I leaned over the desk. "Any sort of book about hoodoo or New Orleans witchcraft."

"Valid photo ID includes the following—" the librarian tried.

"I have my ID. I have it right here. See? Patricia. Carter. Are you blind?"

"Even if you could just point me to the right section," I suggested.

"Will you buzz off?" Patricia asked me.

"Buzz off?" I asked.

"Security," the librarian wheezed. "Security. We have a hooligan. This is a code 090.1167."

A big-knuckled hand settled on my shoulder. This guy was wearing a white shirt with a patch sewn on the sleeves that said DUPAGE PARISH LIBRARY SECURITY. He had on a utility belt with Mace, handcuffs, a nightstick, and a walkie. The weight of the thing was dragging his black trousers down his chicken-bone shanks. He had to be at least a hundred years older than the guy behind the desk.

"Code 090.1167 confirmed," he mumbled. "Hooligan has been restrained."

"I'm being restrained?" I asked.

"Come with me, sir. If you resist, I will have to use commensurate force."

I'm not sure if it was the threat or the unreality of the whole spectacle, but I let myself be manhandled toward the door. As he steered me through the RFID gates, past the bulletin board—with its flyers for FREE POKEMON LESSONS and LEARN HOW TO SING BACKWARD and YOUR DONUTS OR YOUR LIFE: BREAK THE CYCLE, which actually sounded like something I needed to follow up on—the entire library population stared. A real-life Code 090.1167. You don't see that anymore, kids.

When I stumbled through the automatic doors, the guard gave a gasping, "And stay out!" and tottered back inside.

This, I thought. This is why people hate librarians.

Across the street, a jittery guy with thick, curly, shoulder-length blond hair was pacing and smoking a joint. The weed smelled skunky even at that distance. He kept looking over, glaring at me, and then his eyes would skitter away. A fellow Code 090.1167, I figured. This place was turning into hooligan central.

I made my way around the building. It was built on a hill, and the lower parking lot had a separate entrance to the bottom floor. Apparently the Code 090.1167 hadn't resulted in any BOLOs or Most Wanted posters with my picture on them, because no alarms sounded when I walked inside. This section of the library consisted of classrooms and, according to the signs, the DuPage Parish Genealogical Association's headquarters. The hallways were narrow, and the walls alternated between stylish cinderblock and even more stylish beech paneling. I checked doors as I went. I figured eventually I'd find somebody who'd take pity on this poor, dumb, hot piece of meat.

' I struck gold on the fourth door, which opened onto a large multipurpose room. Rows of chairs ran across the center of the room, and many of the seats were already occupied. The population was mostly white women, although I did see some black ladies, and two women I thought might be Mexican. Folding tables lined the walls. On some of the tables, bottles of wine stood next to plastic cups. On other tables, books were on display. On yet other tables, what looked like pieces of stained glass rested on easels. Everybody was chatting and seemed to be having a good time. The white ladies, in particular, seemed to be well on their way to drunk. One woman was flashing a sun hat that had the words SIP BACK AND RELAX embroidered on the brim.

But the real paydirt was Miss Kennedy. She was younger than everyone in the room but me—she probably had five years on me, although that was only a guess—and she was striking in a cornflower-blue halter-neck dress. She'd ditched her braids, and now her hair was short and textured. She had a smile that could have stopped a book truck. On my first visit, she had helped me find important information about the hashok, as well as some truly hot gay vampire books. On previous visits, she had continued to help me, although she was often doing annoyingly time-consuming things like reading to children and helping the elderly.

"Eli," she said as she came across the room. "I'm in the middle of Wine and Windows."

Swing for the fences, I thought. "You've got a smile that could stop a book truck."

"Go away."

A woman who had apparently had a little too much vino whispered loudly, "Look at that very attractive colored boy talking to Kennedy."

I frowned. "You're darker than me. Shouldn't she call you the colored girl?"

"I don't know," Kennedy whispered. "I don't care. Now leave."

"I need help finding a book."

"I'm busy. And you have fines. I had to mark that entire gay-FBI-werewolf series lost."

"I'm still reading it."

"You lost twenty books, Eli!"

"They're not lost. And twenty books are a lot; I'm still reading them. You don't get looks like these and a brain to match."

"I'm going to throw up."

"One really quick question. I promise I'll be so fast."

"No. I'm busy, and I'm doing something, and I've got things to do—"

"Those are all the same thing, which means you don't really have an excuse, which means you're stalling. I was going to ask for some help finding a book, but actually—" I slung the backpack down from my shoulder and opened it. As I pulled out the flannel bag, I continued, "—maybe you could help me with this?"

"Absolutely gorgeous," one of the white ladies was saying.

"He could interrupt me at work any day," another said with a gravelly noise that I realized, too late, was supposed to be a purr.

"Will you put that away?" Kennedy whispered ferociously, shoving the flannel bag into the backpack. She caught my arm and steered me toward the door.

"I've already done this once today," I said. "I'm officially a Code 090.1167."

"Of course that was you," she snapped. "I've already gotten four emails about it. It's going to take me a week to get Lester and Bert to stop strutting around."

"And that perky butt," one of the white ladies said behind us.

"Do you want to tell them that looking is free, but touching is going to cost them?" I asked as Kennedy shoved me into the hall. "Or should I?"

Kennedy answered by yanking the door shut. We were alone in the hallway. "I am so sick of this," she said. "Every damn time."

"Ok, I know I ask you for recommendations, but you really do know all the good gay books. Like that one with the doctor who was also a vampire but also a wizard, and he could do that thing where he changed shape after he'd already, you know, um, put it inside—"

"I'm talking about that!" She accompanied the whisper-shriek with a gesture at the bag. "Not every black woman knows hoodoo. Do you understand that? And not everyone in my family is interested in it. I don't care who my great-great-great-whatever was. I'm a nice, normal person with a nice, normal job, and if one more skinny-assed mixed boy shows up trying to get me to be a witch, I am going to shove a gay tentacle novel right up his return chute."

I blinked.

She took a breath.

Somewhere in the building, a machine kicked on, and its gentle humming filled the lower floor.

"Please don't do that," I said, "because those white ladies really seemed to like my return chute, and if Dag gets fed up with me, I'm going to have to sell this ten-out-of-ten smush machine to the highest bidder."

She let out a breath. "Eli, this is not a good time—"

"Wine and windows. Got it. Wait. Like, actual windows? Or books about windows?"

Her death-stare was level ten.

"Right," I said and swallowed. "Anyway, I didn't know you were secretly a witch or whatever you were yelling at me about. I just—you always help me find books, and something hinky is going on, and I wanted to know about—"

When I reached for the flannel bag, she caught my hand and shook her head. "Give me five minutes," she said with a sigh, "and meet me in the bookbinding room."

"Where's the bookbinding room?"

As she let herself back through the door, she snapped, "Learn how to read and figure it out."

A woman queried, "Miss Kennedy, where did your young friend—" and Kennedy slammed the door, which I figured was my cue.

I found the bookbinding room on the same floor, at the other end of the building. The door was locked, and since I didn't have any of Dag's bad habits, I had to wait for Kennedy. She took seven minutes instead of five, and she was carrying a courier bag over one shoulder. She made an aggravated noise when she saw me still in the hallway.

"It's locked," I protested.

"No talking," she said as she unlocked the door and shoved me inside.

The room was small, and it consisted of a table, two stools, and a wall of cabinets. I wasn't sure what I was expecting, but it smelled like fabric-backed tape and glue. Kennedy pointed to a stool, and I sat.

"If you wanted me to—"

"Does Dag let you get away with stuff like this? I said no talking."

"Most of the time he's a total softie, but—you know what? I'm going to stop talking."

Whatever she muttered under her breath, it didn't sound flattering. She drew out a large book, almost as big as the coffee-table books about windows that I'd seen in the multipurpose room. Unlike those, this one didn't have a glossy dust cover. It was bound in red velveteen, and where the fabric had worn thin, the wooden cover board showed through. A punch-tape label, white letters on black tape, said SAINTE-MARIE – 1860 PEARL STREET – BATON ROUGE, LA.

"This is a family book?" I asked.

"This is a pain in my behind. Let me see that flannel."

I took out the red bag. "I thought it was flannel, but I wasn't sure if that mattered—"

"The fabric is flannel, but the bag itself is also called a flannel. Or a mojo bag, but flannel is more common. Because of the material for the bag. You know, metonymy."

"Right. Metonymy."

"Ask Dag to find it in the encyclopedia for you."

I raised my eyebrows.

She let out a breath. After a moment, she said, "I'm sorry. I don't like...this. Any of it. And I don't like being responsible for it."

"What do you mean?"

Instead of answering, she took the flannel from me. She examined the dime on the string. She opened it and looked at the heart-shaped leaves, which crackled softly under her touch, and the rusted iron nails. "Where'd you find this?"

I told her.

Her expression didn't change. She asked, "Last year, when you came to me with a story about a TV-show monster, what was happening?"

I took a breath, considered the old book and the way she had known, instantly, what the flannel was. Then I told her that too.

Her expression didn't change at this information either, which considering the content—monsters and murder and all of it—really said something for her upbringing. When I'd finished, she nodded slowly. "This is protective work. Cold iron can be a shield or a weapon. In this case, it's a shield—it's meant to keep a spirit from bothering the residents of a home."

I tried to turn that over in my head. "Would it work?"

"It depends on the spirit. For the most part, yes. If they're strong enough, no." She looked physically ill. "If we weren't talking about a murdered woman, I'd ask you to drop this. I'm not looking to get back into the life."

"What kind of spirit? Is it possible that Ivy knew this thing, the hashok, was after her? Was she trying to protect herself?"

"She was certainly trying to protect herself from something. But I can't tell you exactly what—not right now, maybe not ever. Hashok, fifolet, lutin, rougarou, ghost dogs—"

"Ghost dogs?"

"Did I stutter?"

"Um. No. No, you did not."

She sighed. "This isn't exactly a science. I'll look through the book, but coffin nails and High John the Conqueror and a silver dime on a string are pretty common ingredients. A lot of the particular effect depends on the energy that someone puts into the bag, the direction they give it."

"That's pretty woo-woo," I said.

"Tell me about it." Grimacing, she turned the bag inside out. A few brown flakes tumbled onto the table—dried, broken bits from the leaves—and then I saw the symbol that had been brushed onto the inside of the flannel in India ink: a zagging line surrounded by an octagon.

"Does that tell you anything? Is that a lightning bolt? Are octagons powerful symbols?"

She rolled her eyes and turned the bag. "It's an N."

"It could be a Z."

"It's not."

"How do you know?"

"Because I know the witch who made this—by reputation, anyway. She goes by Nelda Pie. The octagon is for the juke joint she runs, the Stoplight."

"A good witch?" I asked in probably too hopeful tones.

"Not exactly," Kennedy said drily as she repacked the flannel. Weighing the dime on her palm, she added, "She might tell you what that woman wanted protection from. She might not. I'd tell you to stay clear of her, but you're already swimming with the current on this one, aren't you?"

"Swimming with the gators is more like it."

"You don't even know." She snapped the thread attaching the dime to the bag, and then she tied it around my neck. She tucked the coin under my shirt. The silver was cold against my chest. "Wear it. And get one for that dummy who hasn't found anyone better yet. Silver. Before 1965."

"Miss Kennedy, I almost think you care."

"Consider it protecting my interests. You owe a lot of money in late fees."

I reached out to touch the worn red velveteen, then I stopped myself. "Could I borrow this? I didn't want to drag you into this mess. I didn't even think you'd believe me, let alone that you were secretly a witch—"

"I'm not a witch," she said, slapping my hand when I reached for the book again. "And I'm not involved. And no, you can't borrow that." With a bracing breath, she shook her head. "But because it's the twenty-first century, I scanned it and have a PDF of the whole thing."

"And you'll send it to me?"

"No, I'm telling you so that you'll appreciate my archival prowess."

"I'm super gay, but I think I might be into you yelling at me."

"Goodbye, Eli."

"Wait, wait, wait. You'll email me a copy of the book?"

Her nod seemed somehow defeated.

"And maybe you could talk to Dag about the yelling thing? I've tried to tell him to be meaner to me, but he just doesn't get it. If you gave him some pointers, like, when he and I were having our special time—Miss Kennedy, hold on, the gay werewolf books, I think there's a spinoff—"

She slammed the door to the bookbinding room so hard that I felt the breeze.

I gave her enough time to get a head start, and then I let myself out. The October sky had hardened to steel, and if anything, the day seemed colder, but I had a tight smile on my face as I made my way around the building. For the first time since Amrey had called Dag, we had a lead. Something to follow. Now I just had to figure out who Nelda Pie was and where the Stoplight—

"Hey, you!"

The tone was asking for a fight, and the words made me stop and look.

His mane of blond hair stirred in the breeze as he marched across the parking lot toward me. It was the guy I'd seen smoking a joint across the street earlier, my fellow Code 090.1167. As he got closer, I could make out a bruise darkening his temple, partially hidden by his hair. I glanced around, but the parking lot was empty aside from the two of us. I looked back, trying to place him. I didn't think I'd met him before, and my brain was suggesting increasingly unlikely possibilities: a former neighbor I didn't remember; somebody whose car I'd accidentally scratched; a guy I'd made out with in a club, in the back-before times.

"Yeah," he shouted, although he was close enough now that he didn't need to. "You!"

Me, master of repartee: "Me?"

"I want to talk to you."

Me, genius conversationalist: "Do we know each—"

Before I could finish the question, he took a swing. I stepped back. My heel hit a parking stop, and my stumble kept me from having my nose flattened. The punch missed my face by an inch.

Adrenaline kicked in, and I reacted. I brought my foot up and got him between the legs, and he made a whuffing noise. His knees turned in slightly, cartoon style, and he stumbled. His hip checked a white Impala. Then he slid down the side, humped the tire, and landed on his ass.

"Lanny?" Running steps underscored Dag's voice, and I looked up to see him sprinting towards us. "E, are you—"

"Fine. I'm fine."

He pulled me into a hug and then shoved me behind him. "Lanny, I knew that was you. What the hell are you doing?"

"I think," I said, studying the gray-green cast to Lanny's face, "he's about to be sick."

I was right.

DAG (4)

"That's assault, Lanny," I said. Eli touched my arm, and out of the corner of my eye, I was aware of library patrons—the Scrabble crowd, to judge by the board games they carried under their arms—milling at the edge of the parking lot and watching us. I tried to bring my voice down. "What in God's name were you thinking? That's ninety days in the parish jail. That's probation. And that's after I beat the shit out of you for laying a finger on Eli."

Lanny moaned and cupped his 'nads.

"Not that I don't appreciate this," Eli said quietly, "and, as a matter of fact, I was just thinking about how you could work on your yelling, but we might want to take this elsewhere."

At his gesture, I glanced up. A centenarian in a security guard's uniform was consulting the Scrabble mob, apparently deciding if he needed to use the Mace that was attached to the utility belt currently dragging his trousers down.

"Get your butt up," I growled, grabbing Lanny's arm and hauling him to his feet. "I honestly cannot believe you."

Lanny did some more groaning, but he stumbled along, managing to stay upright as I gripped his biceps and propelled him down the street. "I think he kicked one of them up inside me," he whimpered.

"Good," I said. "You deserve it."

Eli was looking unbearably satisfied, so I turned to him and said, "Don't think we're not going to talk about this later."

"Me? I'm the victim."

"Don't start with me," I snapped.

Which, in hindsight, I realized should have made him mad, but instead Eli only looked even more pleased.

This was my luck.

These were the men in my life.

Much more of this, I figured, and I would need to start thinking about going that whole ultra-Christian route and getting made a virgin all over again.

My parents' house was half a mile away, but I'd left the Escort parked on the next block. When I'd been dropping Eli off at the library, I'd been sure that I'd seen Lanny following us. The worry in my gut had turned into certainty by the time I was turning onto my parents' street, so I'd doubled back, parked a street over, and walked around the block to see if I'd been right. Which was approximately when I'd seen Eli kick Lanny's junk into orbit.

"Doggo, baby," Lanny said, still probing for damage. "I can't walk."

By then we'd reached the Escort, so I opened the back door and shoved him into the car.

"Baby?" Eli said.

"I told you not to start with me, Eli Prescott Martins."

"Oh," Lanny said from the back seat. "Middle name. You're in trouble."

I slammed the door on him, muffling his cry of outrage.

Eli's eyebrows were up, and they climbed higher as I pulled him against me. For a moment, his body was stiff. Then he relaxed.

I stroked his blowout hair. "Did he hurt you?"

He laughed, and his arms tightened around me.

"What happened?" I asked.

So he told me. Part of it.

"And are you ready to tell me why you were in such a hurry to get rid of me," I asked, "so you could go to the library alone?"

"I told you, I wanted a book—"

"Before you break our rule about lying, I'm going to tell you that I know you have that flannel bag in my backpack."

Eli squirmed out of my arms. The backpack hung from one shoulder, and he clutched it to his chest now.

"Well?" I asked.

"That's really fucking annoying."

"I'm still waiting for an answer."

"Did you ever think I might have a good reason for not telling you? Did that idea ever fucking make its way through your skull?"

"Please don't talk to me like that."

"Why can't we have one fight? Why can't we have one goddamn fight?"

"This feels like a fight to me."

"A big one. A blow-up one. Where you say all sorts of terrible things to me and you rip me to pieces?"

"Why would I do that? I'd never do that to you."

Lanny rapped on the glass and shouted, "He doesn't fight like that."

"Be quiet," I said, and Lanny's face filled with outrage.

Eli threw him the bird. He shrugged the bag higher up his shoulder. Then he wiped his arm across his face.

"Do you want a hug?" I asked.

He nodded, and I drew him close. His head fit in the curve of my shoulder.

"Are we still fighting?" I asked.

He offered a microscopic shake of his head. Then he said, "I was doing it for you, dummy," and he told me the rest of it.

When he finished, I let him wriggle away, but I grabbed his hand before he could go too far. "We're together, Eli. I love you. That means we help each other with our problems. We don't try to do things alone. That's why we have the rules, right? And that's why you're not going to handle this new hashok all by yourself." A tiny grin slipped out. "And that's why when one of us is trying to watch *Shark Week*, the other one doesn't come in and say, 'This is the stupidest thing I've ever seen,' and then try to pick a fight for half an hour because he's feeling neglected."

He wiped his face again, but he rolled his eyes. The green in the hazel caught the light, as bright as the sun through oak leaves. He hadn't shaved, but he barely had any stubble to begin with, and it made him look like somebody had just called, "Cut!" on the set of a CW show, like the kind Sal might be in.

"And him," Eli finally said.

I fought the urge to look over at the car.

"Yes, sir," Eli said. "You know what I mean. If I'm not going to handle a monster on my own, neither are you."

"Fair enough."

"Especially if he's going to assault me in a parking lot."

"I said all right. Don't get me all riled up again."

"The only time I've ever seen you riled up was that night we got the hotel in Baton Rouge and I used those scarves—"

My face caught on fire at approximately that moment, and I made some kind of noise and looked at the car. Lanny made a circling motion with one finger: *keep going*. Eli, mercifully, cleared his throat and finished, "Never mind."

"He likes it when you deep-throat him," Lanny shouted through the glass, hammering on the window a few times for emphasis. "He can come like that."

"Shut up, Lanny," I said.

"Sure," Eli said with what sounded like petulance, "you'll tell him to shut up."

I squeezed his fingers. "I love you."

He rolled his eyes again. He kicked the sidewall of the rear tire. He mumbled something.

"Not a chance," I said. "To my face."

"I love you," he snapped, his eyes coming up to mine just long enough to meet the requirements. "But God, you are really annoying sometimes."

"I can live with that," I said. "So, we need to find this woman, Nelda Pie?"

"I know Nelda Pie!" Lanny shouted.

"I think that makes sense," Eli said. "She made those flannels we found, and she was trying to provide Ivy with some kind of protection."

"From the hashok?"

"From something." Eli shivered, and I chafed his arms.

"I know Nelda Pie," Lanny shouted again. "Hey! Doggo! Hey, Doggo! Baby, I know her!"

"Or we could start with the juke joint," Eli said. "The Stoplight. She owns it or runs it or something."

"Both," Lanny called through the glass. "Hey, can you guys hear me? Hey! Hey! I'm talking to you! She owns it and she runs it."

I was on my phone. "It doesn't show up when I search for it. I could call some of the deputies; it sounds like the kind of place that somebody would have to know about."

"Yeah, you piney-woods-loving, cane-fishing, dick-like-a-fireplug fucking dumbass. I know about it. I'm telling you right now!" He slammed his palm against the glass. "Somebody pay attention to me."

"Please don't make me," I said to Eli.

He was trying to look nice, but he didn't have much practice, and the smile still managed to slip through and shine in his eyes. "I'll handle him."

With a sigh, I opened the rear door. Lanny scooted to the edge of the seat, but when he tried to get out, I put a hand on his head and pushed him back in. He made a noise of protest and swatted my hand away, but he stayed on the bench.

"You wanted to talk," Eli said. "So talk. What do you know about this woman called Nelda Pie, and how do we get to the Stoplight?"

ELI (5)

The problem, I was starting to realize, wasn't getting Lanny Fontenot to talk. The problem was getting him to shut the hell up.

"And that's where Doggo and I took out a couple of pirogues and went fishing but mostly just ended up giving each other fivers—no, wait, you didn't look. Doggo, turn around so E can see what I'm talking about."

Dag hunched lower over the steering wheel, his face grim, and accelerated.

I was trying to be a Good Boyfriend—or whatever we were calling it—which at that moment meant two things: not committing felony manslaughter, and not laughing out loud. I rubbed Dag's back, and he flashed me a grateful look before returning his attention to the road.

"I bet you guys haven't gone fishing, have you?" Lanny asked. He was leaning back against the seat—no seat belt, of course, even after three solid minutes of Dag yelling—and he kept working his hand under his shirt to scratch his stomach and, in the process, flash washboard abs with a scattering of gold hair. He didn't seem very smart, and he definitely wasn't subtle, but God, he was hot. A kind of white-trash gay-boy kryptonite.

"Be quiet," I said.

"You guys want to fuck around?" he asked, and Dag swerved hard.

When I looked over, Dag grunted and had the decency to blush as he muttered, "Chuckhole."

"Eyes on the road," Lanny said with a laugh. "I can't handle that beer can you call a cock without some stretching anyway. But E's real pretty. You want to blow me? I bet we got enough time."

"First you want to knock my block off," I said. "Then you want me to get your rocks off. That's a pass."

In a tone of injured dignity, he said, "I'd'a fingered you. It wouldn't just be me getting off."

"Such a gentleman. Pay attention, Lanny. If you get us lost, we'll drop you off and find our own way back."

"Hey, there's the place we got all that ice, the time we took the fan boat out. Boy, that guy was mad."

"Because you told me you had rented it," Dag said. "Because you tricked me into stealing it."

"Ah, he was fine. He got his boat back, didn't he?"

"Make him stop talking," Dag pleaded in a whisper.

"I like learning about this master criminal I'm involved with," I said. "I had no idea I was sleeping with a felon."

"I'm not a felon!" With an obvious struggle, Dag brought his voice down. "It was a fan boat. It would have been a misdemeanor."

"How long have you two been boyfriends?" Lanny asked.

"Oh Lord, it might have been a felony," Dag said in an underbreath. "It was a pretty nice boat."

"It's kind of cute," Lanny said. "Doggo always wanted a boyfriend."

"Weren't you his boyfriend?" I asked.

Lanny rocked back in his seat. He blinked. "Huh. I never thought about it like that before."

"Really? That didn't occur to you all those times you were stretching yourself for that King Kong dick?"

"Eli, cut it out," Dag said. His voice was tight, and the blush had concentrated to red circles in each cheek. "Lanny, shut up unless you're telling us something useful."

Lanny's expression was injured. "I just asked if you two are boyfriends, and then he got a stick up his ass and you got all butt hurt, and I don't know what I did that's so bad. It's not like I stole somebody's fan boat."

Dag groaned and slammmed his head a few times on the steering wheel.

"Well?" Lanny asked.

"Yes," I said. "We're in a relationship. For almost a year now."

"In a relationship. I'm in a relationship with my mawmaw. I'm in a relationship with Donnie, and he's my dildo. I'm asking if you're boyfriends."

In the gap that followed, the only sound was the thrum of the tires and the old Ford's constant rattling—something loose in the dash, a clinical part of my mind guessed. Hot prickles worked their way across my chest, under my arms, up my neck.

Dag was watching me, and after a moment, he must have decided to take pity because he twisted to look over his shoulder. "We're not putting a label on it. Drop it."

"I don't know why everybody's got to have their dicks out of joint over a simple question—you got to turn right here."

Swearing, Dag braked. The Ford's tires squealed, caught the gravel shoulder, and spun up rocks and dust. He made the turn onto the dirt road, but only barely, and we bounced hard across the baked-in ruts. The Ford's suspension groaned before the road smoothed out—relatively speaking, anyway.

On our right, oaks and bald cypresses shaded the backside of Bayou Pere Rigaud, where the waters were a cement-green color. Spanish moss drifted in the breeze. It was early afternoon, but the shadows seemed long. At Lanny's direction, we had driven to the far side of the parish. Uncomfortably close, in fact, to where I had once lived with Richard. In the same general area where Muriel had lived. And not too far, in a straight line anyway, from Ivy Honsord's trailer.

I kept my gaze on the shadows dappling the water because it was better than looking at Lanny or, to tell the truth, Dag. Something—a wire or a cord—was strung between the cypresses, dropping just below the gray-green surface, and I tried to follow it with my eyes. A blue Clorox bottle floated to mark the submerged line.

"Trotline," Dag said quietly, and it felt like an olive branch. "They've got baited hooks underwater. They're not legal anymore, but a lot of the old-timers still use them. Some young guys too, I guess. It's a way of life."

"Bunch of dumbass rednecks," Lanny said. "What you got to do is hook up some of them yo-yo reels. That's the way to do it."

"Those are illegal too," Dag said. "And stop talking."

"That's all horseshit anyway. Who the hell cares about legal or illegal? It's a goddamn fishing line. It's not like I'm hurting anybody."

"It's hurting a lot of people, actually. Those kinds of fishing techniques contribute to overfishing, which is affecting whole ecosystems—"

"Oh Lord," Lanny said, and I looked back in time to see the roll of his eyes. He smirked at me. "Here we go."

"You know what—" Dag began.

I put a hand on his shoulder. "Why don't you tell us about Nelda?"

"It's Nelda Pie." He stressed the last syllable. "And she'll tell you if you forget."

"All right. What do you know about Nelda Pie?"

"She's one tough cookie, that's what. One time, I seen her use a metal spatula to take the skin off a man's back."

"Jesus," Dag said.

"This poor guy, he couldn't walk right. Something wrong with his feet—looked like he was wearing them shoes the doctor gives poor kids sometimes when their feet ain't straight. Doggo, you know what I mean? And he was stumbling and knocking into things the whole night. Well, finally he came out with a tub full of Cold Duck, iced down for the rednecks, and he dropped it. Broke every damn bottle. And Nelda Pie came flying out of the kitchen. She still had the spatula in her hand, and she started whipping that boy with it. He didn't fight or nothing. Just stayed there on his hands and knees and took it. Just about took his shirt off, and the blood coming up real bad. I bet that boy didn't ever drop a tub of Cold Duck again."

I looked at Dag, who shook his head slowly.

"She's got dog fights," Lanny said wistfully. "She's got music. Nothing good—that old blues crap, delta stuff, and sometimes zydeco or rockabilly, them guys still doing their hair like Elvis. But at least it's live. And you never pay more than a couple dollars for a drink. And you can buy pretty good grass, Oxy, some harder stuff if you want. Oh, and she's got a couple trailers out back, and there's girls if you want, but there's also a couple boys, and one of them got these blue eyes like a Husky, damn near prettiest thing I ever seen." The car bounced over another chuckhole, and Lanny mugged for the rearview mirror, where Dag was glaring at him. "'Cept for you, I mean."

"Shit," I said. "I knew it sounded familiar."

Dag glanced over, then looked ahead again when a low branch scraped the top of the car.

"The Stoplight. Ivy's neighbor, Jeannette, she mentioned it. Remember? She said Roger liked going there for the dog fights."

"Gosh dang it," Dag muttered.

"I never seen 'em," Lanny said wistfully. "You got to get invited, but you can hear 'em sometimes, snarling and yelping. Real crazy noises. You'd think they was killing each other."

"They're trying to," I said. "That's the whole point. That's why it's barbaric and cruel and one of the lowest things you could ever be part of."

Lanny gave a philosophical shrug. "Well, yeah. But it sure gets your blood up, don't it?"

After a moment, I managed to close my mouth and look away.

"Anything else you want to tell us?" Dag asked.

"She got a girl with three titties," Lanny announced promptly. When we both flashed him identical looks, he said, "She do. I never seen her, but my buddy is into that. You know, the pussy. And he told me about it. And the guy who sweeps the floor, he's got them fingers with the skin between them, so he looks like a frog or a fish or something. And one time I gone looking for the trough, but I got the wrong door, and I swear I saw this thing, big old thing like a cat, only it was big as a man and mounting this woman, and she weren't no cat, and it had cut her back to ribbons with its claws." After a moment, he added doubtfully, "I'd done a couple of tabs that night, though, and I was tripping pretty hard."

"You dated this guy?" I asked Dag.

"I don't want to talk about it."

"I'm a great lay," Lanny said. "And Doggo and I got a real connection. Don't we, Doggo?"

"No," he gritted out. "We don't."

"You felt it, though. I could tell. When we was talking. You're with this pretty boy now, but you still felt it. You just about said so last time."

"Are you insane? I didn't say anything like that." Dag turned to me and repeated, "I didn't say anything like that."

"It was more how you said it, I guess."

"No, it wasn't. Shut up."

"I been thinking about what you said. I want you to know that. I'm going to figure out how to make things up to you so we can get together again because I figure you're just about the best thing that ever happened to me."

"We're not getting together again. Ever. In fact, I never want to see you again. Starting right now."

"It's destiny," Lanny told me. "Sorry."

"Thanks" was the only response I could come up with.

Lanny nodded with a kind of bizarrely genteel compassion and said, "Turn in here."

We almost missed the oyster-shell parking lot, which was barely visible in an opening in the weeds to our left. Dag braked hard, swearing again, and shells crunched under the tires. The juke joint was a plank shack on stilts. It sprawled backward, the full extent of the building hidden by the tall grasses and the occasional tree, and it was much larger than I had expected. Whoever had built it had obviously never heard of a level or a square—every plank looked cut by hand, and they fit together poorly, with chinks and gaps everywhere, some of them as big as my thumb. The roof was half wood shingles and half tar paper, with a rotting roll of the paper still up there, as though someone had given up the job partway through and never gone back. The gallery on the front was sunken and slightly slanted, which gave the impression that anyone who risked the rickety benches out front might tumble right off the structure. Instead of a name, the only indication that this was the place was a red octagon painted above the door, the paint flaking and uneven.

"Jesus," I said.

"It don't look like much."

"It looks like I'm going to need a tetanus shot after I walk in there."

"Oh. Yeah, I suppose it wouldn't hurt."

"Come on," Dag said. "I want to get this over with."

"Well, uh, about that," Lanny said.

"Are you kidding me?"

"I wasn't trying to cause any trouble, Doggo. I made a mistake."

"You didn't pay after you tupped the Husky boy."

"Come on."

"You swiped drinks from another table."

Lanny pushed a hand through his thick, golden tangle of hair. He offered a huge smile. "Doggo—"

"Oh my God, I was close. You did a dine and dash."

"I don't think this place qualifies as dining," I said.

"You know what I mean," Dag said. To Lanny, he said, "You didn't pay for your drinks."

"I...Doggo, I just left my tab open, but then things got complicated, and—"

"God damn it." Dag threw open the door too hard, and it rocked back. He had to push it open again as he climbed out of the Ford. "This is why I can't go to half the restaurants I like. Because this—this cheat kept telling me he'd paid the check when I went to the restroom."

He slammed the door to punctuate the sentence.

"Boy," Lanny said, rubbing the back of his neck. He flashed that smile again, and something struck me. A memory. Or something like a memory, but it was gone before I could catch it. "I mean, when he goes on a tear, right?"

"Lanny, I'm not exactly on your side."

His brow wrinkled. "How come?"

I decided that was a good time to get out of the car. Lanny apparently did too, and Dag said, "What are you doing?"

"Oh, well, I heard the last guy who ran out on the check, well, she nailed him to the bar by his sack. I believe it too. It was Jamall Stevens. Or maybe that guy Emile, remember him, who I did coke with a few times?"

Dag stared. Then he turned and started up the steps. The wooden treads flexed under his weight.

"Wait in the car," I said.

"That's what I'm saying." Lanny was staring after Dag, confusion painting his face. "What if somebody sees me? So I think I'll just wander over there—" He gestured to the thick growth of weeds and grasses. "—and play it, you know, safe."

"Fine," I said. "Go pet a water moccasin or something. Just don't blow this."

Dag was waiting for me on the gallery, and before I could say something, he jerked the door open and indicated with his head for me to go inside.

A wall of darkness met me, carrying the smell of rye mash, stagnant dishwater, and sun-hot wood. I stumbled on the first step, where an uneven board caught my tennis shoe. By the time I recovered myself, my eyes had adjusted to the juke, and I could make out my surroundings.

It was bigger than I expected, and the only light came from red bulbs overhead that must have been a play on the Stoplight's name, giving everything a darkroom glamour that only seemed to deepen the shadows everywhere else. A bar ran along one side of the room; on the shelves behind it, bottles glinted and winked, and two ancient aluminum signs suggested buying Dr Pepper and 7 Up for five cents. Spool tables filled most of the rest of the room, with overturned fruit crates for seating. LOUISIANA FIG AND DATE said the one closest to me, with a faded logo on the side that must at one time have meant something to someone. The only open spaces were the stage at the far end, currently unoccupied, and what I guessed was a dance floor directly in front of the platform, marked by peel-and-stick vinyl tiles in checkerboard black and white.

On a Sunday afternoon, the juke was busy but not yet full, the patrons mostly men, a mixture of white, black, and mixed-race people, with a few women who either looked dead-eyed or terrified. A man with cataract-white eyes was spitting into a Skol tin—thick, foamy spit that made it look like he was having a fit of some kind. A woman with hair to her waist clip-clopped across the room in a skirt long enough to hide her feet. A middle-aged woman in hot pants and a Mickey Mouse sweatshirt was waiting tables, looking oddly unbalanced with her chicken legs and heavy top. A kid who had to be younger than me played pinfinger at a table by himself; the tip of his nose had been cut off, and he'd lost two fingers at the first knuckle. Some sort of twanging blues played from hidden speakers. On a CRT television mounted above the bar, what looked like a grainy boxing match was underway. The chyron at the bottom of the screen was boxy and ancient, and I wondered what we were looking at— something from before I was born, I guessed. For the first time I noticed the musty, animal smell. It reminded me of a kennel in need of cleaning, and it underlay everything else.

Dag nudged me toward the bar, and when I took my first step, I saw the man behind it giving us the eye. He was darker than me, fit, with a skin fade that accentuated the powerful muscles in his neck, and he couldn't have been much older than Dag. He had a prosthetic hand. The thumb had been replaced with a bottle opener, and someone had drawn an arrow on the polymer hand toward the tool with the words USE ME! in letters big enough to see while we were still a yard out from the bar.

"We're looking for Nelda Pie," Dag said.

The bartender's eyes stayed on me. He shifted his weight and looked me up and down. Dag put a hand on my shoulder. The expression that flickered around the bartender's mouth wasn't exactly a smile, but there was something amused in it as he picked up a glass and started drying it.

"We're looking for—"

"I heard you. You can buy a drink, or you can get out."

"Fine," I said. "I'll take a beer. Two beers, actually."

He wore that expression again as he reached below the bar and came up with two sweating brown bottles. The white-and-gold label said Jax. Dag stared at them, so I threw down two fives. The bartender scooped them up, tapped them against the wood to line up the edges, and folded them around one finger. He had crinkles around his eyes when he looked up at me again.

As I steered Dag toward an open table, I said, "I hate men. Just so you know."

He took one of the beers from me and turned it in his hand.

"Dag."

"What?"

"I hate men."

"Uh huh."

"That guy was, you know, giving me a look."

He made a noise of agreement and then took a drink.

"Go beat him up," I said, mostly because I hadn't made Dag's life difficult in the last four minutes.

"They don't even make Jax beer anymore," he said, mostly to himself.

I frowned. "What?"

He spun the bottle so that the label faced me. "They haven't made this beer in fifty years."

"Oh. Gross."

"It tastes fine."

I took a drink. "It tastes like beer, so, gross."

"What the hell is this place?"

"Dag, focus. We need to find Nelda Pie, and then I want to get out of here. Before I have to make a decision about switching boyfriends." I hurried to add, "Or whatever we're calling it."

"Uh huh—wait, what?"

I rolled my eyes and studied the room. Behind the stage, an even darker hallway led off the red-lit room, and I remembered the sprawl of the building I had sensed when we'd driven up. I didn't want to go back there. I didn't want to know what was back there; what was up here was enough to give me nightmares and therapy bills for the next decade. Then I saw her.

She sat to the side of the stage, cocooned by shadows, in a black dress that reminded me of Civil War widows in daguerreotypes. Her thick, graying hair was gathered into a massive bun. Her mouth was pinched and oddly distended, as though she were packing chew or had suffered some sort of injury to her jaw. She was watching everything, her gaze unsettled and roving.

"Dag," I said.

He followed my gaze and frowned.

"I'm going to talk to her."

He caught my wrist.

"That's got to be her, right? She's got spooky witch vibes out the wazoo. I mean, in her case, that might be literal."

The Civil War lady had noticed me and was staring now.

"I'll be right back," I said. "You keep an eye—"

"It's not her."

"It won't hurt to ask."

"It might," he said. If anything, his grip tightened. "They're afraid of her. Hell, E, I'm afraid of her. But she's not in charge of this room."

"What?"

"Look around. Who's in charge of this room?"

I looked around. The woman in the long skirt was clip-clopping back across the room, and now I could see that under the long skirt, there was something wrong with her hips and legs—their shape was distorted, disfigured under the fabric. The pinfinger boy had laid down his knife and was crying into his beer. Behind the bar, the bartender was talking to a skinny white boy who wore his golden hair in an undercut and then slicked back. The way they stood, their bodies aligned but not meeting, wrote their whole story into the space around them. Then the white boy turned, and the palest blue eyes I'd ever seen fixed on me with startling ferocity.

Dag squeezed, and I followed his line of sight to the woman in the hot pants and the Mickey Mouse sweatshirt. Top heavy, with bony legs, she had a peroxide-blond bouffant and full, fleshy features striped and highlighted with all the Avon primary colors. Daffy Duck tinkled when she moved.

And Dag was right, I realized. People bobbed their heads when she talked. They looked at the ground. The room's interest and attention followed her like she was guiding them with a road flare. Even the bartender and his little blond boytoy were clearly attuned to her movement as they continued their private spat.

"How did you do that?" I asked.

Dag shrugged. His face looked red, but the whole room looked red, so it might not have meant anything.

"No," I said, "seriously."

"You do that job enough," he said with another shrug, glancing away, "and you start to learn some stuff, I guess. Not that I was any good at it, but even a stopped clock, you know."

I did know. I wanted to kiss him, but I didn't want the taste of this place in our mouths, so I settled for squeezing his hand.

When I looked up, she was standing there. "Now you boys already have drinks, and I like to see that, but how about something else? We've got oysters on the half shell, or an étouffée you'd kill your momma for, but the house specialty," she pronounced the word like a delicacy, each syllable exaggerated, "is the *gratons*, which we make ourselves." Her bright smile caught the glare of red light. "I ought to know; I skinned that pig myself."

"We're looking for Nelda Pie," I said.

"Well, isn't that something?"

"You," Dag said so quietly that it was barely audible over the piped-in music. "We're looking for you."

Her face didn't change, except possibly to grow more rigid. After a moment, she said, "If he sent you boys, thinking I'd pay, you can tell him he's a fool. Get out of my joint before I make you leave."

"I don't know what you're talking about or who you have us confused with," I said as I pulled the flannel out of Dag's backpack. "But I came here for this. Tell us about this. Or, if you want, you can tell the police."

She considered us for a moment. Something warped in her expression—wariness became something else, something she was trying to hide. Something like hunger. That bright smile returned. "Isn't this interesting?" she said to herself, settling at the table. Her eyes fixed on me. "Little half-blood, what are you, exactly?"

I stared at her.

"I don't know what year you think it is," Dag said in that same quiet tone. "And I don't know what year you wish it was, but it's the twenty-first fucking century, and you aren't going to talk to him like that or use language like that again. Do you understand me?"

Nelda Pie's gaze shifted to him. Then she laughed, one hand to her chest, fingers splayed in a pose that would have been some acting coach's wet dream. "Oh my," she said. "I love it when they're protective." Then her gaze slid back to me, and before I could react, she snatched my hand and clutched it. "What are you, little half-breed? What indeed?"

The effect was instantaneous: the silver dime strung around my neck went cold, and frozen fire spread through my neck and shoulder and down one arm. The ice working its way through my body was familiar: the year before, when Richard—the hashok—had attacked me, he had bitten me. Several times, actually. On the shoulder and neck. And each time, he had injected some kind of venom. It had felt like this, burning and numbing, a cold blaze.

With a startled breath, Nelda Pie released my hand almost as quickly as she'd taken it. The sensation of frozen silver vanished, but the echo of the venom continued, a pain that was so intense it was almost anesthetic. Or maybe the other way around.

"Eli?"

I shook my head.

"What happened? Are you ok?"

I found his hand and squeezed it again. The freezing heat was fading.

"What the hell did you do to him?" Dag demanded.

"What are you?" Nelda Pie whispered, and I couldn't tell if the tone was excitement or fear.

I wiped my mouth with my free hand. I expected to find blood; I could taste pennies on my tongue. But my fingers were clean. I nudged the flannel toward her and said, "Us. Or the police."

After a moment, her posture relaxed. She smiled once more, and her lipstick looked cracked and waxy, flakes of it speckling her teeth. Then she opened the flannel and spread its contents out across the table. She turned the bag inside out and inspected the sigil on the inside. She nodded.

"Yes," she said. "I made this."

"Who did you make it for?"

"I have no idea."

"Really?" Dag asked.

"Positutely."

"I find that hard to believe."

"Yes," she said. "You seem rather limited. Unlike this one."

"Don't look at him," Dag said. "I'm talking to you. Look at me. I think you know who bought this bag off you."

"I don't sell them," Nelda Pie said with a roll of one shoulder. "They're gifts. I have a touch of the gift, and so I give freely as well."

"I've heard this before. Favors and gifts and trades. Who was this bag for?"

"I don't know. I'm telling you, I make dozens of these in a year. It's nothing harmful. Little charms. Protection. Attraction. Nothing nasty."

"What's your relationship with Ivy Honsord?"

The fat around her eyes rippled and folded as she frowned. "Who?"

"I think you know who. I think she came to you wanting protection."

"I'm sorry," Nelda Pie said, still frowning. "I just don't know. I have so many friends."

I was suddenly aware of the silence. Not true silence, because someone was still announcing the boxing match in a tinny voice, and a guitar and a harmonica were still competing over the hidden speakers, but relative silence. Every other person in the bar had gone still and was watching us.

"Friends who are worried," Nelda Pie said, "about my well-being. And my peace of mind."

Clutching Dag's hand under the table, I gave it a jerk toward the door.

His expression didn't shift from Nelda Pie's. "Have you ever heard of a hashok?"

The shock in her face was total before the mask dropped into place again. Then she looked at me, her eyes so intent that it felt like she was looking through me. "Well, well, well. The thing in the grass. Is that so?"

"So," Dag said, "you have heard of it?"

"It's time for you to leave," Nelda Pie said.

"What did Ivy Honsord want from you?"

"Either I can walk you out, or my friends can."

"Did she want protection from a hashok?"

Nelda Pie's smile was taut as she rose.

"Did she say she was in danger? Did she tell you anything?"

"I suppose it will be my friends. Rene, Posey. These young men—"

"What is the flannel supposed to protect against?" I asked. "And I'll tell you what you want to know."

Chairs scraped back. Boots hit the boards. But Nelda Pie raised a hand, and the movement stopped. She touched the flannel, and the nails clinked against each other.

"Do you know what a lutin is?"

I shook my head.

"A trickster," Dag said. "Like an elf or a goblin. Something that plays pranks."

"A spirit," she said. "But yes, you're mostly right. They love their games. I don't know anything about this Ivy woman, but this is a flannel designed to...deter a lutin from causing trouble. They don't like cold iron; a lot of spirits don't. There would have been other flannels, one at each corner of the house. That's how I place them. I do it myself, understand? When I do my friends a favor." She turned her whole body to me. "Now you."

I struggled with the words. Richard's arms, tight around me. The helplessness. His teeth puncturing skin. His hands pulling down my pants, fingers spreading me open.

"You don't have to—" Dag began.

"It bit me."

"More than once?" Nelda's voice was sharp, but low and professional.

I nodded.

"And the purge and washings?"

I glanced at Dag, but his expression showed only confusion. When I looked back at Nelda Pie, I said, "I went to the hospital."

Her face went blank with surprise. Then a sickle smile cut across it.

Dag pushed back his chair too hard, and a leg barked against the boards. He was still holding my hand, and he hauled me to my feet, his gaze sweeping left and right.

Nelda Pie followed us to the door. Her smile felt like a heat lamp against my back.

When we stepped out onto the gallery, though, I forgot about Nelda Pie for a moment because a woman was standing there, a shotgun slung around her neck, holding Lanny by the hair the way somebody would grab a dog.

Behind us, Nelda Pie made a hissing sound. "So. You're with her."

"What?" I asked. "No, I don't even know—"

"Very, very, very stupid, trying a stunt like this. And it will only work once." In a whisper, she added, "You've chosen the wrong side, half-blood. When she finds out what you are, she'll put you down, and she won't be gentle."

The door slammed shut behind us.

On the oyster-shell lot below, the woman with the shotgun said in a heavy Cajun accent, "Why don't y'all come down real slow so I don't have to blow this boy's brains out of his pretty head?"

DAG (6)

"We're coming down," I told the woman. My voice sounded high and thin, like an outboard popping out of the water. Lanny had a red mark on the side of his face, not far from the bruise he'd already been sporting on his temple, but otherwise he looked all right. Unconcerned, actually. Which meant he looked pretty much the same as always. But my brain had looped back to the year before when Mason had died, shot on the steps of DuPage First Methodist. They didn't look all that much alike, but they had the same color hair, the same lean, pretty build. I tried to be here and now, but my brain pulled me back to then: the heat of the Indian summer, the smell of piss in the air, the familiarity of Mason's body under mine from years of coonass roughhousing.

On the first step, when the spongy wood flexed under my weight, I stumbled.

Eli caught my arm. His gaze was searching.

"I'm all right," I mumbled.

Those hazel eyes saw too much, so I looked away and tugged my arm free. A moment later, Eli started after me.

The woman was what my dad and my pawpaw would have called a redbone—for all I knew, she might even call herself that. Her brown skin had red undertones, and her high cheekbones and something about her eyes suggested she had Choctaw or Natchez blood. Her hair, shorn close to the scalp, was dark but on its way to gray. The duster she wore over a work shirt and jeans would have been too hot the day before; even on a cool day, it should have looked ridiculous, but she pulled it off. That might have had something to do with the Browning slung on a strap around her neck, the muzzle currently pressed up against the side of Lanny's head.

"Hey guys," Lanny said in a tone that suggested he was more disappointed in himself than we could ever be. I had heard it before. It was ninety-nine percent bullshit and one percent imagination.

"Be quiet," I told him.

"She got the jump on me. It was right after you left, Doggo, and I was still thinking about how good it was to talk to you again, really open up like that, you know, share how we still feel about each other, and I mean, maybe see if we can find a way forward, and I just want you to know how much that meant to me, Doggo, you taking the time to talk to me like that and be honest—"

"Lanny, shut up."

"Oh Lord," Lanny breathed and rolled his eyes.

"That's all right," the woman said. "Right there is fine."

I stopped. I could feel the heat of Eli's body behind me and slightly to the side.

"I'll see your hands first," she said.

I understood the demand, although it wouldn't have made sense to me a year ago. Some creatures—including the hashok—left a mark on the humans they controlled; it usually looked like an injury on the hands or feet. I held out my hands. Eli moved up, his shoulder pressed to mine, and displayed his as well.

"Now your feet."

I began working on my tennis shoes. Eli's breathing was tight, but he did as well. The oyster shells bit into the sensitive skin, and we both tried to stand on top of our empty tennis shoes as much as possible. We took turns, me holding him by the arm so he could expose the soles of his feet for the woman. Then it was my turn. When I brought my feet down, Lanny started to laugh.

"What the hell is going on? You know she made me do that too, with my shoes? I didn't know ladies could be into feet like that, but I guess that's all right, on account of the sexual revolution and whatnot. But do you guys realize how dumb you look? Is this some kind of prank or—"

"Satisfied?" I asked the woman.

She made a noise and lowered the shotgun until it hung from its strap, but she kept a hand on Lanny's hair.

"Let him go," I said.

She didn't respond to that. She had dark eyes, and she was watching Eli and me the way you're supposed to watch when you're lining up a shot—looking through the target, like they're just one stop along the way for the bullet.

"Who are you?" Eli asked.

"You go in places like that?" she asked. "What's that say about the kind of person you are? Plenty of things that aren't what they seem. Dangerous things. You look right at them, think you know what you're dealing with. But plenty of things aren't what they look like, no."

"We'll start with your name. Who are you?"

A breeze whistled through the tall weeds, combing them into lines. It carried a few of the oyster shells, dragging them bouncing and skittering toward the road, and one of them came to rest against my bare feet.

"I heard somebody call her Fen," Lanny said. "He said something like, 'Oh damn, that there's Fen's truck,' and then they got out of here like they had a bad case of the shits."

The woman—Fen—grimaced, and her grip tightened on Lanny.

"All right, Fen," Eli said. "I'm Eli Martins, and this is—"

"I know who you are. And I thought I knew what you are. Now—" She jerked her head at the juke joint. "—I'm sure."

"What does that mean?" I asked.

"Consorting with that kind. I thought I knew, and I was right. So I'll tell you once: you don't bear the mark of the beast, and that's some kind of miracle. Walk away. Whatever you think you want, you ain't gonna get it, but you might end up with a whole heap of trouble. Touch no unclean thing, sayeth the Lord."

"I don't understand what you're saying," I said. "We went in there for information. I walk outside, and you're holding a gun on my friend. Tell me who the bad guy is in that situation."

Her mouth was a thin, hard line. The hand that rested on the Browning's stock could have been carved from stone.

"Nelda Pie thinks we're with you," Eli said. "You think we're with her. We're stumbling around in the dark. You can't be mad at us if you don't tell us what's going on."

"In the dark." Fen made a scoffing noise. "When I heard about the hashok, I came to see. It was dead, sure enough, so I went to find who done it. Me, thinking I'm gonna find someone else to hold up a torch in the night. What do I find instead? You been living with it. You been worshipping it. You been plying your flesh in exchange for the riches of the world." She flashed a yellow smile. "People tellin' me, you're about to make yourself a whole heap more from killing it, so I'll say this much for you: you're smart. But that kind of thing, consorting with them, making deals, using them for your own gain, that puts you on her side of the line." She gestured at the juke joint with the Browning.

"And on your side of the line?" I asked.

Another glint of yellow teeth. "The glory of the Lord, we are told, is like unto a consuming fire. In the land of the shadow of death, a light has dawned." She pushed back the duster to expose an ancient-looking knife tucked behind her belt. "What the Browning don't do for, I got the harvest knife, me."

Eli took a quavering breath, full of something—fear, I thought—that I didn't understand. When I glanced over, though, he shook his head.

"I don't know what you think we did—" I began.

"You don't have its mark, so I'm giving you this one chance, me: walk away from deals with dark powers and the princes of the night."

"—but we don't consort with these creatures, and Eli certainly didn't know what Richard was. What the hashok was, I mean. He was a victim."

"I pulled men out of the embrace of beasts before," she said with that cutting smirk. "I heard it all before, me."

I took a moment, centering myself, examining her body language. It had shifted throughout the conversation. Grabbing my shoes and socks, I nudged Eli, and he copied me. His movements were robotic, but at least he wasn't frozen. "We're leaving," I said and took a ginger step on the oyster shells. "We're done talking. Let him go."

"Information," she said. "What kind of information you need from a witch, you?"

"Lanny, come on."

"I'm asking you—"

Lanny rounded on her, his body turning in towards her, his fist coming up in a wide, roundhouse. Even with the jump on her, he telegraphed the punch. Classic Lanny.

Fen moved faster than anyone I'd ever seen. She knocked the roundhouse aside, sweeping it away with her forearm. Then she threw two jabs, both of them catching Lanny in the face. He stumbled, one knee buckling, and she pivoted at the hips, her upper body generating the force that she directed through her elbow as it connected with the side of Lanny's head. He dropped and hit the shells.

"What the fuck?" I shouted. "Lanny?"

Fen backed up, both hands on the Browning now, but the shotgun remained pointed at the ground. I sprinted over to Lanny, who was flat on his back, moaning, blood streaming down his face.

"Lanny?" I asked again as I crouched next to him.

"You been warned," Fen said, her voice rising as she continued to back away. "You heard the word of the Lord. Next time you are found consorting with beasts, you will be judged."

"Fuck off, you fucking lunatic. Get the fuck out of here. You could have fucking killed him, do you realize that?"

A warm hand on my neck made me start. "I like the swearing," Eli said quietly, "and this protective streak really does something for me, but she's got a gun. Let her go."

"You heard the word of the Lord," Fen called out as she climbed into a battered red Ford pickup. Then the door slammed shut, the engine started, and she rolled out of the oyster-shell lot. Over the truck's rumble, she shouted, "If you want absolution, you come to the Avenue D Rooms. It's never too late to walk in the light." Then she gunned it, and the pickup lurched out onto the state road.

"Doggo," Lanny mumbled. "I got her. Just like you told me."

"I didn't tell you to attack her, dummy," I said, using both hands to turn his head to face me. "I wanted you to walk away."

"And you definitely didn't get her," Eli said. "If anything, she got you."

"Just like you told me," Lanny murmured.

"Lan, how many fingers am I holding up?"

Lanny blinked up at my hand. "Flumpteen," he said with a note of pride. Then he puked all over me.

ELI (7)

Lanny wouldn't go to the hospital or even the urgent care. Refused would have been a gentle way of putting it. He kicked and hollered, heels drumming against the Ford's door, until he made a gagging noise and puked into the footwell. Fortunately, he didn't have much left in his stomach by that point.

Dag agreed not to take him.

"Jesus Christ," I whispered.

"He'll be fine," Dag whispered back as he started the Ford and headed out of the lot. "It's a concussion for sure, and I want him in a hospital, but he's one of those redneck boys you could roll down the hill in an oil drum and they'd crawl out at the bottom and just ask for a shot."

"I'm not worried about him. I'm saying Jesus Christ because he's got you wrapped around his finger."

The change in Dag's expression was instantaneous: his face hardening, his mouth tightening, his eyes cutting back to the road.

"And I guess he's going to be staying with us because he's got a concussion," I said.

Dag yanked on the seat belt across his chest.

"Am I wrong?"

"I feel like you're trying to start something, and I don't want to start something."

"Great; I'll take that as a yes. Glad I was part of that decision."

"Ok. I'll take him to my parents'."

I rubbed my eyes, suddenly too tired for the fight I'd been wanting. All I could manage was to shake my head.

We were on the causeway when Dag reached over and put a hand on my knee. It was barely mid-afternoon, which seemed impossible, the sun slicing the green-brown water. Ahead, the city was a cluster of plaster and brick, copper and steel and glass. Faster drivers whipped past us on the left, the wall of air from their passage stirring the sawgrass growing on the embankment.

"I should have asked you," Dag said quietly.

"Oh my God," I said in an undertone. "Are you even real?"

"I'm trying to say I'm sorry."

"I know, dumbass. I'm the one who should be sorry. You were trying to be nice. You were being a good person. Like always. I was the one being a troublesome prick. Also like always." I let out a breath. "I'm sorry. It was a lot, back there. I didn't handle it well."

He squeezed my leg. "And stubborn."

"What?"

"You were being a stubborn, troublesome prick. You forgot stubborn."

I laughed and kissed his shoulder, and he pulled me by the back of the head for a kiss on the lips.

When I settled back into the seat, he said, "You still haven't said stubborn."

"Oh my God. Stubborn. I was being a stubborn, troublesome prick."

"Well, I didn't want to say anything, but yeah, you were, kind of."

I laced our fingers together. I thought of the look on Dag's face when he'd seen Fen and Lanny, when he'd seen the gun, when he'd understood. It had been terror. The total, pure terror of seeing someone you love in danger. And I'd only seen that expression on his face once before, when he and Mason had fought on the steps outside DuPage First Methodist. I closed my eyes; the sun was too bright on the water.

"Are you all right?" Dag asked.

"I'm not the one who got my ass handed to me by a middle-aged woman in a duster."

"Hey," Lanny protested.

"I meant in the juke," Dag said. "What happened—"

"I don't know what happened."

"You acted like she hurt you. Like she did something to you."

"I said I don't know."

"What she said—"

"Dag, I don't want to talk about it."

My voice rang in the small sedan.

"My head's kind of hurting, Eli," Lanny said from the backseat. "Could you keep it down?"

We drove another mile. The whole world narrowed to the needle of the causeway, the asphalt, the sawgrass, the glitter of the city. Dag worked his hand free of mine and wrapped it around the wheel, and we didn't talk for the rest of the drive.

When we got home, our street didn't have any spots left—it looked like the Hudlins were having their kids and grandkids over, all of them, because the whole block was lined with minivans. Dag had to double park while he helped Lanny inside, and then I drove around for five minutes until I found a spot two streets over.

By the time I got back, Lanny had stripped down to a pair of extremely tight bikini briefs—bright blue, in case anyone's interested—and he was moving around the cramped living room, bumping into Dag, thrusting a sizable bulge in Dag's direction, bending over to rub his legs and, in the process, wave his ass in Dag's face, all while Dag was trying to make up a bed on the sofa.

Dag looked at me, and I saw the request there—a plea for help, even though he was still too angry to put it into words.

"Leave him alone," I told Lanny, catching him by the arm. I steered the pretty dumbass down the hall and to the back of the house, where I sat him down at our tiny kitchen table. I put two ibuprofen in his hand, and then I wrapped an ice pack in a towel.

"These would go down easier with a beer," Lanny said. "Or maybe some of that bourbon. You probably don't know this, but Doggo loves Sugarfield."

"Somehow, I managed to pick that up. You're not getting a beer, Lanny."

"Maybe a Coke, then. Oh, you know what would be good? A lime rickey."

"Water. You get water."

"You don't have to be pissy."

"Take the damn pills, Lanny."

He took them and set the glass back on the table. I pressed the ice pack into his hand. "That'll help with the swelling. Did she break your nose?"

He probed his face for a moment and shook his head.

"Even though you deserved it," I said.

"You don't have to be so mean to me."

"Sorry. I've got this weird thing about pieces of shit who broke Dag's heart and stole all his money. I don't like them. And I really don't like them when they show up and try to take him back." I shrugged. "Like I said, it's weird."

"I messed up."

"Save it."

"I got scared, and I ran, and I did some really stupid stuff."

"Lanny, I feel like I've been pretty chill about you, all things considered. But if you keep talking, I'm going to stop being so chill, and I don't care if you do have a concussion."

"I—"

"Put that fucking ice pack on your fucking nose and shut up."

"You don't have to be so mean," he mumbled around the ice pack.

In the front room, Dag was swearing under his breath, and then steps moved down the hall, and the linen closet door opened. My guess? He'd grabbed his jellyfish sheets by accident and didn't want Lanny ruining them. After a moment, the linen closet door closed, and Dag's steps moved back toward the living room.

"I'm not trying to take him back," Lanny said into the ice pack. "It's not my fault Doggo and I, we got this connection."

I rubbed a spot between my eyes and leaned against the table.

"I done a lot of stupid stuff in my life. I didn't have a dad; did you know that?"

"Oh Lord."

"And I bounced in and out of these stupid foster places."

I rubbed that spot harder.

"And Doggo, he's like, home. You know? He is home. So I gotta come back. That's what you do, right? I mean, that's what home is."

I pushed away from the table and headed for the bathroom. I peed. I washed my hands. I washed my face with cold water and let it drip from my chin and nose. I dried off and fixed my hair.

When I came out of the bathroom, Dag was helping Lanny down the hall. Lanny's boner was pointing the way.

Dag gave me a helpless look.

"Oh no," I said. "I already tried."

In our bedroom, I stretched out on the bed and pretended to read on my phone. The news. Ok, celebrity news. Ok, celebrity gossip, mixed in with some extreme workout videos about how to get abs. When Dag came back, I closed the video and opened my email.

"What were you watching?" he asked as he closed the door and heeled off his tennis shoes.

"News," I said.

He padded across the room.

"Ok," I said. "Celebrity news."

Dropping onto the bed, he let out a contented groan. He smelled like the woodsy aftershave he preferred and the hand soap in the bathroom. After a moment, he rolled onto his side to look at me.

After a moment, the awkwardness of it made me smile, but I kept my eyes on the phone. "What?"

"How mad are you?"

"Not mad."

"Is that a seven or an eight?"

That made me laugh, and I put down the phone and kissed him.

"It's only for a night," he said. "In case he really does need to go to the hospital."

"It's fine."

"Do you want to talk about today?"

"I don't know. Not really."

"Sometimes there's things we've got to talk about."

I picked up my phone.

He put his hand over mine, pinning it to the bed. "E."

"Ok, ok. I promise this isn't me, you know, being Eli. I just don't know what to say."

He cleared his throat. Some of the weight in his hand eased, and he stroked my arm. "Animal bites contain trace amounts of their DNA."

I closed my eyes. "Great. Of course."

Now he laughed, although it sounded forced. "What's that supposed to mean?"

"I'm tired of being the pretty dumb one. Why can't you be the pretty dumb one for a while, and then I can figure things out and you don't have to think about them or worry about them? You could learn something from Lanny, Dagobert. You really could."

He reached to smooth my hair. When I jerked my head away, he let out a sigh. Then he cupped my cheek and turned my face toward him.

"I figured out the bites too," I said. "And you know what a virus is, Dag? A virus is a collection of DNA or RNA that replicates using infected cells."

"See," he whispered. "You're not dumb either. And you're not pretty. You're beautiful. You're the most beautiful person I've ever met in my whole life. And you're kind, when you're not trying to cut the cable on the TV so I'll pay attention to you or pinching my leg when you think I forgot we're cuddling. And you're brave, even if you do some stupid things and try to keep me out of it. And—"

I kissed him.

When I pulled away, he asked throatily, "You tired of me yet?"

"I haven't decided." I squirmed around until we were both propped up by the pillows, and then I said, "Time for you to study, mister. And I'm going to read."

"I didn't know celebrity news told you how many macros to eat so you'd get abs." He smirked as he rolled off the bed. He looked a little too pleased with himself, so when he turned for the door, I smacked him on the ass. His yelp was really satisfying.

After he came back with his school bag, we worked for a while in silence. Or we tried.

First, Lanny got into a quiet shouting match on the phone with someone. He was demanding something back. The quiet shouting turned into loud shouting.

"For Christ's sake, Lanny, shut up!" That was my contribution to the shouting.

The silence managed to sound both wounded and indignant.

"Doggo," Lanny called ten minutes later. "This pillow's hurting my back."

"So move it," I shouted.

"I don't know if I should. My head feels funny. And I'm real tired. I never been this tired in all my life."

"Don't you dare," I whispered as Dag scooted to the edge of the mattress.

"He won't let it go," Dag whispered back as he went to check on the threatening pillow.

Five minutes later, it was "I think I'm all out of crackers. Doggo? Did you hear me?"

"You think you're all out of crackers?" I asked. "Or you're all out of crackers?"

Dag let out a breath; when he set aside the textbook, I grabbed his arm and shook my head.

"I don't know," Lanny shouted to us. "I think. Maybe. I dropped the sleeve, and I can't reach it. Can one of you guys come check? Preferably Doggo because he's the nice one."

"I'll show you the nice one," I screamed back, and then I had to pretend to resist when Dag flattened me against the mattress with one hand.

It went on and on like that. Eventually, I stopped responding. I tried to stay busy. I went through old boxes—junk I'd packed up after my family had died—and lucked into a dime from 1963, and I even managed to drill a hole in it (ok, Dag managed to drill a hole in it) so we could tie it on a string. He even accepted my explanation that he should just *do what I tell you and wear it*, which, if I hadn't known already, would have convinced me that this was perhaps the only man in the universe who would be able to deal with me in a long-term relationship. Eventually, I ran out of other things to do, so I tried to disappear inside my phone, and Dag gave up trying to study and started reading something on his phone as well. I was halfway through an article on Japanese ultra-high-intensity interval training (apparently one guy had died trying it, but you got great results), when an email landed. It was from Kennedy Sainte-Marie. And it had a massive PDF attached.

"Can I borrow your laptop?" I asked.

Dag slid the bag toward me without looking up from his phone.

It was exactly what she had described: a scanned copy of the velveteen-bound book that she had showed me briefly in the binding room at the library. But it also wasn't anything like what I'd expected. The pages were larger than I had realized, and the text was handwritten, often poorly and crabbed. It meant a lot of zooming in and then zooming out again.

But it was more than text. Flowers were glued to the pages. Buttons. Needles. What looked like glassine baggies filled with different kinds of powders. Scraps of cloth. Colored daubs that I thought might have been wax. And drawings—so many drawings. There didn't seem to be any organizing principle. Worse, so much of it sounded like nonsense. Exhibit A, the crone's dishwater spell (soak your clothes in used dishwater, hang them to dry, and then wear them when you need the wisdom of the crone—which, granted, I could probably use, but did I have to smell like a busboy, and also, would I get crow's feet and gray hair? If so, pass). Exhibit B, musky hot oil rub for stamina and potency and fertility (which, fine, if Dag's into it, I'd at least give it a try—he wouldn't have to twist my arm). Exhibit C, Anna's coffeepot ritual (great chicory coffee, plus deeper intimacy and affection with your partner, so, yeah, maybe Anna could help me not be a dick just to get attention).

"How the hell am I supposed to get anything useful out of this?" I muttered.

"What is that?"

I told him.

"Does it have an index?" he asked.

"What?"

"An index." He flipped to the back of a textbook for an example.

"I know what an index is."

"Well, does it have one?"

"No." I hesitated. "I mean, someone wrote it by hand."

"Did you check?"

I dragged the slider all the way to the end of the document, where a handwritten index provided an overview of the contents. It wasn't organized—it looked like entries had been added as the book had been filled—but it was easier to scan than the whole book, especially in PDF format.

"You're getting so much good sex for that," I said as I skimmed the entries.

"Told you it'd have an index."

"Never mind. Good sex is canceled."

Dag rolled his eyes and went back to his phone.

The index had a single page listed for the hashok, which I immediately scrolled back to. But aside from a description of the creature and its abilities and feeding, all of which were consistent with what I knew, it didn't tell me anything I didn't already know. Nothing about infected bites or transmission rates or how to get rid of a monster virus that might be living inside you. Fine. It wasn't exactly like that had been at the top of my worry charts before today. I had bigger issues, like finding a tank top that didn't make me look like I had a freshman beer belly.

I flipped back to the index. The entry for lutins was near the beginning, and it had several pages marked. The first few were references to the creature under other topics—protective flannels, unhexings, money draws. But then I found a description of the creature, which lined up with what Dag and Nelda Pie had discussed: a trickster spirit who liked to cause trouble, which back in prehistoric times, or whenever this book had been written, apparently consisted of spoiling milk, scaring farm animals, and hiding churns and combs. Jesus, save me.

At the bottom of the entry was the description of a ritual: *Drawing the lutin – Your altar you will make out of a child's clothing, something they have played in, which you have not yet washed* (cue a laundry-water spell, I thought—the laundry drudge's wisdom washing, maybe). *On the altar, light a blue taper and lay a beloved toy. Lutins love candy, but they cannot count. You can keep them busy with broken pieces of rock candy, as many as you can pile. Call them with your will and a child's words.*

It sounded both like batshit woo-woo and, at the same time, weirdly banal. Like the dishwater spell. I was really fixated on the dishwater spell.

"What are you reading?" Dag asked. "Still that book?"

"Yeah."

"Find anything?"

The lie came automatically. "Not really. The stuff on the hashok is what we already knew. Nothing about, you know, contagiousness or anything like that."

"Maybe there's some sort of cleansing ritual. Isn't that what Nelda Pie called it?"

I honestly couldn't remember; I had been too freaked out at the feeling of the cold fire running rampant through me. But I shrugged and nodded. "What about you? If you say the Saints, I'm going to remind you about this when you aren't happy with a 99.9% on the test Friday."

"The *Times-Picayune* got the names of the victims."

"What victims? Oh, Jesus. The bodies under Ivy's trailer?"

Dag nodded.

"How many? Do I even want to know?"

"Three."

"Jesus," I said again. "That's awful."

"Two women and a man."

I shook my head.

"Eli, I think I know it's feeding behavior. Part of it, anyway. It's not what I thought."

"What do you mean? It's a hashok, right? The firefly light that Jeannette saw, this creature living off pain and suffering."

"Right." He frowned. "But it's different too. Maybe it's a variant. Or maybe this is...well, Richard and Muriel talked about being different, remember? That they'd left their natural habitat on the lake and the bayou. So maybe this is what a 'normal' one is like, whatever that means."

I honestly couldn't process that thought, so I said, "What's different?"

"Well, I know I've only read one article, but I can't see any links between these people. I mean, the newspaper didn't report any. Last time, they were using the PTSD support group as cattle, but these people came from all over the area—different parishes, different occupations."

"Ok."

"And the rate or schedule or whatever you want to call it seems much steadier. Lorraine Tyer disappeared almost exactly four months ago. July 1. Irma Finck disappeared August 3. George Boutte was reported missing September 1."

"But Ivy was killed October 25."

Dag nodded.

"You think it takes them at the beginning of the month," I said, "and feeds on them for weeks."

"I think it's possible. It could have had Ivy for a month."

My brain was fogged, but I managed to say, "That means we only have a few days before it takes someone else."

"I think that's a safe assumption." He cleared his throat. "Last time, the hashok were...accelerating, remember? More victims, and closer together. But this seems stable."

I nodded.

"Then there's the similarities we already talked about too. Jeannette's story about the firefly. And, well, the pain and suffering. None of these people were happy, stable individuals. Lorraine Tyler was eighteen, and she'd been in foster care her whole life. Police actually looked into her disappearance because one of the foster parents had been accused of molesting children, and they thought maybe he'd done something to Lorraine. Irma was a sex worker and a junkie. And George, well, this was actually the second time he made the news. When he was a kid, he was in the *Times-Picayune* because his mom beat him so bad she put him in the hospital. He's described as homeless in this article, so I guess life didn't get any easier for him."

I shook my head. Then, after a moment, I covered my eyes.

Dag shifted on the bed and pulled me against him. For a moment, I resisted, hitting him with the heel of my hand. His arms tightened, and I gave up and buried my face in his shoulder. My eyes felt hot. Everything felt unnatural, like I was wearing a mask.

"It's ok," he whispered, stroking my back. "We're going to figure this out. Just take some of those good, deep breaths for me, and—"

I pushed hard and got free of him, and by the time Dag had recovered, I was off the bed.

"Hey," he said, rubbing his chest. "E, come on. I'll leave you alone if that's what you want."

Grabbing my wallet and my keys, I shook my head. I shoved my bare feet into a pair of high-tops and stumbled toward the door.

"Eli, we've talked about this."

"I forgot."

"Jeez."

That made me laugh, and I lingered in the doorway and wiped my nose. "I forgot I had a job interview."

"We've got a rule about this."

"It's a bar. Bartender job."

"Will you sit down?"

"No, I'm already going to be late."

"Sure."

"What's that mean?"

Dag looked at me. He rubbed a hand over his head, disturbing the regimental part in his thick, gray hair. Sandalwood eyes held a lot of pain.

"I just didn't know," I said, "that I was such a lying piece of shit you couldn't trust me to go to a job interview."

"You know you do this," Dag said. "You get vulnerable, and then you get scared, and then you hurt people. You hurt me. You know you do it, so why can't you cut it out?"

"Hurt people. Got it. Add it to my list, along with being a lying piece of shit."

"You never said anything about a job interview. You hardly ever talk about looking for jobs. Then all of a sudden you're running out the door, and it sounds really thin, E. What am I supposed to think?"

"Good thing I didn't put you down as a reference," I said over my shoulder and hurried down the hall.

"God damn it," Dag shouted behind me, and I heard the metallic rustle of the miniblinds—probably Dag slapping them or throwing a pillow or something.

"Bye, Eli," Lanny said from the sofa with a wave. "Good luck with your job interview."

"Fuck off, Lanny."

I slammed the door behind me. It was night now, the streetlights spreading a silver canopy over the street. I ran two blocks. Then I stopped, hands on my knees, chest heaving. Pins and needles ran through my face. My eyes welled up, and I had to blink them clear. Fat teardrops fell, darkening the cement. One of them hit a silver gum wrapper hard enough to make the paper tremble. I pressed my hands against my eyes then because I was going to lose it if I saw something like that again.

After a few minutes, I had enough self-control to stand up and start walking. I stopped at the corner market. I bought what I needed. I called an Uber, and I rode back to DuPage Parish and Balmoral Castles, the trailer park where Ivy Honsord had lived. The lake was black under the moonless sky. Amber from the light pollution ruffled the chop. Then Slidell, halide and sodium lights like a thumbtack to the eye. Then the fallow pastures, corn stubble, men and women cutting sugarcane under halogen lamps, miles of dark oak and skeins of moss twisting under the empty sky.

The trailer park huddled under a few flickering lights, and at night, it looked abandoned, post-apocalyptic: the cars on blocks, the forgotten trikes, the sullen flicker of TVs behind aluminum blinds. The Uber driver was a nervy white guy who would have been a cute little twink if he were twenty years younger. When he parked in front of Ivy's trailer, he gave the police tape a long look and then glanced at me.

"Are you sure about this? Because this place looks sketch, and I'm done for the night. My buddy can get us some drinks—"

I closed the door gently, pressing until it clicked, and tipped him. Then I walked along the side of Ivy's trailer. The brake lights flared and then dimmed as the Uber rolled down the block. Then the lights disappeared, and I reached the back of the lot.

The darkness was almost complete back here. I could make out the outline of the trailer steps, the torn sections of lattice that had been removed to access the bodies, even the hump of the riding lawnmower. The air smelled like the bayou—fish and decomposing hyacinth and mud. Water lapped against the shore, and I guessed it was less than a hundred yards downhill, where the shadows of oaks and cypresses bristled. When the breeze picked up, I shivered and realized I had forgotten a jacket.

I wasn't sure if any of Nelda Pie's protective flannels were still hidden around Ivy's trailer, and if they were, I wasn't sure what effect they'd have on the ritual I was about to—stupidly—perform. So, I followed the sloping ground, the smell of the bayou and the sound of the water growing louder with every step, as the oaks and cypresses and their dark shawls of moss climbed above me. The ground was soft when I stopped, and when I knelt, it soaked through my jeans instantly.

I laid down the first item I had bought: a child-sized tee with the Saints branding, because it had made me think of Dag, who had probably been relatively happy before I started fucking up everything in his life. This was my improvised altar cloth, since I didn't have any clothes real children had played in, and I thought asking a neighbor to lend me some might be a quick way to get myself either hauled in or shot in the back of the head.

I opened the top next, tossed the packaging aside, and set the toy on top of the t-shirt. I wasn't sure if kids still played with tops—hell, kids hadn't really played with them when I'd been one—but stores still sold them for a couple of bucks (or more, if you were a New Orleans corner market). More importantly, it was the only thing I'd seen hanging on the pegboard that had looked remotely familiar from childhood. Gard had bought me a top for my birthday when I'd been four or five—in preschool, anyway—and I'd loved it more than anything else I'd gotten that year because it had been from him.

Next, I folded back the cardboard lid of the birthday candles and took out a blue one. I leaned it against the top. I tore open the two paper bags and poured M&Ms into a circle around the candle and toy. I wasn't sure how high a trickster ghost might be able to count, but I hoped it would be enough.

Hearing myself think that sentence made me realize I'd probably already tipped over the edge.

I lit the candle with a lighter, and then I stowed the lighter in the back pocket of my jeans. The light breeze shifted, and for a moment, I caught smells that must have been coming from the prefabbed homes above me: fried chicken, Fabuloso, garbage. My knees were frozen, and I shifted on the damp earth, wincing at the slight suction of mud that told me this pair of jeans might be ruined.

"This is so stupid," I told the night.

Then the breeze shifted again, and the bayou smell of vegetation and stagnant pools of water filled my nose.

"This is so goddamn stupid," I muttered. The next part was my will and a child's words, which I hoped meant something children liked or said, and not baby talk. I'd had plenty of practice with vision boards, so I focused on what I wanted and sang, "Mary had a little lamb—"

Something moved at the edge of my vision. I broke off the song, trying to catch a glimpse of it, but whatever it was, it vanished in a stand of willows. My heart beat a little faster. It was a fox. Or a rabbit. Something small and quick, which is why you didn't hear anything, you just saw that flicker of movement like a light—

I cut off that train of thought. If a hashok were out here—if it had come back—then I'd made a serious mistake. If it wanted to kill me, I couldn't outrun it or outfight it. The last time I'd been lucky because Richard had been overconfident and playing with his food; I didn't think that would happen again.

Blue wax was running down the candle to stain the t-shirt. The clock was ticking. I worked moisture into my mouth and tried again, concentrating on what I wanted to happen, the lutin responding to my call, as I said, "Olly olly oxen—"

This time, there was no mistaking it for a cat or a vole or a coon. Something zipped past me at the corner of my vision, and it was pale and glowing. For a moment, I was sure I heard laughter. A child's laughter. But by the time I'd turned, the light—or whatever it was— was gone, and the sounds of the bayou, frogs and cicadas, kept time with my pounding heart.

"You can go home," I told myself, the words tremulous when I spoke them out loud. "You can go back. You can apologize to Dag. Hell, he's enough of a dope that he'll take you back a few more times."

Instead, I settled myself, dried my hands on my jeans, and took one more deep breath. And then it came to me, as clear as day, and I wanted to laugh. I settled for a grin and poured my will into the words as I called, "Come out, come out, wherever you are."

The effect was instantaneous. The candle flame snapped to the right at a ninety-degree angle, and then it returned to normal and flared so brightly that I had to shield my eyes. I could feel it, the spirit or energy or whatever it really was, lured into the circle by the game I had played. It wasn't trapped; at an intuitive level, I sensed that would have required a lot more preparation and effort, and possibly with less reward. Instead, the lutin was now caught up in the task of counting the chocolate candies. I wanted to giggle. I wanted to tell this thing they sell M&Ms by the pound, now. Too bad you're a lousy counter.

One of the colored discs skittered on the pile, and I jumped.

The laughter was unmistakable, but it had a haloed, insubstantial quality—like the light in front of me. It was like tripping, I realized. Tripping hard. I was starting to understand why mind-altering practices and substances were part of worship around the world.

"You got me," I said shakily, ironing on a smile. "A few times, actually. Didn't you?"

More laughter. It had a swooping quality, rising and falling like the lutin was doing loop-the-loops with glee.

"Yeah, you made me look pretty dumb." Tip of the iceberg, I thought; part of me was still screaming inside that this wasn't real, that this was the inevitable schizoid break that had finally come due. "But they were fun games, right? You like games."

The candle pulsed.

"I thought we could play a game," I said. "Would you like that?"

Another pulse.

"I'm going to ask you some questions, and if you get the answers right, I'll help you count your candy."

The next flare had a slightly dubious quality; it probably didn't sound like the best game, but I was improvising.

"Were you playing tricks on the woman in the trailer up there?"

The answer was hesitant. An affirmative, but slow, as though the lutin weren't quite sure. That threw me; I had thought this was the softball question.

"On lots of people up there?" I asked.

This time, the answer was an immediate yes.

Ok, I thought. So Ivy Honsord wasn't the target of the pranks any more than anyone else. But she'd gone to Nelda Pie for flannels. She'd wanted protection.

"Did you do something that made the woman in the trailer, that one right there, angry?"

The flame stayed low and steady.

"Scared?"

Nothing. The blue wax was spreading across the t-shirt, and I figured I'd gone through more than half my time.

"Did you see what happened the other night when she was—" I wasn't sure if the lutin really was a child, or childlike, or if it was simply a trickster, but I decided to err on the side of caution for once. "—hurt?"

Another moment passed, and I thought I had gotten a no. Then the candle's flame flared so brilliantly that it whited out my vision for a moment. Then the light changed, and it was like I was seeing something else. A skewed version of Balmoral Castles, the angles of the mobile homes slightly off, the structures oversized and looming, the sky a spinning vortex of white and black, like a dead channel on an old TV. Some of the random items left lying on lawns and decks were dark while others—a pink flamingo, the plastic torso of a doll, a catcher's mitt—glowed with rippling fluorescence. My view of the trailer park shifted; I was making my way through it, moving at what felt to me like a sprint.

When Ivy's trailer came into view, it was surrounded by a barrier—a transparent box of sickly brown energy. Then I understood. This was the lutin's memory, how it saw the world. And the transparent box was the protection of the flannels Nelda Pie had placed around the house. The lutin flitted around the barrier, toward the back of the lot and the bayou.

I was still processing this when I saw a man emerge from between the next set of trailers. He was white, his hair in a burr cut, a blue-green tattoo on his neck suggesting prison ink. He wore a white tee, the bulk discount kind, and cargo shorts with black tennis shoes. From the pocket of his shorts dangled the plastic tag of a key, the kind that old motels still used. It had a pink fluorescent sheen, and the lutin zipped toward it. It snagged the key from the man's pocket and hid it in the firewood ricked along the side of the trailer.

A woman's cry made the lutin turn, and in its memory, I saw Jeannette, the neighbor, balanced on a railroad tie. She was staring at something, and the lutin followed her gaze. A man was dragging a woman, who had to be Ivy Honsord, out of the trailer. She was already dead, her body limp, looking thin and hollowed out and strangely at peace. She'd finally escaped, I guessed. Finally found a way out.

The man, though, held my gaze because he was the same man I could see sneaking between the next set of trailers. They could have passed for identical twins except for the neck tattoo. The one with the tattoo was frozen; he still hadn't noticed the missing key. The one without the tattoo was staring at Jeannette, who was screaming again. These were both Roger Shaver, I guessed. The real one, and the thing that had been impersonating him.

Then I watched it happen: the Roger without the neck tattoo dissolved into a cloud of light that condensed into an orb the size of a baseball, which then shot away toward the bayou. The real Roger looked over his shoulder; he was obviously torn between the freak show he'd just witnessed and something he desperately wanted from the trailer. Whatever it was, it won out, and he sprinted toward the trailer's steps.

The vision ended. I was gasping for air, staring down at my makeshift altar. The candle had burned down to a stub, and the flame guttered.

"What about the witch," I asked, "or the hashok? That light you saw at the end, what was—"

The sense of terror was absolute and final, like a door slamming shut. The candle sputtered and then hissed out, and the ring of M&Ms parted as though something had forced its way through, leaving a clear trail behind it.

"Shit," I muttered. "Shit, shit, shit."

I had gotten something. The real Roger Shaver had been here. He had seen what had happened to Ivy, and he had seen the creature that killed her dissolve into a cloud of light. Had it been the hashok? I wasn't sure; I had only ever seen the creatures change between a monstrous form and a human form, but I knew they were capable of taking the shape of firefly lights.

With a grimace for the remains of the altar, I got to my feet. Part of me was already trying to convince myself that I'd imagined the whole thing. The human brain is a resilient thing. It sure as hell didn't want to admit that it had just bartered with a trickster spirit and had an out-of-body experience. But I took deep breaths and tried to be rational about it. If I couldn't trust my own senses—

I turned and jogged up the hill, but instead of heading toward Ivy's trailer, I cut toward the next set of homes, where I had seen— imagined?—Roger Shaver walking. I tripped over a weed whacker, and I swore when my tennis shoe caught a five-gallon gas can and the plastic made a hollow boom and sloshing noise. But the trailer stayed dark; maybe it was abandoned, or maybe I was finally getting a little luck.

I crouched next to the ricked firewood, trying to remember where I had seen the lutin hide the key, and began pulling out pieces of wood. It had been here, this general area, although that had been days ago and someone might have already found it, or, more likely, I had completely gone off my rocker and—

The plastic tag was washed out, colorless in the dim light, but my guess was that it was pink because it had a heart-shaped sticker. It said *L'amoureux - Rooms by the Hour – Bragg, LA – 27.*

"Fuck me," I breathed.

Pocketing the key, I turned back to the altar. I needed to clean up the evidence that I had been here, call Dag, and tell him—

"Hey, good lookin'," a familiar voice called from farther down the hill.

I squinted, trying to pierce the thick shadows. He was about my height, more muscular but also, in a way, thinner. The same trendy, asymmetrical haircut I remembered. He was me. Just a lot hotter.

He grinned up at me, waved, and took another step. He looked left and right. He twisted the hem of his shirt the way I did sometimes, and it was enough to hint at the hard, defined stomach underneath.

"If I'm stroking out," I said, "just make it a good one and let me go. I don't want to eat soup the rest of my life."

"This is what you wanted, right?" he asked, rolling those amazing shoulders. "Backup? A little help?" He shaded his eyes, even though it was almost too dark to see, and said, "A little of your psychic mojo actually being useful for a change?"

"I'm not psychic," I said. "I've got this key here, but I still think I'm having a schizo episode."

"You are," he said. "Psychic, I mean. And you aren't. The schizo thing. Come on; we don't have a lot of time, and I need to show you something." He dropped his hand, flashed a smile, and winked. "On the way, I'll even give you some workout tips for the battle of the bulge."

Maybe it had been the vision with Hope the psychic. Maybe it had been the encounter with Nelda Pie earlier that day. Maybe it was because I'd just called up a spirit and actually had physical proof that the vision had been real. Maybe it was because those Instagram workout videos weren't doing it for me anymore.

I wasn't sure. All I knew was that it didn't sound like the worst idea, so I pocketed the key and headed in pursuit of my best self.

DAG (8)

"Have you tried talking to him?" Lanny asked at a normal volume.

Nominally, this was a stakeout.

"No talking on stakeouts," I whispered.

It had been easy to follow Eli here. His story about the job interview had been a classic deflection—anything to let him escape from feeling vulnerable—and while Eli was creative and intelligent and thoughtful in so many ways, he was fairly predictable when it came to his escape routes. I'd bundled Lanny into the Ford with a little white lie, and we'd spotted Eli on our third sweep, just as he was getting into the Uber. After that, we'd followed him to DuPage Parish and Balmoral Castles. I wasn't sure what he wanted to see behind Ivy's trailer, but I was giving him five more minutes before I went looking for him.

"Because Doggo, sometimes you make assumptions. So maybe you should talk to him."

"I'm the one who's good at communicating," I whispered. "I'm the one who's always making the effort. I'm the one, even when it means dragging things out of him because he wants to say them but he doesn't know how."

"Right, but, I mean, sometimes you do that thing where you're so focused on taking care of the other person that, um, maybe you don't see the big picture."

"No. Talking."

I don't even think we made it thirty seconds before Lanny whispered, "Like with us—"

"No. We are not doing that. We are never doing that. You wouldn't even be here if you hadn't assaulted my boyfriend, I mean, no labels, and if you hadn't snitched on a witch and then tried to attack the scariest-looking woman I've ever seen."

"I was doing what you told me to. You said we were going to find a way to work things out, make things right between us, and then you told me when that lady wasn't ready, I should hit her—"

"I never said any of that." The whistle had a strained, shrill quality, and Dag had to work on his breathing for a moment. "Lanny, I feel like I've been really cool considering you cheated on me and stole all my money and left without any sort of goodbye and basically made me feel like the stupidest, most worthless person in existence, but if you don't stop talking, I am going to lose my mind."

In a surprisingly wounded tone, Lanny said, "I didn't cheat on you, Doggo."

I rolled my eyes. Then I looked at the dashboard clock. Eli got two more minutes before I dragged him into the car.

"I didn't," Lanny said. "Hand to God. And I left you a note."

"A grocery list that only includes your favorite breakfast cereals does not count as a breakup-and-goodbye-and-I-stole-your-life-savings note."

"No, I left you a note. With Bren."

I shook my head.

"I did! He didn't give it to you?"

"No, Lanny. He didn't give it to me. He's the one who told me about all the guys you'd been sleeping with behind my back."

"That's because he wanted to bone you. Well, he wanted you to bone him."

"He was nice to us because I helped him with his fence. He had a girlfriend."

"He was super bi and wanted your dong."

"He—" I forced myself to cut off. "Please be quiet."

"I wouldn't have done that to you, Doggo."

I managed to keep my mouth shut, but I wanted to laugh. The cheating and the leaving without a note, those were a step too far for Lanny Fontenot. Walking off with all my money? Well, he'd have some sort of excuse—a good investment in Mexican tar, or a sweet dirt bike a friend was selling, or underwear that made his junk look good. Not that it ever looked bad. I wanted to rub my eyes. I wanted to talk to Mason. I wanted it more badly than I had at any other point in the last year.

When I'd been fourteen, after a pick-up game at the high school, Mason and I had lain on the gym floor long after the squeak of rubber soles and the thud of the ball had gone silent. Shirts versus skins. Mason had played skins. And with the uneven boards biting into his back, I had let my head roll to the side, had let myself look. Mason had already been getting adult muscles. He had a flat stomach, a hint of pecs, golden down across his chest, more in his pits. He slid one arm behind his head. The curve of his biceps was the swell of a wave. That was when Mason had glanced at me and, in that doofus way of his, asked, "What?" And the confusion had held something else, a kind of foreknowledge that felt like a promise, like Mason was operating on a secret wavelength that only the two of us understood, our bodies keys to each other, to a secret that made me wake, sweating and aroused and ashamed, more nights than not. So I told him.

But I had been wrong. No secret wavelength. No reciprocal words. Mason hadn't hated me, and that was something. Hadn't really seemed to care, although he did tease me about it. There was nothing really special about it at all, I knew now. It happened all the time. Every gay boy's first crush was his straight best friend. I had gotten over it a long time ago. Then my eyes slid to Lanny, who was running a hand through his mane of blond curls, and my face heated.

"I'm done waiting," I said, popping open the door. "Stay here while I get him."

Of course, I was halfway across the street when the passenger door clicked open behind me.

"Back in the car."

Lanny still looked pale from the concussion, and his steps had an uncertainty to them that wasn't usually there. Pale might have been an understatement. He looked drained, as though something vital had been hollowed out of him. But he grinned as he slung an arm around me. "It's like you said, Doggo: we're a team."

"I never said that."

Lanny rolled his eyes. "I'm starting to think you're the one who got hit on the head."

When we reached the other side of Ivy's trailer, I swore. At the bottom of the hill, a familiar silhouette was walking out onto a dock.

"Eli," I shouted.

But the silhouette didn't turn. He was holding something—a lantern, maybe, to judge by the light it put off, although God knew where he'd gotten it from—and bending over something alongside the dock. It was hard to tell the details at a distance, but it was some kind of boat. Then Eli climbed into the boat and pushed away from the dock.

"Eli, stop!"

A light went on in Jeannette's trailer.

"Damn it," I said and hurried down the hill.

A dirt path led between oaks and cypresses. Veils of moss spun in the breeze. Where the ground became boggy and gave way to the bayou, the water looked like spilled oil. My first step onto the dock made the whole structure sway, and I swore and stumbled. Lanny caught my arm.

"Easy, big boy."

It sounded so much like something Mason would say—or, for that matter, Eli—that it gave me a chill. I shook off the echo.

"It's a floater," I said.

Lanny chuckled. "No duh. Cheap-ass peckerwoods. Come on, they've got another pirogue."

"We can't steal a boat."

"Sure we can. We already have, remember?"

"I meant—"

"The fan boat, you know? Honestly, Doggo, your memory. Come on, before a gator gets your boyfriend."

He was already climbing into the pirogue. While I untied the boat, Lanny separated the paddles, and he handed me one once I was settled. Lanny sat with his back to the bayou, which meant I was staring out across the water. No mist, tonight. But no moon either. I thought I saw a flicker of Eli's lantern moving among the trees, so I cut into the water and propelled us out onto the bayou.

For a while, all we did was paddle. Frogs croaked. Cicadas buzzed. The water sloshed against the sides of the pirogue, and sometimes the drops from the raised paddle would patter against the inside of the craft. Lanny helped at first. Then his paddle started dragging, and he slumped on his seat.

"Sorry, Doggo, I think I'm getting seasick."

"You don't get seasick." I helped him get his paddle in the pirogue. Sweat glistened on his face, even though the night was chilly—I was shivering inside my hurricane shirt, and the CPO jacket Lanny had borrowed wasn't much heavier. His breath smelled like bile. "I've been out on the salt with you when you're too drunk to stand, and you've never gotten seasick."

"Maybe I'm growing up," Lanny said, and it was such an odd comment that I glanced at him. He was leaning over, face in his hands.

Two things happened in quick succession. We drifted past the bumps of a submerged log, and my coonass brain remembered too late: gator. Then Lanny leaned over the side and puked.

The gator went crazy. It spun toward us, jaws snapping, and I hauled Lanny back by the shirt. He screamed, arms flailing, and kicked the hull. The pirogue rocked. Water sloshed in over the side.

"Lanny, for God's sake."

He was still screaming.

The gator spun, and its tail cracked against the side of the boat. We rocked again. More water washed in over the side. Lanny was trying to get to his feet, his movements jerky and uncoordinated.

"Stop," I shouted, sliding out of my seat to the center of the pirogue. I pulled Lanny down on top of me. "Stop moving, dumbass! You're going to tip us!"

With our combined weight at the center, and with Lanny no longer trying his best to give the gator a free meal, the pirogue steadied. The gator rammed the boat again, and another heavy thump ran through the hull. Water soaked both of us. Lanny made a startled noise and jerked, but I was holding him tightly now.

The pirogue steadied. The ripple of movement in the water told me that either the gator had gotten bored or had decided to try for an easier meal. A glance confirmed my guess: it was gliding away, barely more than a few bumps and ridges protruding above the waterline.

"Ok," I whispered.

"Holy shit."

"We're fine. It's gone."

"Holy shit. Damn thing about got me." He was shaking. "Did you see it? It almost got me."

"What kind of redneck are you?" I relaxed my arms, squeezed his shoulder, and then poked him in the ribs. "You're supposed to dive in and wrestle that thing, not—"

He kissed me on the neck, and suddenly I was intensely aware of the heat of his body against the cold water of the bayou, the smell of the dark water and the moss and the cypress. I grabbed the side of the pirogue, and the fiberglass was slick under my hand.

"Thanks, Doggo," he whispered.

"Lanny—"

"I know." He rolled his eyes as he steadied himself and got back into his seat. "You're such a dummy sometimes."

The best response I could come up with was "You almost tipped us over."

For some reason, that made Lanny smirk and roll his eyes again.

I stared around the bayou, and after a minute, I could tell which way we'd come—the faint twinkle of lights on the other side of a tangle of branches. But the glimmer from Eli's lamp was gone.

"This is why you should put a tracker on him," Lanny said.

"You're sick. Shouldn't you be quietly feeling sorry for yourself instead of critiquing my relationship with my boyfriend? Not that we're putting labels on things."

"I'm pretty good at relationships, so I can do both."

I shook my head and did another sweep. Under the trees, without a moon, everything existed as only the faintest outline—a sketch of black and the darkest grays. I took a deep breath and tried to reason my way through it. Eli could have gone in any direction. The bayou stretched for miles. And I didn't know why he'd come out here, so I couldn't try to anticipate where he'd gone or what he'd do. In terms of Eli's instinctive need to run, this was a first. Usually I followed him to Bragg, where he made bad choices about food and his body and then wandered around until he was ready for me to pick him up. Once I'd followed him to the Greyhound station, where he had spent forty-five minutes trying to decide on a destination. When I'd approached him and offered to buy him a hamburger while he settled on somewhere, he started crying, and we went home. This, taking a stolen pirogue out into the bayou, was next level.

"Because he's always running away," Lanny said.

"Put your head in your hands so you don't puke on a gator again."

"That's why I'm saying put a tracking collar on him. Oh! Or they can put those microchips in your pets. You could do that."

"Lanny, I told you to stop."

"I was trying to help," he mumbled toward the hull, his tone full of injured adolescence.

"No," I said, "you were trying to get a dig in because you want me to break up with Eli."

"Duh," Lanny said, and he raised his head long enough to roll his eyes.

The sound of splashes interrupted whatever mature response I was about to deliver. It took me a moment to spot where they were coming from, and then I grabbed the paddle. Lanny still looked like he was having trouble with just sitting upright, so I did my best to put on some speed while keeping the noise from the paddle and the water quiet enough to still hear the splashes. They were coming from ahead, where the canopy thinned and more ambient light filtered down to us. The bald cypresses ahead of us leaned in toward each other, branches tangled as though they'd been pleached into an arch. Like a doorway, I thought with a shiver. I shivered again when we passed under the woven branches.

We entered a clearing. The water was still oil dark, but now it reflected the stars, flecks of mercury floating in the slow current. Clumps of arrowwood and buckeye grew on islets, their shapes like India-ink brushes against the thicker darkness.

The splashing came from fifteen feet ahead. Even without a light, I knew it was Eli.

"Jesus Christ," I shouted, and Lanny jerked in his seat. "E, we're coming!"

The only answer was the sound of limbs thrashing in water.

I dug in with the paddle. I kept one eye on Eli while I scanned the surroundings. No gators, although even with more light, I couldn't see far. No sign of anything, really, except fireflies spinning off in the distance. Fireflies. My gut seized, and I paddled harder.

When we reached him, Eli was struggling to keep his chin above water. He kept going down and then forcing his way up, coughing and spitting and gasping for air.

"Keep us steady," I told Lanny as I tossed the paddle into the pirogue.

"How do I—"

"Just do it!" Then I leaned over the side of the boat and caught Eli's arm. He was in a blind panic, still frantically trying to keep himself above water. His hand clipped the side of my head, and he twisted in my grip, almost like he was trying to get away. I dragged the pirogue closer, and then I grabbed Eli with both hands and pulled again. This time, I felt him come free from whatever had been drawing him down. He flopped across the side of the pirogue, and Lanny swore and shifted his weight to balance us. I caught hold of Eli's jeans and hauled him the rest of the way into the boat. My blood hammered in my ears. I looked around. Still no gators, but the fireflies continued to dance, and they seemed closer than ever.

"Eli, can you breathe?"

I pounded him on the back, and he hacked up some water. Then he groaned and sucked in a huge lungful of air. His breathing sounded raspy and labored, but he was definitely getting oxygen. I rubbed between his shoulder blades.

"Lie there. We're getting the fuck out of here."

I grabbed the paddle and set to work. Lanny tried to help, but he was worse than nothing at all, with the paddle dragging and the rhythm off. Finally I told him that his job was to focus on Eli, which, in hindsight was even worse, because Lanny spent the rest of the trip back to shore describing his own qualities that made him better suited for the role of boyfriend.

Eventually, the lines of oaks and cypresses faltered, and then I could make out the outline of the dock bobbing on the water and beyond it, the dark slope of the hill. The mobile homes at the top glowed with yellow lights; after the miles of lapping water, the sooty lines and quicksilver shards that I had just left behind, I felt like I was drifting back into the real world.

The water to my left exploded, and drops sprayed up and stung my face. I thrust the paddle down, more out of instinct than anything else, and swung us around to the side. A spotlight flicked on. For a moment, it cocooned us. I launched us forward. Someone on the hill swore loudly, a woman's voice. The temptation was too strong; I rubbernecked, turning to look over my shoulder. The light stayed stationary, and the pirogue slid out of the spot a moment before the next shot was fired. It looked like someone had fired a thousand BBs into the bayou at the same time. But it wasn't BBs dimpling the water. That was birdshot.

"What the fuck?" Lanny was screaming. "What the fuck?"

"Get down," I shouted.

Eli was trying to sit up, his eyes wide and bloodshot.

"Both of you get down!"

The light swiveled. Where it touched the bayou, the water was green-brown with an electric sheen. The cypresses gleamed like brown glass. The spot pinned a mockingbird to a pine branch.

"Get the fuck down!"

For the first time maybe in his entire life, Lanny did what someone told him: he dropped on top of Eli, bearing both of them down to the bottom of the pirogue.

The light slapped the side of my head. It was so intense that it felt physical, and I would have sworn I could feel its heat. I had to squint against the sudden brilliance. Then the light stopped moving; it was fixed on us, and it cut out my shadow and the shape of the pirogue against the black curtain of the bayou. I paddled faster. I couldn't see her, but she was up there, and she was getting ready to take the shot.

I stretched forward, grabbing the trunk of the bald cypress just ahead, and gave up on the paddle. Instead, I used our momentum and my grip on the tree to swing us around again. This time, I brought the pirogue in line with the tree, so that we were hidden behind the broad trunk. The next shot rang out. The cypress trembled under the impact the way I thought a tin roof might under a hailstorm.

"God damn it," a woman shouted.

I recognized that voice. It was Fen.

"Get out from back there," Fen called down. The light swiveled, but we stayed in the tree's shadow. "You're only making things worse."

"What the fuck, you crazy cunt?" Lanny shouted back at her.

"Fen, what's going on?" I tried to keep my voice level. "There's been a misunderstanding."

"Oh my God," Eli whispered. In the harsh contrast of the xenon light and the bayou's shadows, he looked washed out, and the whites of his eyes were the color of soap.

"I warned you," Fen said. Her voice was closer now. I thought I could hear the suction of her feet where the shoreline was marshy. In my mind, I pictured that ancient, rusty knife she carried on her belt. The harvest knife, she'd called it. "Thou shalt not suffer a witch to live."

"We're not witches," Lanny screamed.

I pressed him back down, the other hand still using the tree to float us in its shadow. The cypress's bark scraped my palms. The smell of gunpowder mixed with the fishiness of gar and bream. The ripple of the water against the pirogue's fiberglass was the only sound, and I realized I couldn't hear Fen's steps anymore.

"I told you," she said, and I couldn't place her voice now among the maze of trees. "I told you, the Lord says, 'Touch no unclean thing.'"

"I don't know what you're talking about," I said. "But whatever you think we did, it's a misunderstanding."

"Shit," Eli whispered. "Shit, shit, shit."

"I saw the altar and the candle and the trap." Fen's voice was unyielding. "Consorting with spirits. I thought I smelled them on you, a touch of the other side y'all carry."

My gaze locked on Eli's face.

"I'm sorry," he whispered.

I closed my eyes. The world shrank to the ridges of the bark, the lapping water, the cicadas.

"Come on out," Fen said. "I'll go easy; you won't feel a thing."

"It was Eli," Lanny shouted. "Eli did it. He's the one you want."

"Lanny, shut up!"

"It's him! He did what you're saying! Not the rest of us!"

"No, he's right," Eli said, trying to sit up. "She wants me—"

"Both of you get down," I said. I shoved them back into the bottom of the pirogue and grabbed the trunk to steady us. "Lanny, shut up. Eli, shut up. Let me think."

"If it's only the one," Fen called, "then he's all I want."

"See?" Eli asked, trying to sit up again. "You and Lanny—"

"Eli Prescott Martins, if I have to put you back down in this boat one more time, I'm going to take a belt to your ass when we get home."

"Middle name," Lanny whispered.

"Shut up," I snapped. "You have no idea the trouble you're in, Lanny."

"The other two can go home," Fen said. "Easy as that. Walk away from the dark and into the light."

"She'll let you go," Eli said. His hazel eyes looked matte and black in the shadows. "It's my fault—"

"She's not going to let us go. Use your brain, E. She's talking about murder; she won't leave witnesses. We're going to have to head back out into the bayou; we'll put in on the other side and find a road, and then—"

The chirrup of a siren broke through my words. A moment later, the light went out, and the bayou's darkness draped us again.

"Down here," I shouted. We're down here! There's a woman with a shotgun. Down here, help, she's got a gun! This is an active-shooter situation. Repeat, she is armed and dangerous!"

Swearing came from the shoreline, and then heavy, running footsteps moving away.

I counted to a hundred. Then I pulled us to one side of the cypress so I could see land. A flashlight—an ordinary one—was sweeping back and forth and coming down toward the dock. I let out a shuddering breath. I wiped my hands on my jeans. My palms were raw from the bark. Then I grabbed the oar, the scraped flesh of my hands stinging, and headed for shore.

Amrey Kimmons was in uniform. In one hand, he held a reinforced flashlight. In the other, he had his .38.

"Dagobert," he said wearily. Then he raised an eyebrow as he played the light over the pirogue. "And friends. I suppose I should have expected them, after hearing about the trouble at the Stoplight. I'm afraid you all are under arrest."

ELI (9)

They kept us overnight in the DuPage Parish jail, which was a cinderblock structure attached to the sheriff's department. Aside from a decorating scheme in line with the color of dried urine, the place really wasn't too bad—it was clean, and the only other person in the holding cell was a middle-aged drunk who grew politely apologetic as he sobered up. Until the point when he passed out, anyway. They even took Lanny to an urgent care, where a PA checked him out and told him he'd been stupid to exert himself with a concussion, but that he was otherwise fine. When Lanny related all of this, I opened my mouth to tell him that he was stupid pretty much all the time, but Dag must have sensed what was coming because he gave me a glare. I shut my mouth. I was too tired for a fight, anyway; I wasn't sure I'd ever been more tired in my life, and after a while I broke down and slept fitfully with my head on Dag's lap.

Monday morning, Amrey released us.

"I won't charge you with obstruction or trespassing this time," he said to Dag, and then he met each of our gazes in turn. "But stay away from Nelda Pie Cheron and the Stoplight. The old days are gone and buried, and we don't put up with that kind of thing anymore."

"Sir, she—" Dag tried.

"Do I make myself clear, Dagobert?"

Dag sighed and nodded. "Yes, sir."

I wasn't entirely sure what Amrey meant, but I nodded when he looked at us, and Lanny scuffed his shoe against the asphalt and mumbled an affirmative.

We drove home.

"Lie down," Dag said to Lanny, pointing to the sofa.

"Doggo, I'm totally—"

"Now!"

Lanny dropped onto the sofa. He took a second, assessing look at Dag and then pulled the sheet up to his chin.

"You," he said, grabbing my arm. "Come on."

He released me once we were inside the bedroom, and he shut the door behind him.

"Dag, I'm sorry. I was embarrassed, and I—"

"I have class, Eli," he said stripping out of the hurricane shirt and jeans. "Now I get to go spend my day smelling like cigarette butts floating in a public toilet."

"Take a really quick shower, and I'll make you something to eat you can take with you—"

"I love you." He jerked a fresh t-shirt over his head. I'd picked it out for him: dark blue, with a stylized anatomical rendering of a shark's mouth. He dug through the drawer until he came up with a pair of camo tech pants. "But I don't know what to do anymore. Am I supposed to spend the rest of my life with you running away every time you're scared or hurt or whatever the hell I did wrong last night?"

"You didn't do anything wrong. It's me. I'm messed up. I didn't—I don't know. I love you too."

"Sure," he said, grabbing his backpack and shoving his laptop into it. He was halfway out the door when he said, "That's why you have to say it to the mirror."

"Dag, wait—"

But he was gone, and a moment later, the Escort grumbled to life on the street outside. The sound softened. When he turned at the block, I lost him.

The silence from the living room was so intense that, of course, I knew Lanny had heard all of it.

I showered. I dried myself. The waves hit me at the worst times—I had to stop, the terrycloth bunched up against my eyes, and hold myself together while I dripped onto the bathmat. When I carried my clothes to the washing machine, I felt the hard, angular plastic of the motel key tag in the pocket of my filthy jeans. I closed one hand around the key and dropped my clothes in the drum. I added Dag's clothes and soap and set the machine. Then I shouted down the hallway, "If you want to wash your clothes, put them in the machine and start it."

"Um, ok. Hey, if you ever want to talk about Doggo, I mean, Dag, I mean, he's got a temper, but—"

I shut the bedroom door. Judging by how the sound rang out in the house, I probably shut it harder than I needed to. Then I crawled into bed.

I tried to sleep. It was like hanging off the edge of a skyscraper and trying to let go. My mind played back flashes of the night before: the lutin, and then finding the key, and then whatever it had been, that other me, leading me out into the bayou, the smothering stillness that hid under the frogs and the cicadas and the splashes of bream and gar and gators. We had paddled out into that emptiness, and I remembered an archway of woven branches, the other me telling me that I needed to see something, needed to understand, and then—

What? Something dragging me down into the water. It was shallow enough that I should have been able to stand, but the ground had been marshy, almost like quicksand, sucking me down, making it impossible to get free. The burning need for air. My vision tunneling. Floating spots of color as my brain panicked and fired every neuron at once.

I sat up and croaked, "Dag."

Flop sweat dampened the sheet under my arms; I could smell myself in the small room. No Dag, of course. I mopped my face with a dry corner of the sheets. I forced myself to release the key. The plastic tag had bitten into my hand and left a bloodless line across my palm. *L'amoureux*. Number 27. I had seen two of Roger Shaver.

And two of me.

I know you're furious with me. I'm sorry for what happened last night. But I think I found Roger Shaver, the real one, and I think we need to talk to him. I also have an idea about how the hashok is operating.

I sent the text. I immediately sent another: *I really am sorry, Dag.*

And then another: *Should we have told Amrey about Fen? We know where she's staying. He could pick her up.*

Dag's reply came a few seconds later: *And tell him what? A crazy monster hunter came after us? We'll talk about it when I get home.*

I was starting to reply when his second text came through.

If you're still there.

I typed out fourteen different replies. I deleted them all, turned the phone facedown, and then, for good measure, slid it under Dag's pillow.

Eventually, I slept, but in the dreams, I was drowning again, or I was wandering the streets of Bragg in those early morning hours of neon lights and Jimmy Buffet and tourists with takeaway daquiris, and in those dreams, Dag never came. When I woke, I felt even more tired—a kind of flickering exhaustion I wasn't sure I'd ever experienced before, rolling waves of it like brownouts you heard about in big cities sometimes in the summer. I made myself get up anyway.

I'd lost most of the day. I used the weights I'd bought to work out in the bedroom. I found the hidden scale. I weighed myself. I hid the scale again. Then I pulled on running shorts and socks and went to the living room.

Lanny was in a pair of briefs, the sheet draped over one leg, watching some ancient show with little green puppets. They were causing all sorts of trouble. One of them was doing something to a stair lift. Lanny seemed fixated on the show, laughing about something I didn't understand, but when I pulled on my running shoes he said, "You're too skinny."

"Ha ha. Tell me another."

"I'm serious. Doggo likes a guy with some beef. Good old American boys, you know? Athletic build, but not like a bodybuilder."

I tied the key in my laces.

"Trust me. I've known him a long time, and I know the kind of guy he checks out."

"Ok."

"I'm just trying to help."

"No," I said. "You're not."

I ran south and followed the levee. The evening sun broke and splintered on the Mississippi. The skeletons of cranes rocked in the wind. It was too cold to be running without a shirt, and I didn't exactly have the body for it, but I liked the air on my bare skin, and I'd felt trapped in the house, suffocating under my own shame and self-pity.

Six miles. Two for every pound I was still over.

I was on the levee when my calf started acting up, and I had to stop. I tried to walk it off. Then I tried to rub it out. Nothing helped, so I limped east, toward the Huey Long Bridge, concrete and steel tacked down across the brown water.

The thing was, I'd never do better than Dag. But he could do so much better than me.

When I got home, I cleaned up. Then I searched Google for psychics in Bragg, and I found Hope's shop. I called her, but the phone rang and rang before going to voicemail. I wanted to talk to her because of the vision she'd shown me. That snippet of the better me, the one who had legit biceps and actual abs, the one who could call Dag in to fuck him, with none of the hesitation, none of the gut-churning memories, none of the terror. She didn't pick up on the second call either.

Next, I called *L'amoureux*. When a woman answered the phone and asked how she could help me, I disconnected; if I was having a psychic break, this was about as real as it could get.

I called the Bragg branch of the DuPage Parish Library and asked for Miss Kennedy.

"Oh, sweetheart, she's at her other job," a woman told me. "Are you her boyfriend?"

I choked a little on that and managed to ask, "What other job?"

"You know, the ghost tours. I think you are her boyfriend. I can't wait to tell Silvia."

"No, don't tell—" was as far as I got before the call disconnected.

Well, add Kennedy to the list of people who wanted to kill me.

At that point, I was down to two options: talk to Lanny and, after a few minutes, stick my head in the oven; or get the house ready for Dag. I chose door number two.

"Go shower, Lanny," I said, pushing on his bare shoulder to get him moving.

"Gizmo's just about to—"

"Now. You stink. Not just like the bayou. It's a whole bouquet you've got going on."

Lanny stomped into the bathroom, and I'll admit I watched him go: those briefs did wonderful things to an already fantastic ass. I stripped the bedding, which also had parfum de redneck, and washed it. I straightened up the living room. We all needed to eat, so I went to the kitchen and got out two cans of Pillsbury crescent roll dough, butter, brown sugar, granulated sugar, and cinnamon. I found the Bundt pan that Gloria had lent me. It was one of her old ones, with a dent on the rim and stains from oil and burnt food. I got the monkey bread in the oven.

By then Lanny was out of the shower. I found him naked in our bedroom, with Dag's clothes thrown all over the room.

"Seriously?"

"I'm trying to find something to wear. It's not like I live here, you know."

"Trust me, I know."

"Where's that Tulane hoodie?"

"That's his favorite one."

"I know. Where is it?"

"You're not wearing his favorite hoodie. You can borrow some of his boxers while your clothes dry."

"You must be one hell of a fuck," Lanny said as he pulled on the boxers. He grimaced. "I look like I'm forty in these."

"You'll survive."

"Which one is your toothbrush?"

"I'm not telling you that."

"I used the purple one."

"Jesus, Lanny."

"I needed to brush my teeth."

"Get out!"

He managed to do an incredible amount of sulking, pouting, glaring, and grumping in the short distance from the dresser to the door. And it just wasn't fair; the man knew how to fill out a pair of boxers almost as well as briefs.

I cleaned up the bedroom. I turned on the LED that sent waves of rippling blue light along one wall. I checked the monkey bread and gave it five more minutes. I set out the Sugarfield and a rocks glass. I went into the living room and turned off the infomercial.

"I was watching that," Lanny protested.

"Too bad. Dag's going to be home soon."

"It was for a waffle-fry machine."

"Lanny, I'm seriously at a ten with you."

"You need to chill; you're wound so tight. No wonder Doggo says it's a relief when you take off like that."

I stopped moving for a moment. Getting shot through the heart does that to you. Then I picked up the Bluetooth speaker and turned it on. My fingers felt numb. I fumbled my phone, picked it up, and set it on the shelf next to the speaker.

"What's that about, anyway?"

I worked my jaw.

"I told Doggo you were probably cheating on him. I never cheated on him."

"No," I said. This time when I picked up my phone, I managed to keep it in my hand. "You just stole all his money and ran away."

"I came back, though. And I'm paying him back. It was basically a loan."

I laughed. Somehow I managed to navigate through my purchased songs and find the beluga collection.

"Doggo and I had a long talk about you while you were still in the juke joint. Do you know how bad you hurt him with stuff like that, running away? I wasn't going to say anything, but then you did it again last night, and I figure somebody ought to tell you."

Something didn't track about the statement, but I couldn't put my finger on it. I settled for "I'm sure you were happy to do it."

"Well, yeah. Doggo's great. You know, after, um, things ended—"

"You stole all his money and ran away."

When I turned around, Lanny's face was red, and he was running both hands through his hair. "—I kept trying to find somebody like him. Everybody's got a type, you know? Like my stepsister is pretty cool, but she goes for the worst guys, like, they're so mean to her and they look like total dogs. Me too, I guess. Older. Tough. But the guys

I picked up, jeez, you wouldn't believe. Nobody's as good as Doggo. So that's when I decided I had to come back."

"You're fucking unbelievable," I said. "And when Dag gets home, I'm telling him I want you out of our house."

Lanny's hands slowed. He raked them one final time through his hair. The look he gave me was strangely hurt, and after a few moments, I broke first and headed into the kitchen.

The door opened a few minutes later, and Lanny said, "Hi, Doggo."

Dag's response was muffled.

"Yeah," Lanny said. "I figured you'd want something nice to come home to."

More quiet words from Dag.

"Especially after everything he put you through last night," Lanny said.

Dag's steps moved down the hall.

"You need a nice night with somebody taking care of you."

I dropped the ice in the rocks glass and poured in two fingers. I took out the monkey bread. My face was hot. The oven, I told myself.

Dag's eyes were dark with exhaustion, and his hair needed washing. He'd managed to get a trail of mustard down the center of the shirt. More of it smudged one corner of his mouth.

"Hi," I said.

He nodded. He looked at the monkey bread. He looked at the Sugarfield on the rocks.

I held out the glass, and he took it. He sipped the bourbon. His eyes came back to me.

"So, um, I wanted to apologize."

He took another sip.

"And tell you I, uh, love you."

He set down the glass.

"And I want to make things right."

"How?"

My eyes stung. I focused on the monkey bread. I picked up a spoon, but then I was holding it too tightly, my knuckles bloodless. The whales were singing their song. Under all that water, and they still talked to each other pretty damn well.

"Ok," Dag said. The glass clinked when he moved it, but he didn't drink again. "Tell me about last night."

So I did. I left out the embarrassing parts—that the hashok's version of me was much more attractive and, apparently, eager to bottom—but I gave him the gist of it.

When I'd finished, he said, "Let me see the key."

I brought it from the bedroom, and he inspected it. Then he set it aside. "This isn't what the hashok did last time," he said. "It's acting differently, taking your appearance, luring you out into the bayou to try to drown you. Why didn't it attack you and kill you?"

"Well, we know they can take human shape, and they use that ability to move around, interact with people, choose victims. For all we know, there's a real Richard out there. And a real Muriel. And the hashoks just chose their shape. Or maybe they killed the real Richard and the real Muriel. But it makes sense, doesn't it? A kind of camouflage? It would give predators an advantage. And I think this might be our way of finding it. If we can figure out which shape it's using now, or if we can figure out the shape it used to choose Ivy as its next victim, we can find it and stop it."

Dag frowned. "I understand why it would look like Roger when it terrorized and eventually killed Ivy. But I don't understand why it would look like you when it came after you."

I gave him a crooked smile.

"Eli," he said softly.

I blinked and shook my head, but the crooked smile was glued on. "I thought about calling Amrey and telling him about the key," I said, "but how do I explain the lutin? And if I just tell him I found it, well, you saw him last night. He already thinks we're too involved. He might even be starting to suspect something. And then I thought about checking out the motel on my own—"

Dag's eyebrows arched.

"—and I realized you wouldn't be happy about that."

"To put it mildly."

"But I also don't feel like we can just let this thing keep killing, Dag. If Roger, the real Roger, can tell us anything—where Ivy might have met this thing, why it chose her as a victim—then we might get our first lead. If nothing else, we can eliminate the real Roger as a suspect and try to figure out who the hashok might be impersonating now."

Dag frowned.

"What?" I asked.

"I don't know. Something doesn't feel right."

"Dag, I know what I saw—"

"No, I believe you. And I think you're right: it makes sense that it's camouflaging itself to choose victims. That fits with what we already knew about the hashok. But there are these weird pieces that don't line up. Do you know what apophenia is? It's when the brain sees patterns where there aren't any. Maybe that's what we're doing. Maybe we're too focused on a few similarities."

"But there are similarities. The fireflies. The pain and suffering. The victims. And Richard and Muriel were outliers; they basically told us that they operated differently from other hashoks."

"That's not what I meant—" Dag began.

"Who do I have to hump," Lanny asked as he came into the kitchen, "to get some of that monkey bread?"

"All right," I said. "Dag's here. It's time for you to go home. Or, since you probably don't have a home, go crawl under a bridge or into a cardboard box or, hey, here's an idea, down a garbage disposal."

"Doggo! Do you hear the kind of shit he says to me?"

"I heard." Dag scratched his ear, considering first me, then Lanny. "Lanny, I think he's right. It's time for you to go home."

The look of shock on Lanny's face made me smile. I tried to hide it, but Lanny jabbed a finger in my direction. "He doesn't treat you right. You wish things were like they used to be; I can see it in your face. Every time we talk, it's like you're telling me what I want to hear, and then when he's around you act totally different."

"I don't know what you're talking about," Dag said. To me, he added, "I really don't. But Lanny, I'm with Eli now, and I love him. You and I aren't going to get back together. Ever."

"I'm paying you back—"

"It's not the money, Lan." His voice softened. "Look, it's been nice to see you again, and I didn't think I'd ever say that. Let's leave it at that. I'll give you a ride—"

"No." Lanny ran the back of his hand across his mouth. He looked close to tears. He shook his head. "You said—you let me think—" After another deep breath, he pushed back his curls. "You never used to play games, Dagobert. If that's what he's teaching you, then you ought to find yourself someone else."

His steps moved away down the hall, and a moment later, the front door crashed shut.

Dag stood there, staring after him, hands balled at his sides.

"If you want—" I said, reaching for the monkey bread.

"Let's get this over with," Dag said. He stepped toward the hall and bumped a chair, and it chittered across the linoleum. The sound was too loud in the suffocating silence. "We'll start with Roger's motel."

DAG (10)

L'amoureux was a pink stucco building on a corner lot in Algiers. It had a double gallery with scrolled ironwork, and morning glory grew so thickly that the streetlights couldn't penetrate the darkness. A good place to get mugged or assaulted, or hide out or hook, which were probably the top four things that happened here. One side of the building was covered in a mural: an eagle with the face of Eddie Van Halen soared against the backdrop of an American flag, and in gothic lettering were the words ONE NATION UNDER ROCK. The other side of the building was attached to a cinderblock car wash.

I parked on the street and held out my hand.

Eli unbuckled himself.

"You're staying here."

The corner of his mouth twitched, and he opened the door and got out of the car.

I caught up with him in the parking lot and took him by the elbow.

"You'll have to drag me," he said. The twitch was a full-blown smile by now. "And then you'll have to tie me up. I'm not into that, but I bet you could make it fun."

"This isn't a debate. And it's definitely not a joke."

"Dag, I know I don't make life easier for you. But do you really think it would be better with Lanny?"

"No. What? No, of course not."

Eli seemed to weigh each syllable. His eyes were distant, focused inward.

"I don't know where he's getting that stuff from," I said. "I've been clear with him from the beginning: I'm with you now."

"Now."

"You know what I mean."

This time, the smile was wry and pained, and it made him look much older. He nodded. "Yeah, I do." His touch on my wrist was gentle as he moved my hand away from his arm and headed for the stairs.

I followed him in silence to the door marked 27.

I knocked. Then, after a minute, I knocked again. Someone in a nearby room was blasting mumble rap. The air smelled like the green dustiness of the morning glory and the perpetually damp rubber door mats and the soap from the car wash next door.

Eli held up the key.

I took it and pointed back toward the stairs. "Wait there. If something happens, call 911."

"I found the key—"

"Eli, don't make me repeat myself."

His eyes were heavily dilated in the green darkness. He rubbed his stomach once, and the movement seemed automatic because his gaze was fixed on mine. Then he took a deep breath, nodded, and moved down the gallery. I could have sworn he muttered something about a boner, but that didn't make any sense, so I turned my focus back to the door.

The key turned easily. I inched open the door. Silence. Darkness. The smell of stale body odor in a closed-up space, and some serious foot funk. I pushed the door open a few more inches. More darkness. A double bed. The weak light that managed to filter through the morning glory gave an impression of rumpled sheets. The breeze shifted, ruffling the morning glory, and a speck of light appeared at the back of the room. A firefly. When I pivoted to look at it dead on, something moved in the darkness, and I took a stumbling step back.

Then the breeze died down. The morning glory settled. And after a moment, I dried my hands on my shirt.

"Dag?" Eli called from the stairs.

"It's a mirror."

"What?"

"Nothing; it's empty. Keep an eye out."

"He chooses now to be decisive."

"What was that?"

"I said be careful."

As I stepped into the room, I caught the double light switches near the door. A lamp next to the bed came on, and then an overhead fluorescent hummed to life above the sink and mirror at the back of the room. Trash covered the floor: empty CVS bags, paper sacks from Rally's—a half-eaten Baconzilla and curly fries still inside—dirty clothes, empty ziplocks, a cup full of brown spit and tobacco flecks, a meth pipe made out of a baby's bottle. I tossed the room as quickly and carefully as I could. Usually it was difficult to do both, but the room was already a mess, so I doubted Roger Shaver would notice minor disturbances. Aside from the obvious drug use and a made-in-China 9mm under the bed, I didn't find anything interesting.

I worked my way through the bathroom next. It was filthy, with urine spattered everywhere and the shower stall encrusted with grime, but it was also empty except for a tiny bar of orange soap. Apparently Roger wasn't one for oral hygiene.

After turning off the lights, I let myself out of the room and locked the door.

When I reached Eli at the end of the gallery, he asked, "Well?"

I shook my head.

"God damn it."

I told him about the meth and the gun as we made our way to the Escort.

"But Ivy wasn't killed with a gun."

"No, she wasn't."

"And we haven't seen any connection to drugs."

"Unless we're both tripping, and that explains what's going on."

Eli looked at me. His hazel eyes were frighteningly intense.

"It was a joke," I said, raising both hands. "A bad one."

He made a disgruntled noise and looked at the pink stucco building. "I want to talk to him."

"He keeps a gun under the bed. I don't think he's happy about late-night visitors."

"I found the key, Dag. That means he was there when the hashok dragged Ivy out of the trailer. And that means maybe he saw something—something that the lutin didn't understand, or something that it was too scared to show me, or something that it missed."

"Maybe."

After a moment, grudgingly: "Maybe."

"All right," I said and settled back into the seat.

He was still looking at L'amoureux, but he had a very expressive face, even in profile.

I laughed.

"What?"

"I don't get you."

"Thanks."

"No," I said, "I meant it in a cute way."

"There isn't a cute way. A cute thing to say would be, 'Gee, Eli, you look hot tonight. I'm getting butterflies in my tummy.'"

"That sounds like a bad episode of *Care Bears*."

"There were good ones?"

"Well, yeah."

He pinched the bridge of his nose. He was trying not to smile. "Of course. Of course I pick the one man in five parishes who knows how to break down a gun, whip my sorry ass into shape, and curate a *Care Bear* watch list."

"I don't remember the titles, but there was a good one about an evil wizard."

"They all have evil wizards. But they're not evil. They're just sad or lonely or frustrated."

I put my hand on his knee.

Instead of pinching the bridge of his nose, now he was covering his eyes. The sound of his breathing was thick in his throat.

"Come here," I said, pulling him against me. He melted into my shoulder. "What's going on?"

He told me about Lanny, about the day while I'd been at class.

"I hope you believe me when I tell you I never said those things to him."

Wiping his face, Eli pulled back. "Yeah."

"Eli, I guess I said something that gave him the impression I wasn't happy. I was...frustrated last night. I probably said things I didn't really mean. But I never told him that you make my life worse or that I want to break up or, God, that I want to get back with him. I mean, Lanny was—I don't know how to explain it, why he has this effect on me, but whatever it is, I'm not dumb enough to let it ruin this amazing thing I have with you."

Even wiping snot with the collar of his t-shirt, Eli Martins knew how to put on a fantastic eyeroll.

"What is that supposed to mean?"

Eli opened his mouth and then snapped it shut again. He pointed at a man—white, late thirties, average height—moving toward the stairs to the second-floor gallery. It took me a moment to recognize Roger Shaver, although the burr cut was the same. His clothes were nondescript: a plain white tee, jeans, and boots that had probably been sold as real leather but that looked plasticky under the sodium lights. The tattoo on his neck was new, and he looked thinner and older, used up by drugs and hard living. He took the stairs two at a time, a flicker of white behind the morning glory.

When Eli reached for the door, I caught his shoulder and shook my head.

"I want to—"

"I know. Hold on."

Three minutes later, Roger came back down the stairs.

"How'd you know?"

I shrugged. "He didn't have a girl. And he hasn't scored yet, so he wasn't going to smoke."

"How can you tell he hasn't scored?"

"The way he moved. He's got ants in his pants."

"That's your tactical assessment, he's got ants in his pants?"

"They didn't send me to the academy for nothing. Of course, they didn't fire me for nothing either."

Eli frowned, but he was still following Roger with his eyes. "I don't like it when you talk about yourself—"

"Come on, I think we're going to have to follow him on foot."

Eli's frown deepened, but he opened the door, and we hurried after Roger.

The night was cool, approaching cold, and Eli—in his almost-see-through-tee and his ass-cupping jeans and his Toms—looked like he was freezing. The smell of the car wash followed us to the end of the block, and then we walked into a wall of weed skunk. Around the corner, two Latino guys and a black guy were passing a joint back and forth, watching a group of kids—presumably theirs—riding tricycles on the sidewalk and running in an overgrown lot. One of the Latino guys gave us a nod; the other two men stared warily until we were past.

Ahead, Roger still had half a block on us, and he was moving with the same nervous energy I had noticed at the motel. I thought about the gun under the mattress. No cash in that place, but a gun. And I wondered if there was a scale for how stupid Eli and I were being.

We went another two blocks, passing low-rent apartments, a strip mall with a tattoo parlor and a fried oyster shop, a Mexican bakery with roll-down security gates over the windows, a thrift store, a Dollar General, a shiny new payday loan store—on and on like that.

Roger turned on the third block. His steps crunched across a crushed-shale parking lot as he approached a converted pole barn. It was set back from the street, the front of the building visible in the light from the streetlamps before darkness swallowed the rest of the structure. A handful of domestic trucks and sedans were scattered across the shale, all of them at least twenty years old, most of them closer to thirty. The corrugated steel of the roof must have been cheap because it was pitted with rust, and although an effort had been made to paint the corrugated steel walls an orangish-brown color, perhaps to conceal the rust, they didn't look much better.

We reached the lot as Roger stepped inside.

"We're going in there?" I asked.

Eli nodded.

The wind tumbled a flattened Swisher Sweets box across our path.

"You're sure?" I asked.

Toeing a used condom half-buried in the shale, Eli sighed and nodded.

"Let's do our best not to catch a bullet in here," I said as we approached the door. A sign said ANNA'S PUBLIC HOUSE, but the bulbs were burned out, which was why I hadn't seen it from the street. As I pulled open the door, I saw more rust scaling the deadbolt. "Or tetanus."

Eli's smile, for one instant, was incandescent, and he squeezed my hand before we stepped inside.

It had the smell of bad bars everywhere: mildewed fabric from mops and bar towels that never dried, the yeastiness of beer, stale smoke from cigarettes and marijuana. Anna's seemed to consist primarily of one enormous room; in the low lighting, the far side was lost in gloom. Empty tables with dirty chrome legs filled most of the space, and a bar ran along one wall, which was where the majority of the patrons seemed to be sitting. They were a mix of men and women, all white, all with the blue-collar look—denim and cotton and stubble on the men, polyester and cheap silver and Mary Kay makeup on the women. They were all either watching each other, watching themselves in the mirror behind the bar, or watching the Insignia flatscreen mounted on the wall, where a white guy in a hairpiece was announcing the pari-mutuel wagers on a horse race.

Roger was sitting at the close end of the bar, leg bouncing on the footrail, both hands wrapped around a schooner of beer.

When I took a step forward, Eli caught my sleeve.

"Let me."

"This isn't exactly your scene."

"It's not your scene either. And I think I might be the lesser of two evils."

I blinked.

"Look." Eli took a breath. "You still kind of scream 'cop' when you get going. It's actually kind of hot, even though I know you don't like to hear that, but when it comes to a conversation, it can be kind of, um, intimidating."

"Huh."

"That's why I had to interrupt you with Jeannette. You were talking to her like you were taking her statement."

"We were taking her statement. We were asking her what she had seen. That's what taking a statement is."

He bit the corner of his smile, and I got the feeling he was fighting hard not to laugh. "Well, the cop thing, I don't think this is the right venue for it."

"I'm not a cop. And I wasn't a very good one even when I had the uniform. All I'm going to do is ask him a few questions—"

"Trust me, Dag. I can handle this."

Before I could answer, he gave a final tug on my sleeve and walked over to the bar. He sat on the stool next to Roger, flagged down the bartender, and ordered something. When the bartender moved off, Eli said something to Roger, who gave a delayed nod before focusing on his drink again.

I sat at the table closest to the door and took out my phone. With the camera app open, I began recording Eli's interaction with Roger. Occasionally I tapped the screen or raised the phone, pretending to read and send messages.

The bartender came back with the drink—what I guessed was an Old Fashioned—and set it in front of Eli. Eli sipped it and set it back down pretty fast. When he drank, Eli usually went for a hard seltzer or, if he was indulging, white wine. He didn't exactly have a coughing fit after that sip of whiskey, but he did look a little red cheeked. He said something to Roger, laughed, and said something else. This time, Roger didn't even nod. His leg was bouncing faster than ever, and from across the room, his hands around the schooner looked blanched and cramped.

When Eli tried to get his attention again, Roger flinched. It was a little thing, but I didn't miss it. And I didn't miss the gravity knife he flipped open and pressed against Eli's side. The blade slid through the thin tee like it was paper, and Eli's whole body stiffened.

I clamped down on my first reaction, which was to pull my gun and put two through the back of Roger's head. It was made slightly easier by the fact that the Sig was currently in a safe under our bed. I sat. I watched. I braced my elbow on the table to keep the video steady. Eli wanted me to trust him, so I was going to trust him, trust that he could handle this. For about five more seconds.

Roger said something. Eli's head bobbed up and down, loose on an invisible string. Roger slid off his stool first, keeping the knife low, where the bar hid it from view. He said something else, and Eli's head wobbled again, and Eli slid off the stool slowly. They moved away from the bar with herky-jerky steps, toy soldiers who had been wound up and pointed in the same direction. Tension showed in Eli's jaw, but he didn't look at me, which meant he was holding himself together. Big surprise; this was the same guy who'd faced down two monsters while dragging my fat ass the length of a house. Roger Shaver was a chump after that.

Still, I had the idea that it was generally frowned upon to sit by and let your boyfriend (not-boyfriend) get stabbed, plus I was, as Eli had none too graciously pointed out, a cop by training. When Roger nudged Eli toward a darkened hallway, I gave them a few seconds lead and went after them. I kept the camera running until Roger and Eli vanished into the darkness. Then I ended the video, made sure it was uploading to the cloud, and went after them.

It was a long, narrow space, with empty cardboard boxes stacked along one wall to make it even narrower. The only light came from the EXIT sign above a door at the far end; it cast everything in a red glare that made me blink as my eyes adjusted. Near the door, two shadowy figures were pressed together against the wall. I didn't bother to quiet my steps. That wasn't how this was going to go down. And while I was shit at essays for zoology class, and I was shit at being a good boyfriend, not that we were labeling things, and I was shit at dealing with the emotional burden of police work, I was actually decent at tactics. I'd known Roger Shaver for a long time, and I had a good idea of how this was going to play out.

As I got closer, I could make out their shapes more clearly. Eli had his cheek to the wall; Roger had one hand tangled in Eli's blowout hair, while the knife was still pressed against his side, the tip hidden by the folds of the shirt. He was muttering questions.

"—he send you? No point lying about it, you little bitch. Or was it her? Because I'm not giving them up without cash money."

I took another step.

His head snapped up and turned toward me. In the darkness, his eyes held tiny points of red light.

"Roger," I said, holding up my hands. "You're about waist-deep in bad choices."

"I got a knife. I'll pop his kidney if you come over here."

"That would be another bad choice. Why don't you put the knife down, and we can talk about whatever's got you so hot?"

He flexed his fingers around the handle. His eyes raked me up and down. "Who are you?"

"LeBlanc." When he didn't say anything, I added, "I took you in a few times for hitting on Ivy."

He made a noise that could have meant anything.

"You can make a smart choice right now," I said. "You can put that knife down and step away from him, and we can talk like normal people."

"Did she send you too? Because I—" He choked up, and he released Eli's head long enough to draw a shaking hand across his mouth. "I'm giving them up for cash. That's all. You tell her she can't throw a scare into me. I don't believe in that voodoo bullshit. And if Fontenot sent you, tell him the same thing. If he comes after me again, I'll track him down and take his dick off."

"Lanny Fontenot?" Eli asked.

"Eli," I said, "not now."

"You've got something Lanny wants? And something— something Nelda Pie wants?"

Roger made that noise again.

"What?" Eli asked. "What do you have that could be—"

Roger caught Eli's hair again, pulled his head back, and slammed him into the wall. Eli let out a cry and sagged against the paneling.

I took deep breaths. The red light from the EXIT sign fogged in my vision and then contracted to crystal clarity. It pulsed like a blinker light. Stop. Stop. Stop. Stop. Stop.

"We're going outside," Roger said, hauling Eli backward by the hair. Eli cried out again. "So we can finish our conversation. And if you follow us, it's going to get nasty. Understand?"

"Understand?" I asked. I felt like I had a conch shell pressed to my ear. I was listening to the rush of my blood, and it sounded like the ocean. "Motherfucker, here's what you need to understand. I've got you on camera abducting him at knifepoint. That's felony assault and kidnapping. That's your third fucking strike, Roger. That's twenty years minimum, and with a piece of shit like you, the judge will probably wipe his ass with the sentencing guidelines and send you up for life. You stupid little bitch, understand that."

Eli was staring at me.

Roger's mouth hung open. The hand with the knife dipped. Then he shoved Eli forward and pivoted toward the exit door. I caught up with him as he hit the crash bar. First, I slammed his head into the doorjamb. Then I got a knee into his kidney. He was already going down, but I didn't want to take any chances, so I stomped on his hand until he squealed and dropped the knife.

Eli swooped in to grab it, and then he backed up again.

"Are you ok?" I asked over my shoulder.

His hazel eyes were enormous.

"Eli?"

He nodded.

"Did he cut you?"

"N-no. I don't think so."

As I crouched, Roger let out a moan. I rolled him onto his back. His nose was a mess—definitely broken, and bleeding everywhere. He had a split lip. A line across his cheek and up to his temple looked like it was going to be a fantastic bruise. I wasn't sure if I'd broken any bones in his hand, but to be honest, by that point, I was too angry to care. When I rocked forward on the balls of my feet, Roger moaned and tried to scuttle backward.

"Uh uh," I said. "Time to talk."

"Just a deal, just trying to make a deal, thought you were putting a pinch on me, wouldn't have hurt the kid—"

"Yeah, sure, you're a saint." I rucked up his shirt. He batted at me, but by then, he was too hurt and defeated to put up much of a fight. When I forced him onto his belly, I found the packet of papers tucked into his waistband. I glanced at them, but they were all handwritten in script, and they looked like letters. I tossed them to Eli. "That's what you're trying to sell to Lanny? Why does he want them?"

Roger glared at me.

"Because they're valuable," Eli said, flipping through them. "These look like love letters. To Nelda Pie. From Nelda Pie."

And then it made sense: Lanny refusing to go inside Stoplight, Lanny's weak story about his trouble at the juke joint, Lanny needing money, Lanny's big score, Lanny holding the Louisiana state record for being a dumbass for the longest continuous stretch of time. Amrey had even warned us to keep him away from Nelda Pie; she must have called in a complaint about us and about Lanny, which Amery had assumed were connected, although apparently she hadn't reported the theft.

"He stole them from her," I said. "From the Stoplight. That's why he told us that story about running out on the check; that's why he didn't want to go inside."

"Jesus," Eli said. "That was stupid."

Roger made a noise that I took for a laugh.

"You're just as dumb," I told him. "Where do you come in?"

"I went there to score. Friday. Fontenot was there. I know him from around, and he wanted to buy me a drink. I was fresh off of a ninety-day, dry as a fucking bone, so I said sure. I mean, I knew him from around, so I knew he was a queer, but he's not faggy, and he never tries anything. He wanted to buy me another drink. He started talking big. He was about to pull in this big score. Sure, I thought. He's a queer who talks big. But then he must have realized he'd said too much, and he got real quiet. But he didn't leave. And he was watching the place. Asked if Nelda Pie was in, and he got real happy when they said she was out, even though he tried to play it cool. Sure enough, when the zydeco started up, he went off to use the can. I followed him. Saw him bump the lock into the office. So I settled up and went outside, and when Fontenot came out like he had a rocket up his chute, I cracked him on the side of the head. He went down, and what the hell did I get? A bunch of papers and—"

He cut off so suddenly that his teeth clicked.

"And what?" I asked. I'd seen the bruise on Lanny's temple, and so far, the whole story sounded disappointingly close to the truth.

He stared at me. Under the blood from his broken nose, in the weak glow of the EXIT sign, he looked like a corpse.

"You're terrified," Eli said. "Why?"

"Because he stole from Nelda Pie," I said. "You met her. I wouldn't want to be on her bad side."

"But it's more than that. What's going on?"

Roger's jaw tightened.

"Why don't we call the Stoplight?" I asked. "If we yell real loud, they'll hear us even over that zydeco crap."

"No," Roger moaned. "Look, I called her. I told her I'd sell them back. The letters. And then I started—I started seeing things."

"What?" Eli asked.

"Things!" Roger took a few hyperventilated breaths. "I wake up, and the room is crawling with shadows. Or I see them coming after me on the sidewalk. Middle of the day, they're there. And if I turn on the light, or if I turn around, they're gone. But I know I saw them. And one time, I'm going to be too slow, and they're going to get me. Shadows, man. Fucking shadows." He let out a noise that started as a laugh and dissolved into a sob.

"What do these shadows—" Eli began, but when I shook my head, he cut off.

I let Roger cry for half a minute. Then I shook him by his shirt. "You were at the trailer the night Ivy got killed."

Roger let out a wet noise. Snot mixed with the blood on his face.

"You were there."

He nodded.

"You killed Ivy."

"No!"

"You did. We've got an eyewitness who saw you dragging the body out of the trailer."

"That wasn't me, man."

"Sure, it was. You've been hitting on her for years. Beating the hell out of her whenever you needed to feel a little better about yourself. And it's been worse, the last few months. You've been getting real nasty."

"Swear to God, no. There's no way. I did a ninety. They put me up for a ninety, Deputy. I haven't touched her."

I glanced at Eli.

Roger must have sensed the opening because he blurted, "You call the Orleans Parish Jail. Call and ask. They'll tell you. I got out Friday."

"That's funny," I said. "Ivy got her head bashed in on Friday."

Moaning, Roger shook his head and tried to twist away. I hauled him back by the shirt. "You won't believe me," he said. "Nobody's going to believe me. It wasn't me. It just looked like me. Don't you see? I got sent up, but you ask around that trailer park, and everybody will tell you Roger Shaver's been scratching his balls and drinking his beers and blowing Ivy's money at the Stoplight. It wasn't me, man. It looked like me. You ever see that movie about the blue girl that can look like anybody she wants?"

"No," Eli said. "Nobody knows what you're—"

"Mystique," I said.

Eli groaned.

"You're telling me this thing just happened to look like you."

"Yeah, man. Yeah. That's all. It looked like me. But it wasn't me. Call the jail; they'll tell you."

"But you were there. You watched that thing kill her."

"No."

"Yes, you did. You saw it. You stood there and watched it beat her to death."

"No, no!" His voice yipped on the last word. After a moment, with what looked like a great deal of struggle, he managed to bring it down. "No," he said hoarsely. "I got there. I saw that—that thing." His voice began to thin with his efforts to control it, but emotion made it slip. "It had my face, man. That thing had my fucking face. And then it dissolved. Turned into this light. I've done some hard stuff. I think my brain is seriously fucked up."

"What about after?"

Licking his lips, Roger tried for innocent. "After?"

"You went inside the trailer. And don't lie; we've got a witness for that too."

He gave a jerky nod.

"Why?"

"I thought maybe someone else was hurt. I knew Ivy was dead, and I couldn't do anything for her. But I thought—"

"Do not try pulling my leg on this one, Roger. I'm at the end of my rope tonight. You went in there, but it wasn't to look for more victims."

"We always kept a stash. I was sick, man. I'd gotten one hit after I got out, and then I was broke, and I needed something to take the edge off. But it was gone. So I went to the Stoplight to score, and that's when I saw Fontenot, and it's like I told you."

"All right," I said. I threw another look at Eli, and he nodded. "Let's get you on your feet, Roger, and then we're taking a ride to see our old buddy Sergeant Kimmons. It'll be like a family reunion."

As I dragged Roger to his feet, a man barked behind us, "What's this? What's going on?"

I turned automatically at the sound. That was my mistake.

Roger hit me in the back of the head. It wasn't much of a blow, clipping me along the back of the skull, but it was enough to make me stagger. Eli reached out to catch me. Roger turned and threw himself into the crash bar, and he ran out into the night.

"Hey!" the man shouted from the end of the hall. "Stop right there!"

When I had my balance, I caught the door on my shoulder and pulled Eli outside after me. The streetlights were spaced far apart, hanging cottony spheres of light too weak to dispel the darkness. Roger was gone, but I ran anyway, heading back to L'amoureux and the Escort.

Eli had to yank twice before I realized he wanted to stop. He was favoring one leg, as though he'd pulled something in his calf running, but his breathing was deep and even in spite of our pace. Perfect hair, perfect face, perfect body, and the jerk could run flat out and not break a sweat.

"Your leg—" I started.

But he pulled out his phone and pressed it to his ear. Then, after a moment, he pulled it away and placed the call on speaker.

The woman's voice sounded strained. Panicked, even. "—friend, an acquaintance, someone who has recently come into your life—"

"Hope," Eli said. "Hope, slow down."

"I can't slow down. That's what I'm trying to tell you. It's a man, I'm almost sure of it, and he's—he's like—the impression I'm getting is lazy Sunday mornings and breakfast cereal with marshmallows and sex like coals that burn long and low. Oh my God, why can't I just see his face?"

"Lanny," Eli whispered.

My face was hot, but I nodded. The description sounded like Lanny. It was uncomfortably accurate.

"We know who it is, Hope," Eli said. "We think we know who you're talking about."

"Then you need to find him. Right now. Because he's about to do something very stupid." Her voice hitched, and even with the frantic need propelling her, she stumbled. "I think he's about to kill someone."

ELI (11)

In the true fashion of all psychics, Hope had been absolutely zero fucking help at all.

"Why can't she tell us where he is?" Dag asked as we got in the car.

"I don't know."

"How can she possibly know that he's about to do something like that?"

"I don't know."

"Lanny wouldn't kill someone."

I was too busy fighting the need to massage my calf to respond to that. I grabbed Dag's school bag and shoved the stolen letters inside so that I wouldn't lose any of them.

"He wouldn't," Dag insisted. "He's a pig, and he's a thief, and he's got the maturity of a jar of grape jelly. But he's not dangerous, and he's not a killer."

"Dag, I hear what you're saying." I gave up and leaned down to rub my leg. "Let's just try to find him for now. Do you know where he might be?"

"You hear what I'm saying, but, what? I'm wrong?"

"Does he have places he likes to go—"

"Don't do that. I don't like when you treat me like I'm too dumb to know what you're doing. You think I'm wrong about Lanny."

L'amoureux's pink stucco glistened in the humidity and the glare of the sodium lamps. A woman in a fur stole, a cami, and a rainbow skirt sashayed past us. She was laughing into her phone, adjusting the cami as she walked, a cigarillo hanging from her lips. It wasn't until one of her boobs slipped out that I realized she was in drag.

"You know, I'm the dumb one," I said. "You get that mixed up sometimes. You're the smart one. You're the one who's going to be the scientist."

"Yeah? Could have fooled me with the grades I'm pulling. And don't change the subject."

"I know you've got these complicated feelings for Lanny—"

"I don't. He stole from me. He ran out on me. That's pretty simple."

I bit my lip and kept my gaze fixed on the sweating stucco. I thought about the time he had moved a garter snake off the sidewalk. Or the time he had bandaged my knee after I'd fallen on a run. Or the Sunday at his parents', turning around to find the two of us alone in the kitchen, and he'd kissed my ear and whispered, *I love you* before taking another brownie. I thought about his face when Fen had held a gun on Lanny. When I trusted my voice not to break, I said, "All right. I think it's a strange coincidence that Lanny showed up in your life at the same time that we encountered another hashok. I think hashoks are creatures who like taking apart people's lives seam by seam, feeding off the pain and suffering they cause before they move on to their next victim. I think it's strange that Lanny was at the Stoplight, that he stole those letters from Nelda Pie, and that it all happened the same night the hashok killed Ivy."

Up the street, someone was playing "Hot Girl Summer." A little late for that, I thought. It was too mellow. Didn't anybody have any cannons they could set off?

"You think Lanny's the hashok?"

"It's a possibility."

"And what—he has this grand plan to pretend to pay me back so that he can somehow ruin my life?"

"He's not in your life to pay you back, Dag. He's here because he wants to replace me."

It was a mistake; I heard it as soon as my words faded into the Escort's perpetual fug of Big Macs and French fries.

What was worse was the tenderness in Dag's voice. "Eli—"

"Oh my God, no. Please don't." My eyes were hot, and I closed them. The nap of the upholstery felt pebbly as I clutched it.

"E." He touched my cheek.

I jerked my head away. And, of course, I hit the window. And then I couldn't help it: I started to laugh, and Dag started to laugh too. I opened my eyes, and a few tears leaked out before Dag brushed them away. Then he kissed me.

"Please don't," I whispered.

His dark eyes looked deep and still. Then he nodded.

"I don't think he's the hashok. For one, he's...Lanny. I don't know how else to say it. I don't think a supernatural creature could impersonate him. Not and fool the people who know him. He's too..."

"Lanny?"

"Yeah, let's go with that."

"Dumb?"

"Eli."

"Horny and dumb?"

Dag grinned and thumbed another tear away. "It's not Lanny."

"It's somebody, Dag. And it's going to get another victim. I know you don't like the idea, but I think it's Lanny."

"Ok." He pulled out his phone.

"What are you doing? He's not going to confess."

"Jeez, if Lanny really were a monster, he actually might. One time, a security guard caught us on this golf course, and when he asked what we were doing—the kind of question that nobody really answers—Lanny told him he was going to get me really drunk and then have me fuck him on the eighteenth hole. He kept saying it was going to be a hole in one; I don't even know what he meant."

"Uh huh."

"Don't judge me."

"I mean, you did date him. For a surprisingly long time."

"I was going through a phase," he said, rubbing a spot between his eyebrows. "I don't even know what kind of phase it was. At least it's over."

But I did. It was called your first love. And it wasn't Lanny. And nobody ever got over it, not really.

"If he tells you—"

But Dag frowned at me and shook his head, about to say something to me before he cut himself off and said, "Hi, Mom, I need to ask you something—no, we don't have time for that." He listened for a moment and then broke in with, "Oh my God, oh my God, oh my God. Fine." He tapped the screen. "There. You're on speaker."

"Hello, Eli," Gloria LeBlanc cooed.

"Mom, do you have—"

"How are you?"

"Fine. When Lanny was over—"

"And Eli, how are you?"

"I'm wonderful, Gloria."

Dag's dad, Hubert LeBlanc, bellowed in the background, "How's Eli?"

"He says he's wonderful," Gloria shouted back at him.

"Has he been doing those Kegels we talked about?"

"Never mind," Dag said. "I'm going to let this monster kill all of us because it's better than this."

"He's feeling unappreciated today," I said.

"Oh, have you tried changing positions?"

Dag groaned and reached for the handle. "Goodbye. I'm going to walk into traffic."

"Tell them about pony play," Hubert shouted in the background.

When Dag tried to wrench the door open, I caught his arm and whispered. "This is one of the top five reasons I love you."

"I think it's called bareback, Hubert," Gloria was shouting away from the phone. Then her voice came back more clearly. "Have you boys tried bareback? With the masks and the stirrups?"

"It's pony play." Hubert's voice was growing louder, presumably as he moved toward the phone. "I read an article in *Cosmopolitan*. I was looking for something about squirting, which is when—"

"This is how I die," Dag shouted into the phone. "I'm going to die because my parents can't keep it in their pants."

"Dagobert, you say such horrible things sometimes," Gloria said. "Now, I wanted to talk to you about having Eli make some of those bukkake videos."

She caught me at a bad time, and I choked on my spit, which turned into a coughing fit.

"Serves you right," Dag muttered.

"And then your father wants to talk to both of you about anal fissures. We were going to have this conversation on Sunday—"

"Perfect conversation material for Sunday dinner," Dag said.

"—but you canceled. And do not take that tone with me, young man."

"Safe is sexy, Dagobert," his father shouted.

"He's right, Dagobert. A doctor on TV said if you aren't using enough lube—"

"Mom, we are really running out of time here. I know you've talked to Lanny. I know he went to the house and you gave him my number and told him where to find me. But I need to know, when Lanny showed up at the house, did he give you his phone number? A way to contact him?"

Gloria trilled a nervous little laugh. "I don't know why he would— I mean, how did you—Dagobert, you sometimes ask the silliest—"

"Oh my God," Dag moaned. He put his head in his hands. "How long?"

Gloria sounded a little breathless now. "I don't know what you mean."

"How long has he been coming over for dinner?"

"Well," Hubert said with grumpy satisfaction. "They trained him right at the academy. You can't say they didn't. He saw through you right away."

"This has nothing to do with being a cop. Every time I wonder what my parents are doing, I just imagine the worst, most humiliating thing possible, and I'm always right."

"Dagobert, what a terrible thing to say," Gloria said.

"Apologize to your mother right now," Hubert said.

"How long?"

"Since you moved out." Gloria sniffled. "I saw him in the Quartier. He was panhandling, Dagobert. The poor thing. I know the breakup was bad, but he was always so sweet, and you had Eli now, and I couldn't very well leave him there—"

"Every night?"

"Don't be silly."

"Every Monday," Hubert said. "He's a lovely young man. Not a perfect ten like Eli—"

"Thank you, Hubert," I put in.

"—but he's a very fine specimen. And you're welcome, Eli."

"Of course," Dag said. He was talking to the dashboard. The clock, in particular, it seemed. "Of course my parents are aiding and abetting my ex."

"Did he tell you where he was staying?" I asked. "A friend, a relative?"

"Well, no," Gloria said. "He kept moving around. He said they were his boyfriends, but Eli—" Her voice lowered discreetly. "—I think they might have been hookups."

I made the most politely noncommittal sound I could manage.

"And since I didn't know where he would be, I had to call him on his cell phone every week."

"You've been calling him every week?" The words exploded out of Dag. "For a year?"

"Do not take that tone with your mother," Hubert shouted.

"Of course, sweetheart," Gloria said. "I had to ask him what he wanted to eat that week. And then I needed to know where to pick him up, and—"

Dag was making a noise somewhere between a kettle and an emergency siren, and a vein was throbbing in his temple.

"Gloria," I asked, "can you please text us that number?"

"Of course, dear. If you'd called half an hour ago, you could have talked to him here."

Dag's hands tightened around the steering wheel. The vinyl made squeaking noises.

"Take a breath," I whispered to him. To Gloria, I said, "He was there? Tonight?"

"Yes, of course. It's a Monday. Of course, I had to pick him up in New Orleans, tonight, and the poor thing looked absolutely miserable. He'd had his heart broken. I think that's why he ate all the beignets and three of the custards—"

"Did he talk about anything? Say anything that you can remember?"

"He'd had his heart broken, Eli. The poor thing could barely finish his étouffée."

"You made him étouffée?" Dag shouted.

I leaned closer to the phone. "If he said anything, Gloria, it could be really important."

"I don't know. He wanted to talk about this young man. He said he was really his type. He said this young man had everything he wanted in a relationship. What he'd been looking for his whole life. And—oh. He did ask your father about that club out by where your father used to work."

"It's not a club," Hubert shouted. "It's a juke joint."

"I don't think the gays have juke joints," Gloria screeched back at him.

"It's not for the gays."

"They can go anywhere they want, Hubert. It's the twenty-first century—"

"The Stoplight?" I broke in. "He asked about the Stoplight?"

"That's it, dear. Is that a BDSM thing? Because he kept asking if they had a back door."

DAG (12)

The causeway was almost empty as we shot across the lake toward DuPage Parish. Behind us, New Orleans flickered, a crescent flame like a candle about to be blown out. Ahead, Slidell guttered on the horizon. No moon tonight. Only a glaze of stardust on the dark waters.

"He's not answering," Eli said.

"Of course he's not answering. The dumbass finally geared up to do something really, truly stupid." I tried to stop there, but the words had a momentum of their own. "He's not going to hurt anyone. Lanny wouldn't hurt anyone. He's going to rob the place. Or he's going to try to marry that pretty boy they've got doing sex work. Or, hell, maybe he's not going after anyone in the juke, but there's a dealer nearby, and he's trying to hit his stash."

The faint light from the dash painted Eli's face. He squeezed my hand, which was worse than arguing, and placed another call to Lanny's cell.

"That psychic might be full of shit."

Eli took a deep breath. He shook his head. "When I talked to her, I saw something, Dag. I think she's legit."

"But she doesn't know what he's going to do. She said someone new in our life. Someone who might do something stupid. We're the ones who said it was Lanny. And she said she thinks he's going to kill someone. She thinks. She doesn't know."

With a slow exhalation, Eli dropped the phone in his lap. He started to squeeze my hand again.

I pulled free and hammered on the dash. "God fucking damn it, Lanny. What the fuck is wrong with you?"

The sound of the causeway under our tires changed when we reached land. I wiped my face and looked over at Eli. He was watching me. His hazel eyes were a maze.

"What?" I asked.

"I'm really sorry."

"What the fuck is that supposed to mean?"

He blinked a few times and shook his head and looked away.

We drove past the bristles of empty corn fields. We drove past cotton fields that hadn't been touched yet, the bolls as bright as bone in the starlight. A mile later, they were burning the stubble in a canebrake, and the air was smoky and sweet, like caramelized sugar, as embers spun up against the sky.

Bragg met us, old and crouched under a quilt of sodium light.

Then we were past Bragg, driving along the willows and oaks and cypresses at the edge of Bayou Pere Rigaud. The darkness settled deeper here. Only the faintest light made it through the trees, and it glimmered on the ripples and troughs of black water. Something moved, an explosion that broke the bayou's surface and threw a spray that glinted in the Escort's headlights. An owl streaked in front of us, and by the time I'd hit the brakes, it was gone. I was shaking as I pressed the gas pedal again.

The red exterior lights of the Stoplight were visible long before the juke joint itself, a hazy column that rose above the tall grass and the weeds. It was like a beacon. Summoning. Warning. Maybe both. I slowed just in time to spot the oyster-shell lot, but I kept going. Half a mile farther, I turned onto a dirt road and drove until the tall grasses hid us. I let the Escort roll to a stop on the shoulder.

We hiked back. Two cars—sedans, a Chevy and a Saturn—were parked at the far end of the lot, in a section I guessed was intended for the juke's employees. The parking close to the joint was meant for customers. But the rest of the lot was empty aside from an ancient red Ford pickup. It was the truck Fen had been driving the day she confronted us here.

"Lanny doesn't have a car," I said.

"He might have stolen one."

I shook my head and pointed at the truck. "He came with her."

"We don't know that."

I turned off the Escort and got out. Oyster shells crunched underfoot as I started toward the side of the juke joint. Behind me, Eli's door opened, and then his steps moved after me.

"Stay here," I said. "He asked about the back door, so I'll go around back and see—"

Eli's hand, warm and firm, closed around my upper arm. I could have kept going, but I let him drag me to a stop.

"Something bad happened here," he said quietly. "I need you to face that before we go inside. The lot's empty—"

"It's a Monday night."

"It's a Monday night in a parish where a third of the men drink themselves under the table every Monday night. The lot shouldn't be empty. You know that."

After a moment, I gave a savage nod. "Wait in the car and keep your phone ready to call the police."

Eli smiled. His fingers tightened around my arm, once, and then his thumb stroked a line up and down the skin there. My eyes stung, and I turned my attention to the Stoplight, with its plank walls and its sagging steps and the red security lights making me feel like I was on the set of a horror movie.

"I'll go around back," Eli said. "I think—"

"No. You're staying here."

"Dag, I'm not—"

"Then do what you want, Eli. You always do." I ripped free of his grip and started around the side of the joint. Behind me, he let out a sharp breath, and then a spray of oyster shells rattled against the juke's stilts, and he swore savagely.

I parted the wall of grass and weeds and plunged into the overgrown field. The vegetation closed behind me, and all of a sudden, I couldn't hear Eli anymore. Cicadas buzzed. A mockingbird sang. Stalks of grass whispered against my jeans. I could even hear the rasp of the planks under my fingers as I followed the outline of the building with one hand. I could hear my heart, my pulse quickening until it was a drumbeat inside my skull.

The grass and weeds ended as abruptly as they had begun, and I found myself in a small clearing at the back of the juke joint. The ground cover here was mostly clover. There was a boarded-up well with a sun-bleached plastic bucket on the ground next to it. A brick firebox—sloppy construction, with the mortar oozing out between the bricks—supported a barbeque grill that was black with old burnt meat and char. Two aluminum pull-behind trailers were set on cinderblock piers; both were dark. A plank-wall privy stood at the far end of the yard.

But the only thing that could hold my interest were the steps up into the juke joint, where a door stood open, and light—normal, warm, yellow light—spilled out into the night.

I hurried up the steps and went inside. I stood in the kitchen. Bare bulbs hung overhead, illuminating worn checkerboard linoleum and white-enamel appliances—a three-quarters-sized fridge, a reinforced door that led to what I thought was a walk-in freezer, a stove that was pulled out from the wall and not in use, and farther down, a second stove, this one with a pot simmering above a blue flame. The air smelled like gumbo—garlic and shrimp and sausage—

and clove cigarettes and too-hot frying oil and marijuana. My stomach turned. Sweat popped out on my face like spatters of hot grease. A hole had been blown in the door on the other side of the kitchen with what I guessed was a shotgun, and to judge by the splinters all over the linoleum, it had happened recently.

I took a step toward the door. What sounded like Jerry Lee Lewis was coming from the front of the juke joint. Great balls of fire. I fought a giggle and another wave of nausea, and I almost missed the faint scraping noise that came from the walk-in freezer. I stopped. Then I backed up a few steps. When I tried the handle, it opened partially before catching, and someone—something—inside moved. I positioned myself to the side of the door.

"This is Dagobert LeBlanc. I'm with—I'm trying to help. Is someone in there?"

This time, only silence met me.

"Lanny, if you did something stupid, we can figure it out."

A short, sharp disagreement broke out—two voices, the words so quiet I couldn't hear. Then something rattled, and the door popped free of the seal and swung open a few inches. Cold air misted out into the warmth of the kitchen.

"Just move real slow," a man said. His voice was familiar, but I couldn't place it. "He startles easy."

I caught the door and opened it. LED lights filled the freezer with white clarity. Frost bloomed on stainless steel panels. Shelves lined three walls, heavy with meat and bagged produce. More fog licked across the floor as warm air rolled in.

All of that registered at a distance. What I focused on was the pair of the palest blue eyes I'd ever seen, and the skinny white boy they belonged to. He was holding a chef's knife that had to have been twelve inches long, and he was naked. Every bit of him was as pretty as his face, and I figured this was the kid Lanny had paid to spend time with. He looked like he wasn't out of high school yet.

Behind him stood the bartender who had served Eli and me on our first visit. He was missing his prosthetic hand, and I caught a glimpse of something that didn't look like a stump before he moved the limb behind his back. He had a hand on the boy's neck, and he was whispering in his ear.

"—see? Nothing to worry about. He's not going to do anything."

The white boy's chest rose and fell like he was still running a marathon. The knife trembled. Light made a sickle along the edge.

The bartender petted his neck and shoulder. "Go on, baby. Put it down. We don't want anybody to get hurt. Good. That's real good. You did so good keeping us safe, and now you can relax, because everything's ok, right?"

The last was directed to me. It took me a moment to catch up, and then I nodded. "Back door is clear. You can get out of here."

"Hear that?" Slowly, the bartender's hand closed around the boy's, easing the fingers back from the wooden handle of the knife. "You did so good. Now we're going to go home."

With one final, deft movement, he slid the knife from the boy's hand and passed it to me handle first. The boy stumbled in a circle, pressing his face into the bartender's chest, and began shivering uncontrollably.

In a subdued voice, as he stroked the boy's back, the bartender asked, "Is it really clear?"

I nodded.

"I've got to get him out of here."

"What happened?"

"You know Lanny?"

I nodded again.

"That coonass came in here with a redbone woman. She shot out half the lights in the bar while Lanny was screaming for everybody to leave."

"How'd you end up in there?"

"I know who that woman is. I wasn't going to let her have him." His hand pressed possessively against the boy's back.

"I don't think she's interested in him, but you'd better go anyway. Call the cops."

"She's after all of us," the bartender said, but his hand moved up to squeeze the boy's shoulder, and the boy nodded and made a snuffling noise. "Not that Nelda Pie's any better."

"Where would she be?"

"Counting cash in her office. I heard something like an explosion, though. Different from the shots, I mean. Not sure what you're going to find."

"Jeez."

"Dag?" That was Eli's voice, and it came from the front of the bar.

I gave the bartender a last look; when the man nodded, I moved toward the kitchen door again. I emerged into the hall just as Eli appeared at the other end.

"Somebody shot that place to hell," Eli said. He was carrying a broom cocked over one shoulder like a baseball bat, and his head swiveled as he examined the doorways he passed. "I checked the bathrooms. Nobody's up front."

"It was Fen and Lanny," I said. "The bartender and that boy were holed up in the freezer; they told me. They said Nelda Pie was in her office when Fen and Lanny got here. I sent them out the back."

We converged where another hallway branched off. Eli opened his mouth, but he must have seen what I saw at the same moment: blackened planks, a chunk ripped out of the doorway, a reinforced door hanging open, a hole blown in the floor. The smell of whatever had been used in the explosive charge lingered in the air.

"Shit," Eli muttered.

I pressed a hand to his chest, holding him back so I could take the lead. I adjusted my grip on the knife so I held it low, with the edge up. You stab up to do the most damage. To get under the ribcage. That had been part of my job, knowing that. Someone had paid me to know that. Someone had paid me to know how to—

Eli's hand found the small of my back. I stilled. Then I pulled myself together and crept forward again.

I heard Lanny before I saw him.

"—just gotta do this, gotta do it and get it over with, do what matters, just gotta do it, come on, come on, come on you fucking coward just do it—"

"Lan," I called ahead. "Hey, Lanny, it's me. Dag. Doggo. Can you hear me?"

His mumbling cut off. He was panting like he was sick.

"Lanny, why don't you tell me what's going on?"

"Doggo?"

"Yeah, it's me."

The hesitation had a snapped-tight quality to it. "For real? Because sometimes it's you, and you say things, and sometimes— sometimes I don't think it's you, but I want it to be."

"It's me." More of that cable-taut tension. "The same guy who cleaned you up after you snorted all those Smarties, remember? You thought they were Adderall."

His laugh sounded wet, gasping, the bottom of it ripped out. "Doggo."

"Yeah. I'm going to come around the door now, all right? Is that all right?"

He sounded like he was crying. "Yeah. Doggo—Doggo, I really messed up."

"It's ok. We're going to figure it out, just like we did those Smarties. I'm coming through the door now, ok?"

Eli caught my arm, and I had a glimpse of his face, eyes wide, before I shook him off. Then I stepped around the corner and through the door.

It was bad. It was worse than I'd thought. Fen lay on the floor in a pool of blood, the duster flapped open beneath her, the blood almost the same color as the leather. She looked washed out, and her eyes were half closed and empty. She was breathing, but only barely. Nelda Pie was breathing too—harsh, grating noises interspersed with hacking coughs. She lay near a desk on the other side of the room, curled up on her side, one hand to her throat. The peroxide bouffant was limp and flat. Lanny stood between them. Fen's shotgun rested in the crook of his arm. The ancient, rusted harvest knife was tucked into his waistband. He looked untouched—his mane of golden curls; a threadbare tank top with rainbow-lettered words across the front that said IN MY PAST LIFE, I WAS EVEN GAYER; jean shorts; white Vans. His eyes were red, and I guessed it was a mix of crying and some seriously strong grass.

"Oh, Lan."

"I didn't do it. I was going to do it, just like you wanted me to, but I knew I was going to pussy out. So I found her," he nodded at Fen, "just like she said, the Avenue D Rooms. I told her what you wanted, and she said she'd help. Only it all went wrong. We got here, and people were scared, and I about peed myself, and she did something to the door to make it explode, and when we came inside, Nelda Pie stabbed her, but she hit Nelda Pie in the throat, and—and I want to do it, Doggo. I want to keep you safe. He won't." He jerked his head at Eli, who stood in the doorway. "He won't do anything for you. But I will, and if this is what you need—" His jaw trembled. He sucked in a breath and set the stock of the shotgun to his shoulder. "—I can do it. I can do it, Doggo. I'll do it because it means you'll be safe."

"No! Lan, Lanny. Put it down. I don't want you to do this. Whatever I said, I don't want you to do this. You don't hurt people. That's not Lanny Fontenot."

"But you said—" The stock flattened Lanny's cheek. It made his face childlike. "Sometimes my head's real fuzzy, Doggo. And I'm tired all the time."

"I changed my mind," I said. "That's all. I changed my mind, Lanny. Put the gun down, would you? You're making me nervous."

After a moment, he let the shotgun fall into the crook of his arm. He looked around. The childlike look hadn't left his face, and a worry line creased his forehead. "I'm not going to get in trouble, Doggo? Because this looks real bad."

"We'll figure it out. Put that all the way down, Lan. On the ground."

Lanny set the shotgun awkwardly on the boards. He stepped back and rubbed his face. He did look tired, I saw now. Drained. He hadn't slept well on the couch, I told myself. He'd been through a lot the last few days.

Lowering the knife, I beckoned him over. I kept my movements slow as I plucked the harvest knife from his waistband and slid it under my belt. "Let's get out of here. They need an ambulance."

"Dag," Eli said.

When I looked over, his head was cocked. Then I heard it too. Sirens.

"No way," Lanny said. He shied away from my touch. "No way, I didn't do nothing, Doggo. They're going to fit me up for this, and I didn't do nothing."

"Dag," Eli said. He was staring at something behind me, but I was trying to settle Lanny, who kept pulling away.

"You're fine, Lan. Let's just walk out of here for now. We'll figure the rest of it—"

"Dag!" Eli shouted.

I glanced over my shoulder in time to see Nelda Pie grabbing the shotgun, her mountain of bleached hair wobbling with the movement.

Two things happened at the same time. Eli threw himself past me and landed on top of the witch, and the force of the collision sent both of them rolling away from the gun. Lanny launched himself in the other direction, barreling out into the hall, and I had a vision of Lanny charging a sheriff's department cruiser and getting himself shot.

"Go after him!" Eli shouted as he and Nelda Pie crashed into a wall of filing cabinets. The metal shivered and chimed. "Go! I've got her!"

"Like fuck you do," Nelda Pie rasped as she bucked and tried to claw at Eli's face.

"Go!" Eli screamed.

I took off after Lanny, but he was lithe and fast, and he had a head start. The juke joint's front room was dark and the shot-out glass from the broken lights crunched under my tennis shoes as I ran. Ahead of me, a rectangle of relatively lighter darkness opened, and a silhouette darted out into the night. The door slammed shut. I hit a table, and my leg went numb. I swore as I ping-ponged through the maze. The sirens wailed.

I crashed into the door and tumbled outside. Night. A few drowned stars. The smell of the grass, the bayou, the gar and mud and moss. Blue lights streaked down the road.

Lanny stood at the edge of the oyster-shell lot. He was talking to someone. My brain went into cop mode: white, slightly above average height, muscular build, short hair. Gray hair.

And then, from the opposite direction of the cruisers, a semi blew into view. Its headlights picked out Lanny and the other man.

It was me.

And I watched myself as I kissed Lanny, caught his hand, and tugged him out onto the asphalt.

The blare of horns. Sirens screaming. The shriek of brakes. A thump.

The force of the impact threw Lanny into a cypress, and if he wasn't dead already, that did it. I heard his body break against the old tree. He fell out of sight, into cattails and darkness. My legs weren't working, so I watched from the gallery of the stilt-shack juke. Because you hit that table, my brain told me. Just a bad case of dead leg.

The semi screeched to a stop down the road. A cruiser braked hard on the shoulder, tires throwing up grass and dirt.

"He ran right out in front of me," the driver was saying. He was an old guy, and he pulled at his long hair. "He ran right out."

Where was I? Gone.

Something palely luminescent drifted out over the bayou's water. Lanny was dead.

A deputy got out of the cruiser. It was Maxwell, the coonass drunk, and he was screaming into his shoulder walkie, "It was LeBlanc, it was LeBlanc, I seen him do it with my own eyes!"

"Dag?"

A hand touched my shoulder, and I startled. I couldn't tell if my heart was beating anymore.

"Dag?" Eli asked again.

"I seen LeBlanc do it," the deputy was repeating into the walkie.

"They run right out in front of me!" the driver was shouting.

"Lanny's dead," I said. "The semi. I. Someone. He was running— it looked like me."

"Jesus Christ," Eli said, pushing me toward the back of the juke. "I need you to stay with me, Dag, because we've got to go now."

My legs still weren't working right, so I held on to Eli and staggered as we ran.

III

When I was a teenager, there was a spot where young couples went in hopes of getting a look at the fifolet lights—known elsewhere as the will o' the wisp, or just plain ol' swamp gas. For the most part, the only fire out there was the sparks of young love.

– *Cajun Folktales*, J. J. Reneaux.

ELI (1)

We hid in a Slidell motel called the Magnolia Rooms. Outside, it was the color of dried toothpaste, with a roof so old the shingles looked like cigarette ash. Inside, it had mustard-colored carpet, maroon drapes, and parakeet wallpaper that had been picked away in long strips. The ancient television got one channel, which was an English-language broadcast out of Mexico of a preacher who promised treasures from heaven if you'd wire him just five American dollars. The bathroom's shower stall had a cracked pan, so we had to shower in thirty-second increments to avoid flooding the room. We ate out of the Texaco on the corner—prepackaged sandwiches and shelf-stable trays of unidentifiable meat and something that some marketing genius had decided to call gravy. I bought dime baggies from a white boy with a cleft lip who spent all day smoking his own product and sitting on the curb of the radiator shop a street over. Dag ate when I forced him to eat. Otherwise, he stayed in bed and slept. Sometimes he watched the preacher out of Mexico, who healed people by beating them with the sole of his shoe. By Thursday, I was ready to kill myself.

Instead, I called Gloria and then smoked weed on the cement pad outside our room. Not in a chair, in case you were wondering. The Magnolia Rooms didn't offer those kinds of amenities. October 31 was cold by early evening, and although I'd tried washing my jeans and underwear and tee in the sink, all I'd managed to do was shift the funk from BO to waterlogged BO, and no matter what I did, the clothes were now perpetually damp. So I smoked. And I shivered.

The sky was clear and darkening quickly. To the west, the sun was swollen, the sky striped with orange. But to the south, the horizon became a clean white cut. It was a relief. There was something moving there, where my eyes rested. A shape that bobbed. The aluminum skin of a plane, maybe. Or an early star. I closed my eyes, and that was even better. I'd always thought being a fugitive would be fun. Better than this, anyway. More frantic sex. Less mildew and despair. Zero moments where my nerve broke and I yelled, "You need to get your ass out of bed because I don't know what to do anymore."

The dream came on me so suddenly that I thought I was still awake at first, only I was outside my body, watching. Dag knelt on the bed. He was naked, his powerful body exposed, the chiseled lines of muscle on display. He was hard. He was touching himself, and his face was fixed with what I took for anger at first, only to recognize an instant later as an intensity that was unusual in the sex that Dag and I shared.

A moment later, I watched myself emerge from the bathroom. I was naked. I was perfect. If Dag was chiseled, I was sculpted. Muscle, sure, but beautiful muscle. Lean muscle. The carved lines of my Adonis belt. The rippling saw of serratus muscles. A better haircut. Whiter teeth when I smiled, when I kissed him, when I laughed as he pushed me onto my back and inched closer, his knees dimpling the mattress.

He entered me without asking, without prepping, without the whispered worries, without all the concern. The better me arched his back, his eight-pack popping into sharp relief, and the noise he made signaled an overload of pleasure.

"Fuck yeah," Dag said, grabbing my ankles to haul me closer. He thrust again, spreading me, lifting me, and the me on the bed squealed. "Yeah, bitch. You like that?"

I guess I did, because I babbled something, and I made noises that I could barely believe, and Dag pounded into me—steady, unyielding, a fuck that matched the unwavering intensity of his focus. And then I watched the me on the bed buck and writhe again, every muscle on display as my body tensed, and then as that version of me came untouched. Came just from the fuck. Came just from Dag.

"—son, are you ok?"

I blinked the sunspots out of my eyes. The sky was indigo, almost black now. I tried to hold on to the dream or the vision or whatever it had been, but it was like trying to hold on to air. Exhaustion washed over me.

For a moment, all I wanted was to talk to Hope. She had helped me see it once; I wanted to see it again. I wanted to know how I could have it—if it was even possible, no matter how much exercise, how many hours, how many meals of boiled eggs and sweet potatoes.

"Eli?"

I tried to adjust to the darkness so that I could make out the face hovering in front of me.

Hubert LeBlanc frowned and shifted the gym bag he was carrying.

"He was having a fit," Gloria said. She stood behind him, even less distinct—barely more than a shadow, although I could tell she was carrying something, and I smelled bacon.

"I don't know," Hubert said doubtfully. "That's quite an erection."

"Oh my God," I groaned and rubbed my eyes. But I didn't die or spontaneously combust or even wake from this second nightmare, so apparently, the universe was back to her old tricks. "Hi, Hubert. Hi, Gloria. How'd you get here so quickly? The police must have been watching you."

Hubert snorted. "Morris Maxwell was passed out in his cruiser with a bottle of Wild Turkey. I could have bumped his fender backing out of the garage, and he wouldn't have noticed."

"I'll just check on Dagobert—" Gloria took a step toward the door.

"Here," I got to my feet, recovered the roach, realized they were looking at me—at it—and shoved it into a pocket. "Let's go inside."

Seeing it through their eyes was a lot worse. The smell of microwaved food, body funk, and the stink of the weed. Trash overflowing the tiny wastebasket. Dag had the polyester coverlet wrapped around him like a shawl, part of it pulled over his head in a hood, and he was watching the preacher from Mexico do the foxtrot with a woman who looked close to ninety. In the background, a cane-back wheelchair suggested her recent change of status. Dag looked gray in the light from the TV, his face puffy and washed out, and his eyes were like those plastic discs they sew on stuffed animals. Gloria let out a cry of distress and set aside the covered casserole. Hubert cleared his throat and lowered the gym bag onto the lone chair.

"Baby," Gloria whispered as she settled on the bed next to Dag. Then she made another of those pained noises and pulled Dag to her shoulder. His body heaved, and he turned into her.

"I'm sorry," I said. I couldn't look at Hubert, so I directed the words to an empty spot at the middle of the room. "I should have made him get up." I began grabbing the coated-cardboard trays from past meals. Sweet and sour chicken. Salisbury steak. I looked around for another place to put the trash. No luck, so I balanced them in one hand as I stacked more. "I should have made him walk around. Exercise is really good for depression, and—"

Hubert took my arm in a firm grip and pulled me to my feet.

"If he needs me—"

In answer, Hubert grabbed the wastebasket with the remaining garbage and steered me outside.

We wandered around the back of the motel, dropped the trash in a dumpster, and stood there. Hubert released my arm. He was looking south too. The lake was black and flat now, with chalky smears of light. Crickets were going mad, and then, somewhere nearby, a car alarm went off.

"Did you get my son involved in this?" Hubert asked in a voice I'd never heard from him.

I opened my mouth.

"Sergeant Kimmons told me they think Dagobert killed Lanny. They think he might have hurt some other women. A man named Roger something; I think they found him later. They believe you're involved too. Let me tell you something, Eli: my boy, the one I know, couldn't have done those things."

"He didn't do any of it."

"A deputy says he saw Dag pull Lanny in front of that tractor-trailer."

"It was...someone who looked like Dag. Or was trying to look like him, I should say. Dag was with me." The weed had dried out my throat, and I still felt like my head was floating on a string that was a little too long. "Someone wanted the police to think Dag did it."

"He was framed?" Hubert picked up a flattened PBR can and tossed it in the dumpster. He wiped his hand on his jeans. "Why would someone want to do that? And why would someone want to hurt Lanny or those women?"

"I don't know," I said. "We were trying to figure out what happened to a woman Dag had helped when he was a deputy. Who killed her, I mean. And I think maybe we were getting close. And I think maybe Lanny knew something. Those women, too. Or they were a threat, somehow, all three of them."

"The killer was trying to cover his tracks."

"Maybe." I rubbed my eyes. The weed had been a bad choice; the shadows were like waterfalls, and when a spotlight flickered to life, I was back in the bayou, watching that pale light float away from Lanny's dead body. I tried to clear my throat. My mouth was still too dry. "Lots of maybes."

"Gloria's the one who watches 20/20," Hubert said. He dug a blunt out of his front pocket, patted his other front pocket, and frowned. "Eli, son, do you have a light?"

"What?"

"A lighter." When I didn't react fast enough, Hubert twirled the blunt for emphasis.

I fumbled the lighter out of my jeans.

After sparking the blunt, Hubert puffed on it a few times until the ember was bright, and then he held in the smoke. He rubbed his nose as he lowered his head and let out a breath. The smoke wreathed him, twining through his graying hair.

"I bet we've got some of the episodes on the DVR, though," he said and took another hit. Then, holding his breath again, he passed the blunt. I took it automatically. When he gestured, I took a short pull and immediately began to cough.

"That is some strong shit," I wheezed before another round of coughing hit me.

Hubert grinned. He was nice enough not to call me a lightweight, but he did pluck the blunt out of my hand.

His grin faded as he stared off into the distance. "I bet you can order the DVDs. Maybe some of those mystery books, too. They're different, you know. You got to be able to think both ways. That's what I'm thinking right now. *20/20* and Agatha Christie. How's that sound?"

"It sounds like one of us is really high," I said. "And I'm not sure who. What are you talking about with all this *20/20* business?"

"Solving the murder, Eli. Lord knows you're a ten out of ten for looks, but I'm starting to think Dagobert likes them simple. Lanny was simple too, and Dagobert loved him like you wouldn't believe."

"Trust me, I know." I thought again about Lanny: the lean, golden muscle; the blond locks; the way he rocked the straight-guy-who's-into-dudes vibe. My eyes stung, so I took the blunt back and held in the hit until I felt like I was wearing a mask of bees. As I blew it out, I rasped, "Does he even know why he's so into him? Into that type, I mean."

"It's a hard thing to stand outside yourself." Hubert's gaze was mild. He squeezed my shoulder. "And loving someone, half the time it means going crazy trying to get them to see themselves for what they are, and the other half, it means fighting because you don't want to do it yourself."

A tabby crept out of the shadows. Its eyes glinted when it turned its head. It watched us, stretched out one paw, froze. It must have smelled something good because it couldn't bring itself to pad off into the shadows again, but it wasn't going to risk two shady characters like Hubert and me. The thump of a basshead echoed down the street, and sixty-thousand dollars' worth of Dodge Ram rolled past the lot. The truck was jumping with the beat. The cat spun and darted back into the night, and I let out a breath I hadn't realized I'd been holding. The gleam of the cat's eyes mixed in my vision with the glare of halogen headlights. The world looked streaky, like someone had run a cheap squeegee over it.

"Oh shit," I said. "That stuff is really, really strong."

Laughing, Hubert took my arm. He was talking again, mostly to himself, and I tuned in for parts of it. "—they just follow the evidence, and it's all logical, with the forensics, that kind of thing—" That was when my legs decided sideways was up, and I had to focus on not falling against the motel wall. "—the other kind, there's a twist, because you didn't realize they were twins, or you thought it was the wrong twin, or they weren't twins at all, well, it's a lot about twins, I think—"

Somehow, we got back to the room.

Gloria was waiting by the door. Her eyes were red, and she rolled them when she saw the blunt.

"He'll need lots of special attention," she said to me. "Dagobert looks strong, but he's really very gentle."

"I'll do better."

"Physical intimacy isn't always possible during intense grief. I was reading an article about it in *Mommy's Waiting Room* the other day."

"Sex is important, Gloria," Hubert said, pausing to puff on the blunt. "And it's a survival response. The boys have probably been at it like rabbits after everything they've been through this week. Two young men in a small motel room. Both of them randy as sin. I can imagine the mess the housekeeper has to deal with."

"Oh my God," I whispered.

"If you boys need extra towels, you should ask—I read that's a good way to keep the sheets clean during anal."

"Oh my actual God."

"I'm not saying sex isn't important, Hubert," Gloria huffed. "I'm the one who picked out that double-sided dildo for the boys for Christmas. Oh, darn, I'm sorry I spoiled it, Eli."

I shook my head because I didn't have any words.

"But I'm talking about performance issues," she continued. "Intense emotions might make it difficult for Dagobert to perform."

"No one's talking about performance, Gloria. Dagobert is a healthy young man." Then Hubert lowered the blunt. Smoke curled from the corner of his mouth. "He is healthy, isn't he? He's still able to maintain an erection?"

I opened my mouth. "I don't—"

"It's not just Dagobert, Hubert." Gloria waved in my direction. "What about Eli? He might be having his own trouble."

"I don't think so," Hubert said. "You saw him when we got here. The boy could have called an elevator with that thing."

"I'm just going to check on Dag," I said, cracking the motel door. As I slipped into the room, I added, "Thank you for stopping by. I'm going to do better."

"Some sort of cock ring might help—" Gloria began.

I shut the door.

The bed was empty. The TV was off. In the tiny bathroom, the shower ran in intervals as Dag, ever considerate, tried not to recreate Noah's Flood, and the perfume of the hotel soap filtered out to me. Someone, probably Gloria, had straightened the quilt. The casserole dish was on the TV stand, and when I checked it, I saw that it was actually one of those divided food carriers—on one side, with its own lid, some sort of shrimp pasta in a white sauce that was, knowing Gloria, mostly butter and cream; and on the other side, in a separate section, bread pudding in a sauce that was, knowing Gloria, mostly butter and sugar. I sighed and decided future me was going to have to wait another month.

Lying on the bed, I considered the cracked plaster ceiling. The shower's rhythm was strangely soothing. When I closed my eyes, I could still see those sunspots dancing there. I was still exhausted—beyond exhaustion, so tired I thought I might close my eyes and never open them again. I wanted to fall into that dream forever, the one where everything was so easy, where I was who I was supposed to be, and Dag was who he was supposed to be. But I felt wrung out. Empty. Too tired even for a dream, I guess.

But I must have slept because I woke to Dag's hand on my forehead, smoothing away my hair.

"Hi," he said.

"Hi." Then my stomach grumbled.

Dag laughed. It was a quiet laugh, all the stuffing knocked out of it, but it sounded real. "I guess that answers one question."

His hand lingered on the side of my face. I could smell the soap. Warm skin underneath it. I let my eyes rove over his face, the gray hair heavy with water but already neatly parted, the cut of his jaw. He was wearing only a towel, I realized now, and it was one of those thin, tiny scraps that didn't hide anything. I turned my head slightly. Just enough to kiss his palm.

"Let's eat," he said, his voice rough. "Before it gets cold."

I tried to remember how I'd said it in those dreams. "Dagobert, fuck me."

His pupils dilated. His hand pressed more tightly against my face.

I raised my eyebrows.

"No using sex to get out of eating," he said. "That's going to be a rule."

"If you're feeling back-to-normal enough that you can make up rules, then you're definitely back-to-normal enough to fuck."

"Eli, I'm serious, we can—"

I rolled my head and took his thumb into my mouth, sucking lightly, and then sucking harder. He let out a noise that was part groan and part protest. I tugged, and the towel came free. I ran my hand up the inside of one hard, thick thigh. His dick was iron when I cupped it.

Instead of protesting again, though, Dag stood. The towel fell to the floor, and he crawled onto the bed. He reached past me, and when he settled back again, he was holding a travel-sized bottle of lube. I rolled my eyes at Gloria's—or possibly Hubert's—level of dedication to their only child. Dag must have seen because he curled his thumb, hooking it behind my bottom teeth, and rocked my head from side to side. He pulled, and my head and shoulders came up off the pillow. The whole time he stared down at me, his face fixed in that mask of intensity I had seen in the dream. My whole body was flushed, and sweat was starting to stick the cotton of my shirt under my arms.

"Get out of those clothes," Dag said.

I stripped awkwardly, flopping around on the bed. He watched. His dick bobbed when the mattress bounced. The tip was wet. When I reached for it again, he caught my wrist and shoved me down.

"Oh fuck," I whispered.

Every inch of my body felt hot, but when he caught me below the knees, his touch was fire. He hauled me forward and then pushed my legs back. He ran a dry finger around my balls and then lower, the friction a fresh kind of heat. He pressed lightly. Then he pressed a little harder, the rub of skin burning now.

The night my family died, I had been on my stomach. A hand around my neck, choking me. The fuckboy I'd picked up at the club had smelled like fried catfish, and he'd pounded me into the bed, his weight pinning me, while my world fell apart without me even realizing it.

I came back to the motel room in fragments, aware of Dag stroking my calves, my thighs, my belly. I blinked my eyes clear, turned into the pillow, and wiped my face. My breath kept coming in jittery gasps. But looking at myself, down the length of my body, all the sag and all the flab, and at Dag kneeling between my legs, was worse in its own way. I had to squeeze my eyes shut.

"Can you—" I had to stop when my chest seized. "Can you just go outside for a few minutes?"

He must have shaken his head because a moment later he answered, "No. I don't think so."

I pressed fingertips to my eyes. "Please?"

The cap on the bottle of lube made a popping noise.

"I can't, Dag. I want to. Oh my God, I want to, because I know you want to and I love you and—God, I am so fucked up."

He shushed me. A hand cool with lube closed around my dick. I wasn't hard—cue Gloria—but Dag manipulated me slowly, his fingers sliding and opening and closing. "I don't care about that. I like being with you. That's what I want."

"You don't have to do that," I said. I put an arm across my face. "I don't need you to feel sorry for me."

"You know how I like rules?"

I cleared my throat. "Yeah, I picked up on that."

"Here's the rule for tonight: say anything that's not my name, and I'm going to turn you over and spank your ass. Starting now. No complaints. No objections. No clarifications. No negotiations. Say anything that's not my name, and you're not going to sit for a week."

I dropped my arm from my eyes.

His hair was drying, the color more like steel now. His eyes were dark, the pupils swollen. His face looked the way it did when he bottomed, as though everything else in the universe had been wiped away except me.

"Good boy," he whispered, and that's when I realized I was hard as a rock.

"Oh f—" I had to bite my lip, and when he raised an eyebrow, I blurted, "Dag."

"Good," he said in that same low, encouraging tone. His hand moved faster.

Maybe it was the weed. Maybe it was just a backup from the sexless days and nights we'd been trapped here. Maybe it was like Hubert said, a vital reaction, the body responding to the threat of death.

"Dag." I said it like a warning and grabbed his wrist.

"Let go."

"Dag."

"I said let go, Eli."

I clutched the bedding with both hands, writhing. "Dag. Dag. Dag!" My head thrashed from side to side, and something took over, and I tried to scoot away. "Dag!"

He threw a knee over me. His hand was flying.

"Dag!" When I bucked this time, my head cracked against the wall. I barely felt it. And then I was coming as I screamed, "Dag!"

Then, my voice a grunt, "Dag." Then the name torn from me: "Dag." And then I was falling. "Dag."

His clean hand stroked my side. His lips brushed mine. I tried to kiss him, but he'd just hand-jobbed me halfway to Mars, and he chuckled. I was still halfway out of it when he grunted and sprayed across my belly.

With a little wriggling and contorting, Dag lay down and pulled me to his chest. He kissed my cheek. He kissed me on the lips. I was on my way back to Planet Earth by that point, so I did some kissing of my own. Then I raised my hand.

"Keep it short and sweet," he said, pulling me back down against his chest. "Or I'll change my mind."

"I love you," I whispered into his arm.

Seconds ticked by. His stubble scratched the back of my neck. He shifted, the hair on his legs tickled mine.

When he said, "I love you too," he was crying.

I twisted around to face him.

"I'm sorry," he said. "I feel so messed up. I don't even know why I'm crying. It's not like I loved him. I love you. Lanny was—I mean, he ruined my life."

He cried into my shoulder for a while. I carded his hair. It was still wet in places. It smelled like his pillow at home.

"Sorry," he said. "I don't know what's going on with me. He didn't deserve that, you know?"

"And you cared about him."

Dag rolled his eyes, which was impressive considering how puffy they were. "I mean, he was like a big, dumb puppy."

"I guess you've got a type, then," I said with a smile. "I'm pretty dumb myself. I'm sorry I—I'm sorry I didn't know how to help you. I'm sorry I didn't try more."

"My mom hugged me and told me she loved me and then said she'd brought a wooden spoon in her purse and she was going to smack my bum if I didn't get out of bed and start living again."

"That was not on my list of ideas."

Dag grinned.

"But it is now," I said.

Dag rolled his eyes again.

"Do they make purse-sized wooden spoons?" I asked. "Asking for a friend."

Smoothing my hair, Dag said, "You're not dumb, you know. You're smart and you're handsome and you're the bravest person I've ever met. I dated...well, you know I didn't date much, and not at all after Lanny, but they were always like that. These blond guys, gaybros, not a lot going on besides the gym and the next lay. Buck bunnies, all of them. And you know what? I'm glad Lanny did what he did, because I wouldn't have found you if he hadn't. I just wish—I don't know. I feel stupid that I feel so messed up inside."

"Can I say something?" I asked. "And you won't get mad? You don't have to say anything, actually. And I won't say it again. If you think I'm wrong, just ignore me."

"That's a lot of windup."

"I think maybe you were in love with Mason."

Dag closed his eyes. I wasn't counting the seconds, but it had to be close to a full minute before he spoke again. His voice was locked down. Neutral. "And because Mason was straight, Lanny was the substitute?"

"Not exactly. Not like that. But I noticed that they were pretty similar right from the start. They've got a lot of physical similarities, but it was more than that. The bro vibe. The way Lanny liked to give you shit. The dumb puppy routine. I know they aren't identical, but there was overlap, and I was kind of...curious. Then Lanny said something that made me start thinking about it more. He was talking about his sister. How she went for the same guys over and over again. And how he did it too, kept trying to find someone like you, only what he really wanted was you, which was why he came back."

"And because my best friend from high school was straight and is now dead, Lanny got to fill in. Great. That doesn't sound like I'm psycho at all."

"Never mind," I said. "That was really inappropriate of me. I just thought—I don't know. I'm sorry."

His eyes were still closed, but he was crying again.

I thumbed away one of the tears. "That was so stupid. I'm sorry, Dag."

"No," he said thickly. "I mean, it's not exactly that. I mean, I did love Mase. But it's not like I was trying to replace him. It just—I just liked those guys. And yeah, now I can see it. They were like him. They looked like him. I mean, it's pretty messed up."

"It's not messed up; everybody does it, Dag. Or a lot of us, anyway. We want our relationship in the present to...answer, I guess, something from the past." I smoothed his thick, gray hair. "I might, um, have a thing for older guys. Not because I wanted to fuck my dad, but because, well, I don't know. Lots of things. Stability. Maturity. I didn't have those things in my life when I was a kid. Plus I know I'm a lot to handle."

"You?" he murmured.

I pinched his nip.

His eyes snapped open. "Eli, jeez!"

"I didn't bring it up because I think it's weird. The opposite, actually. But I said it because—well, I think part of you is really grieving Mason all over again, and I thought maybe it would help if you could untangle the two. Grieve for both of them. But, you know, separately."

He followed the curve of my cheek with one finger. "You're pretty good at this stuff."

"I watch a lot of Dr. Phil," I said, sitting up and cupping a hand on my belly as two loads ran down me.

"I'm serious. Have you thought about giving school another try? You'd be great as a therapist. You could help so many people."

"But then I'd have to read all those big books with all those big words," I said. "And if I did, I'd be busy, and who would cook and clean and pretty up all your notecards?"

"I actually had to explain that in the middle of class because I was getting glitter everywhere. I don't think anybody believed me when I said my boyfriend, uh, no labels, did it."

"That's because you go to a school full of basic bitches," I said, chin raised with what I hoped passed for justified outrage.

"Come here," Dag said.

"I'm going to shower."

"Lie down, Eli."

"Make me," I said and clambered over him in a race to the shower.

Dag caught up with me, and the water was warm, and the soap was slippery, and I didn't even mind when we got out of the stall later and I remembered why we'd been taking short showers for all those days.

We ate the pasta on the bed, which was the only unflooded portion of the room, and even though Gloria had provided two forks, we ended up just using one. I'd take a bite. And then Dag would take a really big bite. And then the fork would dangle in his hand, and I'd decide if I needed to clean the corner of his mouth after every round. Dag's other arm, the one that wasn't occasionally busy with the fork, was around my bare shoulders. The whole situation was the kind of thing that, when I saw it in shows, made me turn off TVs and walk out of theaters.

"I can't do dessert," Dag said as he took the lid off the bread pudding. Then his arm tightened, crushing me against him. "Stop laughing at me."

"Usually people say that when they're not going to eat dessert," I managed to say into his shoulder.

He squeezed me tighter.

"You're killing me," I said into his neck.

"Good. More bread pudding for me."

He let me fight him off. And then, miracle of miracles, he let me off easy and didn't try to force the dessert on me. Then we lay there, my head on his chest, his arm against the curve of my spine. He turned on the TV and, our second miracle, the static parted enough that we got the local news, sports, the highlights from the Saints game on Sunday. Dag made a contented noise. I nibbled at his chest hair.

"Do not get me going again, Eli Prescott."

I cupped his dick. "Say something about spanking again."

"You're a brat."

"Yeah, that's a good start."

Grinning, he sat up and dug out a pair of shorts from the gym bag his dad had brought. He dragged them on.

"Rookie move," I said. "You think that's going to stop me?"

"Eli."

"Fine. I'm sorry I'm bothering you."

"You have all that werewolf porn on your phone. Read that."

"It's not werewolf porn. They're mystery novels. About werewolves. And they have some sexy times, which is more than I can say—ok, ok, ok." The look on his face made me mime zipping my lips. Dagobert LeBlanc had the patience of the saints, but apparently even saints reached a point when they just wanted to watch the news in peace.

But after an FBI werewolf fuck-a-thon in the Seattle office, and with a boyfriend—or whatever we were calling it—who was patently ignoring the boner jutting into his thigh, I said, "Dag, what are we going to do?"

"Good Lord," he muttered and wrapped a hand around my dick.

Laughing, I stopped him. "I mean—your parents said we're suspects in a murder investigation."

Dag sighed. He ran fingers through his thick gray hair. It had a slight wave that he usually combed out of it.

"Dag?"

"I don't know."

"Dagobert!"

"Don't yell at me. I don't know what to do. I mean, I can't call Amrey and tell him a shape-shifting monster that feeds on pain and hunger is behind all of this, oh, and remember last year when you found that thing that everyone pretended was a bear, that was one of these monsters too."

"I can't be the brains and the body," I said, pinching my gut. "I need you to think of something."

"Cut it out. I don't like those jokes."

"You were a deputy. You're supposed to have an idea. I'm the dumb, pretty one."

"I was a bad one, and I told you to cut it out."

I rolled my eyes.

"We'll figure it out," Dag said, stroking my back.

"Soon, though. We're almost out of money."

"My parents brought some."

"How much?"

He made a face, already looking at the TV again, and made a gesture with two fingers to indicate the size of the bundle of bills.

"Were they ones? Fives? Tens? Hundreds?"

He shrugged.

"Mary, Mother of God," I said, "protect me from daddies who can't balance their checkbooks."

I rolled onto my stomach, grabbed our clothes and belongings that we'd piled on the room's sole chair, and then shrieked when a slap landed on my bare ass. I stared over my shoulder at Dagobert LeBlanc, who was staring back at me.

"Got something to say?" he asked.

I decided not to dignify that with a response.

Inventory time. In my wallet: zero dollars, zero cents, a patron card for the DuPage Parish Library, a MasterCard, two Visas, and my insurance and dental cards. In Dag's wallet: a condom that felt brittle inside packaging with the label worn off ("What?" he asked with a tone.), a matching MasterCard that was connected to the same account as mine, a sandwich-shop club card with eight of the twelve punches completed, a 2017 pocket-sized cheat sheet for Louisiana fish and game regulations, a laminated picture of his parents, a foil-wrapped packet of lube ("I didn't even know those were in there," he protested. "I bet my mom put them there."), and four hundred dollars in twenties.

Four hundred dollars could keep us going—in this place, eating microwave shit—for a chunk of time. But it wasn't going to last forever.

I kept going with my inventory. We had the creepy, rusty knife that Dag had taken from Lanny, who had taken it from Fen. We had the gym bag that Dag's dad had brought. I went through it and saw that Gloria had packed enough of Dag's old clothes for both of us, along with a vibrator ("I swear to God, I'm going to kill them.") and an unopened package of silicone butt plugs in different sizes (at this point, Dag put the pillow against the side of his face so he could watch TV without having to look at me). Then I grabbed Dag's backpack, which we'd brought in from the car when we'd started hiding out. It had been stupid to keep the car; I was starting to realize that—and starting to realize, too, how lucky we'd been that the cops hadn't spotted it yet. But I hadn't exactly been thinking clearly over the last few days. Neither of us had. In the backpack, I found Dag's laptop, which was great because I was sure he wanted to study for his midterm tomorrow. Then I pulled out a wad of paper, which I proceeded to unwad.

"Dagobert LeBlanc."

He shifted the pillow to look and groaned before making a swipe at the pages.

I pulled them out of reach.

"Pretend you didn't see it," he said, hiding his face again. "Oh my God, this is actually worse than the butt plugs."

"A 69.5?"

"I said pretend you didn't see it."

I studied the paper. It was an analysis of something called energy pyramids. And, while I was admittedly not the expert on school, what I remembered from Ms. Milton's Senior Composition course told me I wasn't seeing a lot of analysis. The paper basically consisted of a series of factual statements. *Phytoplankton are autotrophic organisms. They contain chlorophyll. When producing energy, they use carbon dioxide and sunlight and release oxygen.*

When I checked the rubric at the end, I saw I'd been right about my guess.

"Why didn't you tell me about this?"

Dag pressed the pillow completely over his face. After a moment, he asked, "If I change the channel back to the preacher who was whipping that lady with his shoe, can we stop talking about this?"

"Hey," I said, touching his leg.

Something exciting happened on the game highlights, and the recorded crowd was roaring. Dag inched the pillow down to peek.

"Mister."

He squeezed his eyes shut.

"Nice try," I said.

Rolling to face me, he let out a breath. Then he opened his eyes. "It's humiliating, all right? I mean, I talked this big talk about going back to school, and I read all those books, and I can't believe I thought I was actually, you know, maybe good at something, and Sal got a ninety-nine or something because of course he did, and I'm going to end up failing out, and that's when you're going to realize you need someone who can actually provide for you so you'll leave. That's all."

My eyebrows went up.

"That, um." He cleared his throat. "That might be a little bit of an exaggeration."

"You are smart."

"Please don't do this."

"No, we're doing this. You're extremely smart. And this stuff, it's something you love and you're interested in. And you've worked harder than anyone this semester."

"Yeah, well, it doesn't matter if you work hard if you're not smart—"

"Stop saying that! And yes, I understand the irony because I say it about myself all the time, but I am beyond irritated right now, and I also don't want to give you the high ground."

"Is that why you're yelling?"

"You're goddamn right that's why I'm yelling!"

A tiny smile cracked the corner of his mouth.

"Dag," I said in a softer tone, "you are smart. You do great on the tests and exams, right?"

"I do all right."

"You literally got over a hundred percent on one of them."

A blush came into his cheeks, and he mumbled something.

"Did you read the comments your professor wrote?" I asked.

"I glanced at them."

"You know what you're doing wrong?"

"I don't know. She doesn't really—"

"You're writing these reports like a cop. 'Suspect was a male anemone, approximately thirty-five years old, last seen swimming toward the Gulf.'"

"Actually, a lot of anemones are asexual, and they don't swim because they're attached to whatever's beneath them by this little foot that's called—"

"Dagobert!"

"What?" He blinked a few times. "Stop yelling at me!"

"I'm trying to tell you this is an easy fix. I'll help you."

He cleared his throat.

"The look on your face makes me feel attacked," I said. "For your information, I got an A in my Senior Composition class."

"Oh." He brightened. "I mean, I knew you were smart—"

"He was this hot, young dude, totally hung, and I'd blow him in the classroom after school."

His face was the classic Dagobert LeBlanc mix of shock, worry, and anger.

"Oh my God," I muttered.

He tried to sit up. "I knew it was a joke."

"Oh my God."

"I knew you were just saying that."

"Worst boyfriend ever."

"Eli, I knew! I was just playing along! Wait, boyfriend?"

"Or whatever we're calling it." I shoved his essay in the backpack, and my hand brushed more paper. Since I figured I was on a roll, I pulled these pages out too. And then I stared at them: lined paper, the kind kids take to school in shrink-wrapped packs, pages and pages of it covered in two very different handwritings. One was a looping script that suggested—to my sexist mind—a woman. The other was blocky print letters that—raise the sexist flag—made me think of a man. And then I remembered shoving them into the backpack after we'd taken them from Roger.

"Nelda Pie's letters," I said. "The ones Lanny stole."

"And that Roger stole from Lanny," Dag said. He propped himself up on an elbow and scanned one. "They look like regular letters. 'How are you?' 'I miss you.' That kind of thing."

I propped pillows against the wall, scooped the letters next to me, and lay back with one in my hand.

"You're going to read those?"

"Right now is when that preacher out of Mexico starts speaking in tongues, and I've already got blue balls from my werewolves."

"But you won't watch *Star Trek*."

"One of my werewolves spit-roasted his supposed-to-be-tough-and-straight partner with their best friend, also a werewolf. When Picard and Scotty and whoever do that, call me and I'll watch *Star Trek*."

"You're mixing up the shows. Picard is on *Next Generation*, and Scotty is on the original—" Something on my face stopped him. "You know what? I'm going to watch the rest of the news."

"Do that," I said, shaking the first letter open. "Before I have to break up with you."

Although there had to be at least twenty different letters, they all looked relatively recent—none of the paper was yellowing, and it didn't have the smell that paper gets when it's old. Nobody had bothered to date their correspondence, so I read them at random. Dag was right: at first, they looked like ordinary letters. The ones written in a woman's hand, which I assumed had been written by Nelda Pie, were longer, often beginning with recaps of recent events in her life.

But then the tone shifted. *I miss you* became *I miss your touch. I think about you all the time. I'll do anything not to lose you again.*

The letters done in print were shorter. Choppier. In fact, if I had to guess, I would have suspected that their author had also passed Senior Composition through the oral exam method. The phrases that seemed strange at first—*It's a miracle we're together again. I had forgotten what it was like to be with you.*—became disturbing—*They will try to keep us apart. We can't let anyone separate us again.*—and then downright scary—*The Hunter will kill me if she knows. You will have to remove her. Please don't let her take me. Kill her. Kill her. Kill her.*

I stared at the words. Whoever had written the letter, they had pressed hard on the pencil. The graphite tracks were deep, almost tearing the paper in places. And my brain went, of course, to the Stoplight, where Nelda Pie had stabbed Fen and then tried to finish the job with the shotgun. To be fair, it seemed like Lanny and Fen had gone there in the first place to kill Nelda Pie, so it wasn't exactly like they were innocent. But I didn't understand why any of it was happening. Why had Lanny been so focused on Nelda Pie? Why had he recruited Fen to help him kill her, Only to let himself be dragged out in front of a semi by someone who looked a lot like my boyfriend—or whatever we were calling it? And why, at the same time, was Nelda Pie writing love letters to someone—something?—that wanted her to kill this hunter, who had to be Fen?

And then it all came together: all the things that hadn't made sense, all the pieces of the puzzle I'd forced to fit when they weren't from the same puzzle at all.

Bundling the letters together, I said, "Get up and get dressed. We have to go."

"What? Where? Now?"

"Now. Put a shirt on. And bring your flashcards. Or your textbook. Or both."

I grabbed clothes out of the gym bag, a hoodie and joggers, and squirmed into them. "Dagobert! Right now!"

"Jeez," he said, pulling out a sweater. "Can you tell me what's going on?"

"It's not a hashok," I said as I yanked on the zipper. "We need to talk to Jeannette."

DAG (2)

As we drove into DuPage Parish, I kept trying to figure out what was going on. Eli was talking over himself, stumbling on his own words. A flush glowed under the soft brown of his skin. His eyes were wide and bright with excitement.

Finally I clamped a hand on his knee and said, "One deep breath, and start from the beginning."

He told me about the letters.

"Ok, I get the major weirdo vibe. But what—"

He shook his head. "Let's talk to Jeannette first. I want to see if I'm right."

But when we made our way up the duckboards and past the trellis covered in morning glory, Kevin answered the door. His stringy hair was either greasier than usual or wet, and today he was wearing a shirt that said FREE HYRULE and then boxer shorts printed with original Gameboys.

"What do you want?"

"We need to talk to—"

"Oh no," he said. "No more witchcraft. I told her, and I told you: we're a Christian family. No astrology, no terror cards, no wedgie boards."

"Please," Eli said. "We only have a few questions. Just a minute, that's all it'll take."

"No witchcraft," Kevin said firmly.

"That's the whole point. It's not witchcraft, it's—"

But Kevin was closing the door.

I'd dealt with a lot of Kevins in my life. I put a hand on the fiberglass and the peeling paint, and I leaned into it. I was taller than Kevin. I weighed a lot more than Kevin. The door stopped moving.

"You can't do that," Kevin hollered. "You can't do that. You can't—"

"This is a police investigation," I said. "The way I see it, sir, you can either let us talk to your wife for a few minutes, and we'll be on our way, or we'll come back here and arrest her as a material witness. We'll take her into custody. And then we'll get another warrant to search for any photographic or video evidence relevant to the murder of Ivy Honsord. And then, sir? I'm going to tell my team to take as long as they need. It might take three days. It might take five. It might take a week. We'll just keep coming back until I'm convinced we've checked every possible hiding spot. Heck, it might take a month."

Kevin flushed. He was one of those white guys who got blotchy. He dug a thumb under the waistband of the boxer shorts and mumbled, "She's sorting the hammy downs."

"Then I suggest you go get her. And put on a pair of pants next time you answer the door, sir, or I may have to add a public indecency charge."

With a glare, Kevin marched back into the trailer, mumbling, "— pouring salt in the womb—" as he went. Then he shouted Jeannette's name.

"What?" she called back.

"You brought them cops to the door again with the witchcraft and all that." His steps moved farther. In what must have been the kitchen, cabinet doors slammed. "And why the hell don't we have any of the jalapeño Cheetos when you been to the store twice this week?"

"Ok," Eli whispered. "I take back everything I ever said about the cop thing."

I shrugged.

"From now on, you're the tough one."

"From now on?" I asked, and then I grunted when he elbowed me.

Jeannette appeared a moment later. She had her hair tied in rag curlers, and today, the book was Calvino, *If on a Winter's Night a Traveler*. She paused when she saw us, glanced in the direction Kevin had gone, and let out a heavy breath. Then she trudged over to the doorway.

"I can't talk to you. Kevin doesn't like it."

"What happened the night you tried to help Ivy?" Eli asked. "Last week, I mean."

"That? You already saw for yourself." She touched the bruise on her face.

"But what happened?"

"She went crazy. I thought I was helping her. She was out on the lawn sobbing. He'd let her have it. So I grabbed her arm, and I started walking her this away, telling her how she'd never have to see him again, and she went insane. Hitting me. Spitting. Screaming. Using the Lord's name in vain. Once she whomped me, I let her go. You can't help someone who doesn't want to be helped."

Tension eased from Eli's body. He had a weak smile on his face as he asked, "She wanted to go back to him?"

"She was desperate to get back there. Messed up. Abuse does that to you, messes with your head. She'd tell anyone who'd listen she was in love with Roger Shaver, but I call it Stockholm syndrome."

Eli nodded and said, "When the witch—"

"She wasn't a witch," Jeannette said with a note of asperity. "I told him that a hundred times. A psychic's not the same thing as a witch." She lowered her voice. "But you heard him. He says half his words wrong anyway. He's a good man, but the Lord didn't give him the brains of a socket wrench."

Pale, Eli stared at her.

The wind rustled the morning glory, and it carried the smell of char from the oil-drum grill at the end of the duckboards.

Jeannette frowned. "Is that all—"

"You're sure?" I found my voice first. "You're sure it wasn't a witch? A woman named Nelda Pie?"

"Oh, she came around. Plenty of times, mostly when Ivy was gone. She was giving Roger the eye, and maybe a little more. Brought him those little bags she makes because something was bothering Roger, I think. And she was here the night Ivy died. But Kevin's talking about last week. I thought maybe Hope could help Ivy. Give her some perspective. So I called her and asked her to come out. She's sweet like that; she'll do house calls. She walked over there, only Roger answered the door. I don't know what he said to her, but I've never seen a woman move so fast. She stopped here long enough to tell me to stay away from him, and that's the last I heard from her. She hasn't answered any of my calls, and I haven't had my reading this week. The next time Kevin has a shift, I'll catch a ride into town and see if I can find her at her shop."

"In Moulinbas," Eli said. His voice sounded dead.

"That's right," Jeannette said. "You know it?"

He managed a jerky nod.

Taking his arm, I said, "We're going to talk in the car for a minute. If we have more questions, we'll be back."

"Kevin won't like that," she said as she eased the door shut.

After I got Eli in the passenger seat, I went around and got behind the wheel.

"Hope," he said. And then he laughed, and it was a broken, ugly sound. "I know the name was just chance, but oh my God. I am so stupid."

"E, you figured something out, but I don't know what's going on. I need you to pull it together."

"I'm fine." He wiped his mouth and laughed again. "I'm fine."

And then he told me.

"I don't understand. These visions, or whatever they are, of us having sex—"

"Please don't make me spell it out for you." A windsock snapped taut from where it hung on the front of a trailer down the road. The wind reached us a moment later, whistling along the Escort's shell. "I want it. I want to look like that. I want to be able to do that." He swallowed. "With you."

"I don't care if you—"

"You're missing the point."

"I'm not worried about a monster right now, Eli. I'm worried about my boyfriend." He cleared his throat. "Not that we're putting labels on things."

He groaned. "Can you stop being impossibly pure and sweet for, I don't know, five minutes?"

I thought about that. "Two minutes."

"I ought to break all your pencils and leave the caps off all your pens. That would get a reaction out of you."

I rubbed his leg.

"This thing, whatever it is, isn't a hashok. Hashoks feed on pain and suffering. They inspire these cycles of violence. And what we couldn't figure out was why there wasn't a cycle of violence. Why we didn't see people's lives imploding. But we're not seeing it because this thing isn't doing any of that. No cycle of violence. No pain and suffering—at least, nothing that wasn't already happening."

"Because it's not a hashok."

"Exactly."

"So, what is it?"

"I have no idea. But we know a few things about it. We know it can look like someone else, maybe someone important to you. We know it still looks like a firefly or a light. We know it feeds on people, and they end up dead. But it doesn't feed on pain and suffering, it feeds on—"

"Love," I said.

Eli nodded.

"No," I corrected myself. "Not love, I don't think. But desire? Something along those lines. What people want deeply, maybe what they want more than anything else—what they want more than is good for them." Then I realized what Eli had told me moments before, and my face heated.

"Trust me," he said with a wry grin. "I know." His smile faded as he said, "It seems unreal, right? Two monsters that look like fireflies? I mean, that should be impossible."

"Not really, actually. Not if you think that monsters, or whatever we're calling them, still follow some of the same patterns and principles you see in standard zoology. A lot of animals imitate the appearance of other, more harmful animals." I grabbed my flashcards, flipped through them, and displayed one for Eli. "See? It's called Batesian mimicry. The hashok is like an apex predator, I think. Whatever we're facing, it doesn't have the same physical power, so it camouflages itself to look more dangerous."

"This is why I told you to bring the flashcards."

"So instead of a physically unstoppable killing machine, we're dealing with a mind-reading killing machine?"

"Something like that. I think—I think it must be able to pick up details. Not everything. It can't read minds, I don't think. But it can sense what's on the surface. When I met Hope, she—it—picked up on what I was feeling, what I wanted. She tried to promise it to me. When I saw her again, I thought I was worried about the hashok, but really, I was fixated on you and Lanny, on how things seemed like they'd been so much easier for you with Lanny. So she showed me—well, me. This better me. And—"

"Not better."

He rolled his eyes.

"No," I said, "I want you to quit talking like that."

"Ok. But do you get what I'm saying? And then, when the lutin was helping us follow this thing's trail, it decided to get rid of me. That's what I saw—that's what lured me out into the bayou. Me. This better—I mean, this other me. And tonight, at the motel. God. That's why I've felt so exhausted. And Lanny too. Because it was feeding on us. Remember how Lanny wanted to sleep all the time? It must have started feeding on him earlier. It hasn't been working on me for long, but I feel like I could sleep for a week."

"But this psychic, isn't it—" I tried to put it into words. "Isn't it a coincidence that you met her?"

"I kept going out there." He made a face. "I kept going to Bragg...wandering. I didn't know why. I think it must have been watching me. Or us. And last week, someone gave me Hope's card. That's how I ended up there. I don't think it was coincidence at all; I think it was a setup. I don't know why, if it was something like Fen's reason—maybe this thing knew we were responsible for killing the hashok and wanted to keep an eye on us—or maybe it was something else."

"Forget that for a minute," I said. "So this thing, whatever it is, takes over Roger's life. Around the time Roger goes into the parish jail, it either meets Ivy, or it met her previously and decides now is the perfect time to feed on her. And because it can take shapes, it looks like Roger, and it lives with her, beating on her, feeding on her, and she puts up with it. Because that's what she wanted?"

"You've seen lots of domestic abuse, Dag." A frown creased Eli's cheeks. "You know that's not how it works."

"Part of her wanted something that he was offering her," I said. "Ok, I can believe that. The rest of it was, well, the whole messed-up psychology behind those situations. And meanwhile, it was feeding on other people too. People who wanted something."

"We all want something. And we usually want something we can't have. And this thing is a master at figuring out what we want and promising to give it to us."

"And then Jeannette gets spooked, so she calls Hope, the real Hope, to come over and try to help Ivy self-actualize or whatever, and instead, Hope comes face to face with this monster." I paused. "She must have known what it was, right? Because Jeannette said she took off running."

Eli nodded. "And I think that's why this thing had to kill Hope and replace her."

"No. That's why it had to kill her. It chose to replace her because—because that's what psychics do, right? The fakes, anyways. They sell people hope. A promise of whatever they want the most. That's what this thing does too, only the price is your life. It's like this monster hit the career jackpot."

"That's an unbelievably cynical way to see the world."

"I'm sorry. I was a cop for a lot of years; you start to see the world a certain way."

"It was super hot. If we weren't sitting in a trailer park, I'd—you know what? Screw it. I'm going to do it anyway."

Laughing, I pushed him back into his seat. Then I wrapped a hand around the steering wheel and drew a deep breath. "What about Lanny?"

"I don't know where this thing caught him, but I'm guessing it had to do with Nelda Pie. We know she was in its web; my guess is that she met it when she took the flannels to Ivy's trailer. She might have some power or ability, but I don't think she's particularly self-aware, and it must have caught her. You saw the letters. She thought this thing was her long-lost love. After that, Lanny might have run into this thing at the Stoplight. Maybe when he was stealing the letters."

"Maybe," I said. "He definitely saw it at the Stoplight later, when we went there together. Remember, he kept talking about something I'd said to him while you were still inside? But that never happened. I was in there with you the whole time. I thought he was just—I don't know, making it up, or living a fantasy. Really, though, it was this thing. It looked like me to get to him. It used—it used whatever he felt for me to hurt him and control him."

Compassion wrote itself across Eli's features. His voice was carefully neutral when he spoke again. "It needed Nelda Pie to eliminate Fen, and then it wanted Lanny to get rid of Nelda Pie. Only things went wrong. It didn't count on Lanny hesitating or on us showing up."

"If it knew anything about Lanny," my voice was on the edge of breaking, "if it knew anything about him at all, it would have known. He wouldn't have hurt a fly. It used my face to kill him, Eli. He trusted me, and I killed him."

"You didn't kill him."

"What is this thing? I want to find it, and I want to fucking murder it."

"I don't know," Eli said. "I guess I could read hundreds and hundreds of digitized pages and bad handwriting. Or—"

"You could call a librarian?"

"Yes, please, that."

He placed the call on speaker. I hadn't met Kennedy Sainte-Marie, but Eli had talked about her plenty. The voice on the phone sounded young, educated, and self-assured. "What in the hell kind of trouble did you get yourself into? They're talking about murders, Eli. What the fuck happened?"

"Polite young ladies don't use that kind of—"

Most of what she whisper-screamed at him wasn't really a sentence. Not after you took out all the swears.

"And Happy Halloween to you too," Eli said when she finished. "I'm here with Dag."

"Hi, Kennedy," I said. "Nice to meet you."

"Why do you put up with him? Why haven't you tied him up on the train tracks? Why haven't you thrown him into a tank full of piranhas?"

"It's interesting that all your solutions come from old cartoons," Eli said, "but unfortunately, we don't have time for me to work my therapist magic on your childhood trauma. I need your help."

"Of course you do. Brenniyah, do not chase her with the spaghetti! Charlotte, absolutely not! Put that down!"

"Threesome?" Eli asked. "Don't worry. They're always awkward at the beginning, but things will smooth out once the first, well, tab goes in, um, the first slot."

Kennedy's breathing sounded dangerously accelerated. "I'm watching my nieces. I'm trying to get them ready to trick-or-treat."

"Really? While you're having a threesome?"

She legit growled this time.

"I'm going to jump in here," I said. "Kennedy, we need your help." I explained everything I knew about the creature we were following. "Does that sound like anything—"

"Fifolet."

"Is that a shrimp restaurant?" Eli asked.

"Brenniyah, I'm taking away the Switch if you don't put that lamp down right now! Charlotte, you cannot ride the vacuum cleaner down the stairs." Her voice came back to the phone as she snapped, "No, you idiot, that's the name for this thing. And if you're smart, you'll run away from it as fast as you can. Charlotte, no!" From the other end came a series of thumps and then a child's pained cry. Kennedy let out a sigh. "Well, I warned you." To us, she said, "Since Eli is an idiot, and I assume you must be an idiot because you're dating him, I'm going to guess you're not going to run away. In fact, I'm going to guess your next question is how to kill it."

"Dag's very smart," Eli said. "He makes the flashcards, and I pretty them up."

"I actually do want to know how to kill it, Kennedy."

"Cold iron. But if you get that close, you'll be too focused on what it's offering you, on the whole wish-fulfillment fantasy, to do it any harm." Her voice shifted. "All right, Brenniyah. That's it. No Switch for the weekend; wait until I talk to your mom."

Belligerent child screams answered her.

"I have to go drown them in the bathtub," she said. "Goodbye."

"No, no, no, wait!" Eli said. "What can you tell us about it?"

"Primarily, they stay in the bayous where they can lure people into marshy areas—usually the victims drown, or a gator gets them. Occasionally they'll get bold enough to go on land. They'll look like dead relatives. Or they'll promise to lead you to a treasure. The MO, when they're dealing with groups, is to make people turn on each other. But they don't do that often, and they won't stay long. If you wait this one out, it'll go back into the bayou." A vacuum roared to life on the other end of the call, and a girl shrieked. "Mother of God," Kennedy swore, "it's got her hair." Then the call disconnected.

"Just wait for it to leave," I said. "I like the sound of that."

"But it's been months." Eli shook his head. "This thing has been on land for months. Maybe longer. It's not going to leave. I don't know why, but it's not going to leave."

"Predator-prey systems shift, Eli. Sometimes it's only temporary. If there's an abundance of prey, or if a predator—" I cut off. My tongue felt too thick to continue.

"If a predator what?" he asked.

I rifled through the flashcards and held one out to him. "If a predator is displaced. Food pyramids, right? Apex predator at the top. All the way down to the plants that support the prey animals. But if you remove the apex predator—if it's hunted into extinction, or if it's displaced—then the pyramid changes." I flicked the card. "Trophic cascade."

"Ok. So, like, a cascade of changes. That makes sense. The prey animals aren't getting eaten, or not as many of them. That kind of thing."

"It's more than that. Removing an apex predator affects the other predators as well. Apex predators are at the top, right? Well, then you have what are called mesopredators. They're in the middle. Apex predators might be timber wolves, for example. Mesopredators are coyotes. They can't compete with apex predators. In fact, the presence of the apex predators keeps the mesopredators in check, up to a point."

"But if you take out the apex predators—"

"The mesopredator populations explode. It's called mesopredator release. That means a lot of pressure on the rest of the pyramid. Another round of trophic cascade—maybe multiple cascades before things settle. It happens in the ocean, too. As large sharks have been hunted, smaller sharks and ray populations have increased. The cownose ray decimated the North Carolina scallop populations in the '80s and '90s."

"I knew all those stupid books were going to be useful one day."

"They're not stupid books, they're—"

"Now we just need to figure out how to kill it."

"She told us," I said. "Cold iron." Then I reached into the back seat, shifted our bags, and lifted the knife I'd taken from Lanny. The blade was slightly longer than four inches, the metal rippling with toolmarks from when it had been worked by hand. How long ago? A hundred years? Two hundred? The handle was wood, a dark reddish-brown. It was smooth and gleaming from decades of cleaning and oiling and, of course, use. "Fen carried this for a reason."

"Ok. And I've got an idea of something else we can try," Eli said. "A backup plan. It means trying one of those flannels that Kennedy's book talks about; I don't know if you're comfortable with that. I've got Nelda Pie's flannel in the car, and I could make the changes pretty easily."

"If it stops this thing, I'm comfortable with it."

Eli flipped the pull on the hoodie's zipper. Up. Down. Up. Down. Up. Down. He teased out his hair, which was looking decidedly less windswept and significantly more one-sidedly fluffy. "That's it? That's our plan? We're going to do this?"

"We're going to do this," I said and started the car.

ELI (3)

The psychic's store sat on an unremarkable block of Moulinbas. This section of Bragg, the Creole townhouses with their chipped plaster and their rusting iron scrollwork, looked like the older, strung-out sister of New Orleans's French Quarter. It had its touches of lingering beauty: bougainvillea flaming along a widow's walk, a hint of copper among the verdigris on the steeply pitched roofs, the smell of fried oysters, the twang of Delta blues from the next block. And, of course, the laughter of drunken white girls stumbling past on the other side of the street, two of them supporting a third, who was puking as she walked while trying to maintain a death grip on her piña colada, served in a novelty coconut. I could practically hear Don Middlebrook's ghost.

"Caribbean cowboys and señoritas," Dag said with a snort.

"God, I love you."

The door was closed, but the sign with the Eye of Horus was flipped to OPEN. It was evening. The light was powdery and blue. One of the white girls stumbled, and the coconut went flying. It hit the cobbles on the old street, bounced, bounced again, and then clattered down the hill. Then one of the white girls started crying. The whole thing was giving me flashbacks of a *Flintstones* episode: Fred bowling while Wilma got wasted and bitched all night to Betty. That probably hadn't actually happened in any of the episodes, so consider that Exhibit F of my messed-up childhood.

On the other side of the door, Hope's shop glowed with soft, yellow light.

I pulled, and the door swung open.

It smelled like the incense that girls I knew in high school would buy, and I coughed. The décor hadn't changed: scarves and veils and curtains, an epergne that might have been silver but looked plasticky and spray-painted, the IKEA chairs, the table, the brass ornaments, the crystal ball. Small speakers were hidden somewhere in the room, and somebody was playing Track 9 on a CD that was probably called

Ocean Surf and Sighs. Maybe it was just the blood rushing in my ears. I remembered last time thinking that all the little details were meant to up the woo-woo factor. Well, mission accomplished. I tried to swallow and couldn't, so instead, I shifted my grip on the flannel.

"You can come out," Dag said, and God bless him, his voice was calm and firm. "We know what you are."

Nothing.

"The game's over," he said. "No more tricks. No more illusions."

"There's another room back there," I whispered, pointing to the curtain opposite us.

The ocean breathed back at us.

After a moment, Dag let the backpack slide forward. He drew out the harvest knife and held it low as he took the first step. I came behind him. The white hiss of beach noise built in my head like steam.

When he reached the curtain, something moved on the other side, and we both stopped. Dag realized his mistake and started to lunge, but then the curtain parted, and he stopped.

I was staring back at us. Me. Not the better me. Not the me with the eight pack and the better hair. This was Eli Prescott Martins. Present day asshole version. Right down to the gay cowboys t-shirt he was wearing, with its grunge print in red and blue. Right down to my new Adidas. The motherfucker had raided my closet. The only new addition was a steel cuff around one wrist; a broken length of chain hung from it. His face was bruised, his lip split, another weal running across the bridge of his nose.

"Thank God," he said and started to cry. Then he froze when he saw me. He reached for Dag's arm as he said, "Dag, get away from that thing."

Dag flinched back. He kept his eyes on Other Eli, but I could tell he wanted to look. Wanted to check. Make sure.

"Don't listen to it," I said.

"Don't listen to it," Other Eli said. In the same voice. In the same timbre.

"It's a trick," I said. The flannel clinked and rattled as I shifted its weight in my hands. "I'm the real Eli. You know me."

"What day is it?" Other Eli asked. "How long have I been gone? The last thing I remember was coming here Thursday night. To Bragg, I mean. And I wandered around, and I met this psychic. She chained me up. And then she looked like me." Its voice rose in pitch. "Dag, why aren't you saying anything?"

"Yeah," I said. "Why aren't you saying anything?"

Dag shifted his weight. His whole hand blanched from the pressure of his grip on the harvest knife.

"You know I'm telling you the truth," Other Eli said. "You knew something had been wrong for a while now. He hasn't seemed normal, has he? He hasn't seemed like me. Has he acted strangely? Done anything different? Kept secrets? Not told you where he was going?" Other Eli's voice broke as he added, "I love you. If you loved me too, you'd be able to tell which one of us is real."

"The real Eli," Dag said, his voice thick, his gaze still locked on Other Eli. He cleared his throat. "The real Eli is a heck of a lot snarkier."

Other Eli relaxed; I hadn't even noticed the tension until it was gone. Then it laughed. "It's hard to pick up on everything at once. The more time I have, the better I do."

"You're out of time, motherfucker," I said.

Other Eli didn't seem to hear me. It was staring at Dag, and Dag was staring back.

"Dag," I said, "stab that fucking thing."

Dag flexed his fingers around the harvest knife. His mouth hung open slightly. He was breathing too fast.

"I can be so much better than him," Other Eli—the fifolet, Kennedy had called it—said. "I can be snarky. I can be sweet. I'll look you in the eyes when I tell you I love you, and I'll mean it." A smirk that was a mirror image of my own lit up the fifolet's face. My face. "I can ride your dick like a champ."

Dag made a distressed noise. He looked bloodless.

"Dag, what the fuck?" I shouted. "Stick that knife in that motherfucking monster!"

"It looks like you," he snapped, his head turning toward me. "How am I supposed to—"

The fifolet leaped forward and clubbed a fist against the side of Dag's head. The sound was like a cantaloupe hitting the floor. Dag's eyes emptied, and he bounced off a chair before he hit the carpet. The knife tumbled under the tiny table.

"No!"

I took a step forward.

The fifolet lunged at me, and I stumbled back. It slowed, its movements becoming predatory. When I clutched the flannel to my chest, it laughed.

"You didn't make it right. It was a nice try, but it won't save you."

"You try making one of these fucking things without a recipe card," I said. My voice sounded thready in my ears. I followed the table, trying to put it between me and the fifolet as I made my way around the perimeter of the room toward Dag, but then the monster changed course, moving back toward Dag. I stopped as it crouched next to him.

"You feel so many things for him." The fifolet touched the back of Dag's head and raised a hand—my hand. Its fingertips were red with blood, and it licked each digit slowly. The cuts and bruises on its face were fading. Its hair was changing. When it wiped blood from the back of Dag's head again, it was Better Eli—better hair, better shoulders, better abs peeking out from behind a ripped tee. As it sucked each finger clean, its erection was a hard outline under mesh shorts. Better cock, too—at least, to judge by the bulge. "Resentment. Frustration. Desire. Quite the tangle."

"Yeah, my brain is one fucked up playground. Let me know if you figure it out."

"Why waste your time with him? His nagging. His worrying. All his rules. He's building a cage around you, one bar at a time, to keep you fat and ugly, so that you'll stay with him. You know it's true. You think about it at night. It sends you out walking. He won't let you go, and so he'll sabotage you. He'll bring you sweets. He'll laugh at your fears. He'll lie to you and tell you what he thinks will keep you trapped." It straightened. The erection was even more noticeable now. My face felt flushed. My throat was hot. My chest prickled. "I can give you what you want. I can give you this. What you deserve to be. You've worked so hard. Sacrificed so much. And I can make it yours."

I took a stumbling step forward. My hands fell, and the flannel hung limply at my side. The drawstring had slipped open, and the sound of the clinking and rattling of the bag's contents competed with the whoosh and rush of ocean noises from the speakers. I managed to get out one word: "Why?"

The fifolet cocked its head. My head. "Why?"

"Why us?

"You mean, 'why me'?"

I swallowed and nodded.

"You killed the hashok. I watched for a long time, trying to understand how you managed. I could feel it inside you, its trace, and I had to know if you were like it. But you didn't sense me, as the hashok would have. I crossed your path a dozen times, and you never looked twice. When I grew bold enough, I called you."

"All those times I ran away. All those times I came to Bragg, even though it was far, even though it didn't make any sense."

"You came when I called. And then I knew: you were not a threat. You had killed two hashok, but they had grown careless, foolish, too bold. You were nothing; you had gotten lucky."

"Big talk." I cleared my throat. "You're pretty bold yourself."

It laughed.

"I won't let you hurt Dag," I said. "That was the real mistake. You shouldn't have touched him."

"You can have this body," the fifolet whispered. It was taking on the quality of the beach sounds, a hissing white noise that made it difficult to think. Better Eli's face was dissolving into a diffuse white light. I dragged myself toward it. "You can make it your own. Come with me. We'll run away together."

A last, faltering step brought me within its reach. A hand touched my arm. The light was too bright now for me to see anything except a kind of afterimage of Better Eli, but what touched me didn't feel human. Cold fire swept through me—the hashok's venom, whatever it had injected into me, lit up again, a frozen brilliance that made my whole body feel like light shining through ice.

"Yes," the fifolet whispered, that sound of rushing water, white noise obliterating thought. "You will be beautiful."

My hand slid inside the flannel.

"You will be confident."

My fingers closed around one of the coffin nails.

"You will have what you deserve," it whispered to me, and the sound was bliss.

I brought the nail up and drove it into the fifolet's body. I couldn't see, so I went by feel. The inhuman hand clutched my arm, and the cold fire inside me burned more fiercely. The fifolet made a wet, gasping noise as I twisted the coffin nail, trying to bury the cold iron deeper in its body. The light blinding me began to dim, and I could make out a watery, translucent version of Better Eli—no longer quite my face, no longer solid, already starting to dissolve.

"I might be stupid," I gritted out, forcing the coffin nail into the creature. "And I might be selfish. I might be royally fucked up. And I am certainly the world's worst boyfriend. But do you know what my superpower is?" I thrust again with the nail. And again. Every time the iron went home, the fifolet shrieked. It was as clear as water now, with only glimmers of light to suggest my face or shape. The hand on my arm had dissolved. I kept stabbing with the iron as I spoke, my voice rising into a scream. "My superpower, motherfucker, is that I really don't like myself."

The screeching rose to an intensity that made me stumble back. The fifolet's brilliance had faded. It was now just a translucid outline, vaguely humanoid, staggering in its death throes. Its light flared, filling a clear shell. Then it faded again. It flared one last time, and then, with a shriek that had me clapping my hands over my ears, it melted away—a blurring of lines and light against the air, and then nothing. The coffin nail made a muffled thump when it hit the carpet.

As I crawled to Dag, digging my phone out of my pocket, I mumbled into the wake of the fifolet's death, "But I sure as fuck love Dag."

DAG (4)

I woke up in a hospital. Again. The smell came first, a lemony disinfectant smell that overlay the odors of unwashed bodies and bleach. My head hurt, but the hurt was wrapped in gauze and set high up on a shelf. I let myself drift. Eventually, the voices reached me.

"—won't at least try Bear Week."

That was my mom.

Eli said, "I really don't think—"

"Lots of bears have nipple rings." That was my dad. "Have you talked to him about getting his nipples pierced?"

"I'm not sure Dag is a bear," Eli said.

"Well, he's not a twink," my dad said. "Is he a wolf?"

"Eli is definitely a twink," my mom said. "Or do you shave? Maybe he's really an otter, but he hasn't grown into it yet. Eli, are you really an otter?"

Eli laughed like a man looking for the first window to jump out of. "I don't know."

"You don't know?" my dad asked. It was the same tone he'd used when I'd told him I didn't know what kind of porn I liked. When I was thirteen.

"I mean, not every gay guy has to have a label."

The silence had the quality of secondhand embarrassment. "That's very sweet, Eli," my mom said. I was pretty sure she was patting his hand. "But just so you know, they're called tribes."

"And it's very important to know your tribe," my dad said.

"Or your tribes, Hubert. They can be in more than one tribe."

"I know, dear. I'm trying to simplify it. Eli doesn't know the first thing about the gays, and if you start telling him that he's a furry chaser with a daddy kink and that he's a twink who might be a twunk if he went to the gym more, and based on the state of the bedroom, he might need a dom top—"

Eli was doing that laugh again.

At that point, I decided I was being cruel—and that I needed to check the room for any windows he might be able to open—so I opened my eyes. Just a slit.

Eli was looking right back at me.

"Oh my God," he whispered. "Oh my God! Dag!"

Then he was crushing himself against me, and then he was whispering apologies, and then he was hugging me again, and I realized he was crying. My mom hugged me and cried. My dad hugged me and cried. It was a lot.

When they'd all settled down, my mom said, "Dagobert, we were just telling Eli about Bear Week and how you might be a bear but also a daddy, and we didn't get to this part, yet, but we think Eli might have an age kink."

"Sorry," I mumbled. "So sleepy."

"Don't you fucking dare," Eli whispered in my ear.

I shut my eyes, but I couldn't quite get rid of my grin.

I was only in the hospital for another day. That took us into the weekend, which mostly consisted of Eli babying me—poorly, with a surprising amount of bullying and an unsurprising amount of attention-seeking behavior like turning the TV to face the wall when he felt like I wasn't paying enough attention to him. Amrey stopped by to tell us that we were no longer suspects in their investigations. Apparently the bartender and his boyfriend had convinced the police that Eli and I had been busy saving their lives—as well as Nelda Pie's— while somebody else, somebody who might have looked like me, dragged Lanny into traffic. That pretty much put me in the clear. Amrey did say they wanted to talk to Fen, who had escaped from the hospital and disappeared. He also told us Nelda Pie had already been released from the hospital and gone back to the Stoplight. She was, somewhat unsurprisingly, threatening to sue the parish.

On Monday, I went to class and talked to Dr. Delanuville, and after she saw the hospital paperwork, she let me pick when I wanted to take the test.

When I got home, I told Eli, "I got my worst grade on a test yet."

He was on the couch in one of my old Braxton Bragg Memorial High sweatshirts, which he had pulled down over his knees as he read a magazine. His head came up. His eyebrows drew together. His mouth opened.

Then he frowned. His eyebrows sharpened a little more.

"What?" he asked. "You got a 96%?"

"97%."

"Next time we have a date night planned and you cancel because you tell me you have to study, I'm going to put your textbooks through a woodchipper."

"We don't own a woodchipper," I said as I headed into the bedroom to drop off my bag.

"Then I'll buy one just to fuck up your textbooks," Eli shouted down the hall. "And you'd better put that midterm on the fridge because I am so motherfucking proud of you!"

The yelling and the swearing were a nice touch, I decided as I grabbed a Café du Monde magnet to hold the test.

We went to Lanny's funeral. His mom was there, and his stepsister, and my parents, and a few of his friends from high school. It was a beautiful November day. Not a cloud in the sky. The St. Augustine grass was still green, and the air smelled like hothouse lilies and freshly turned earth. Next to the grave stood an easel with a blown-up picture of Lanny. He was in a tux, and he looked young. I figured it had to have been from prom. He was beautiful. He'd been happy and sweet and for the most part kind. He'd been a liar and a thief and a heck of a lot of trouble. When the service was over, I decided to walk for a while, and Eli kept me company. The cemetery looked out over the lake, and the water was green-gray and ruffled. A houseboat was trundling over the waves. I started to cry.

Eli slid an arm around me.

"He would have really liked to steal that boat," I managed to say through the tears.

Eli rubbed my back, and I cried harder.

And then, somehow, daily life carried us back into something like normalcy. I went to school. Eli pretended to look for a job. At the end of the day, we ate dinner together, and I studied (tried to study) or read (tried to read) or watched TV (tried to watch TV), while Eli found spontaneous opportunities to run the vacuum in front of the sofa or bang pots in the kitchen or, not that I'm complaining, seduce me.

I was reading about scavenger population decline when he sat on the couch next to me.

"We have a quiz," I said around the highlighter clamped between my teeth.

He grabbed the waistband of my sweats.

"Eli Prescott Martins, I've got homework."

His thumb traced the head of my dick.

I groaned. When I looked up from the book, I was surprised to see his face serious, his expression pinched, almost angry. His thumb continued its steady, insistent friction.

"What happened?" I asked. "Are you ok?"

After a moment, he shook his head.

"What?"

He gave my (rapidly hardening) dick a squeeze, stood, and walked into the bedroom.

With another groan, I rolled myself off the sofa and followed.

By the time I reached the room, he stood naked near the bed. His windswept hair was mussed from pulling off his shirt. He was biting a full bottom lip. My eyes followed broad shoulders, a toned chest and arms, the slight curve of his belly. He was soft, but (and I know this sounds strange), even soft, he had a beautiful dick. He had strong thighs and slenderly muscled calves; he complained that it looked like he skipped leg days, but Eli had never skipped anything in his life except dessert. His feet were long and narrow, and so were his toes.

When my eyes came up to his face again, he was blushing, and his hazel eyes were full of tears.

"Eli, babe, what's wrong?"

It took him a moment. When he spoke, his voice was thick. "I'm just—I'm having, you know, like a thing. Right now."

I nodded. I sat on the bed, and he turned so that he was facing me. He folded his arms across his chest, and his shoulders curved in. When I patted the mattress next to me, he didn't move, so I put my hands on his waist. He was warm. His soft brown skin felt electric under my touch. I pulled. He resisted, and I put a little effort into it, and he half-fell into my lap. He made a noise and buried his face in my neck. I kept one arm around his waist. I rested my other hand on the inside of his thigh.

"I'm trying to handle it," he mumbled. "Better than I normally do, I mean."

I ran my hand up and down his thigh. My whole hand. Then fingertips. Then just blunt, trimmed nails. Goose bumps ran all over him. I kissed the side of his head. I kept my hand moving. He hardened slowly. He spread his knees. I kept my hand on his thigh. He made a noise in his throat.

"You're beautiful," I whispered. Then I thought about what I'd read, about what was important. "But you're more than that, right? You're smart. You're brave. You killed a monster. You managed not to murder my parents."

He gave a wet laugh into my neck. His body relaxed into the curve of mine.

"I've got gray hair," I said. "And I'm twenty-eight."

"You're hot with gray hair," he said into my shoulder. "I'd break up with you if you had brown hair."

I laughed. My hand continued to chafe his thigh. "I'm kind of, uh, block shaped."

This time, he laughed for real, and he raised his head enough to say, "What does that mean?"

"I mean, I'm like a cube or a rectangle or whatever."

"You're literally all muscle. You have an insane chest. Your arms, I'd kill for your arms."

I kissed the side of his head again. Then I nuzzled his cheek until he lifted his head, and I kissed him on the mouth.

He was crying again. Just a little. "I know it's in my head. I mean, I've got a gut—that's just a fact. But I know feeling this way, it's in my head. I'm messed up."

"You're healthy, right? You're strong. You used a fucking nail to murder a monster. You can run a six-minute mile. You've got lots of energy." I let a grin slide into my voice at the end, and I tapped the head of his dick. It flew back up and hit his belly with a wet smack. "Right?"

He made that noise in his throat again.

I kissed him again.

"Ok," he whispered. "Thank you."

"Anytime," I whispered back, brushing his hair away. "Thank you for telling me."

His smile looked tired, and I could feel it: the exhaustion of struggling with this day after day, of trying not to give in.

"Let's lie down," I said. "And just be together for a minute."

"Fuck no."

I raised my eyebrows.

"You never swear. And it's hot. So I want to have some crazy, frantic sex while you talk dirty to me."

I nodded slowly. "I think that can be arranged."

He undressed me, his mouth moving across my chest, warm and wet and sucking at my nipples, laving my abs. When he pulled down my sweats, he stayed there for a while, licking, caressing, rubbing my dick on his face. He suckled on the head, and I had to catch a handful of his hair and pull him off me. My breathing sounded like a band saw.

With a smirk, he pulled the sweats off the rest of the way.

He climbed onto the bed, and I straddled him, a bottle of lube in one hand. I prepped myself while he ran his hands over my chest. Then I scooted back and said, "Flip. I want to lie down."

Eli frowned. He stretched. Brown skin shifted over lean muscle, and when I growled, he rolled his eyes. But he got onto his knees, and I lay down.

"You're going to fuck me," I told him. "You're going to use that fucking beautiful dick and that fucking beautiful body to fuck me out of my mind."

Now he was the one breathing fast. His lips were pink and parted.

"Did you hear me?" I asked.

He nodded.

He took my legs below the knees and shifted me. He spread my legs. He rubbed a finger, checking my prep work, and then he slid a thumb inside me. I gasped, and his pupils dilated. A flush ran from my crotch to my face. He rotated his hand, dilating me. Then his thumb curved up, back toward himself, and I swore. My hips jerked up from the bed. Pre dribbled from my dick. He kept the pressure there as I bucked, and then he released me, kissing a circle around my dick, lapping at the drops of pre.

"E," I said raggedly.

The head of his cock rested against me, and he pushed in slowly. I closed my eyes, relaxing into the resistance my body offered. Then, a few moments, later, it was over. He was inside me, and I was full with him.

"All those muscles." My whisper sounded hoarse even to me. "Let's see you get some good use out of them."

He started off like a jackhammer, and he only went at it harder after that. I wrapped my legs around his waist, trying to pull him deeper into me. Then I couldn't even do that. I moaned. I rocked, trying to take as much of him as I could on every stroke. I lost myself, until all I could feel was the throb of his dick raking through me. My orgasm uncoiled slowly in my gut, in my chest. Fuck me, I thought I could feel it in my face.

"Now," he grunted, the hair at his temples damp with sweat.

I grabbed my dick, and I came. A rush of feeling that was like a waterfall, like a wall of noise, the Millennium-fucking-Falcon going into hyperspace. When I dropped back into my body, he was grunting, thrusting, churning his come inside me. I gasped at the sudden rush of sensitivity, and his grin was wicked as he met my eyes and kept going.

He let us both down from that barbed-wire overstimulation by degrees. He pulled out of me slowly, and then he collapsed against my side. For a moment, both of us lay there. Then I smoothed his sweat-soaked hair against his face. I laughed, but I was so tired that it was barely a sound, mostly just a rumble in my chest.

"What?" he asked, the sound annoyed and petulant and slightly offended.

I kept laughing.

He elbowed me. "What's so fucking funny?"

Smoothing his hair again, I managed to say, "Be careful what you wish for."

He bit my nipple, which made me shout, but then I just laughed harder. When I'd stopped, he was propping himself up, studying my face.

I smiled at him. I followed the slice of his jaw with my fingers.

Eli's hazel eyes locked on mine, and he said, "When I saw the fifolet come out of that back room, when I saw the shape it had taken..." He shook his head. "Me. Regular me. I didn't understand. I still don't. I don't know how I'm supposed to be that version of me, whatever you saw, whatever you want. I don't even know what you want."

"I want you to be happy," I said, stretching up to kiss him.

His eyes were full again and shining. "I am," he said in a wobbly voice. "It doesn't make any sense, but I think I am. Happy, I mean. With you."

I smiled and pulled him against me. "So am I."

But he was still tense, and he squirmed to put distance between us. When I saw his face, I realized he was afraid. Maybe more afraid than I'd ever seen him.

"It's ok," I whispered. "Whatever you're feeling, it's going to be ok. I love you, and—"

He snorted and wiped his cheeks. "I know you love me. I'm not worried about you loving me. And yes, Dagobert LeBlanc, I love you too." He blew out a wet breath and gave a funny laugh. "I'm worried you're going to say no."

"To what?"

"When I ask you to be my boyfriend."

I ran my hand through his hair. "Oh."

He made an aggravated noise. "Well?"

"You have to ask me first."

"Will you?"

"Will I what?"

"Oh my God, never mind. I don't even care anymore."

I grabbed him, and we wrestled across the bed until I had him pinned under me. I ran my thumb under his eyes. He was blinking as fast as he could, but he couldn't stop crying.

"Now, you're not going anywhere," I said. "Right?"

"Right," he managed in a broken voice.

"So you might as well ask me."

"Will you—" He sucked in a deep breath and looked away. I turned his face back with my index finger. He struggled for another moment before he burst out, "Will you please be my boyfriend?"

"Hmm. Let me think about it."

He sucker punched me in the ribs, which turned into more wrestling, which turned into us tangled around each other on the mattress.

When I got up on one elbow, he was grinning and trying to dry his eyes.

"I thought about it," I said, "and I decided I would like that very much."

"It's about time," he said and kissed me.

Acknowledgments

My deepest thanks go out to:

Cheryl Oakley, who helped me keep track of murders (and murderers!), who pressed me to make the first chapter clearer, and who caught so many other errors—all those he's and him's that should have been I's and me's!

Dianne Thies, who made sure everyone had the right number of hands, who caught so many proofing errors (see coonass-self vs coonass self), and who helped me hide the Escort in a much better place!

Wendy Wickett, for catching the errors nobody else did, for counting sodium lamps, and for being so encouraging (the crone's wisdom! the India-ink brushes!)!

About the Author

Learn more about Gregory Ashe and forthcoming works at
www.gregoryashe.com.

For advanced access, exclusive content, limited-time promotions,
and insider information, please sign up for my mailing list at
http://bit.ly/ashemailinglist.

Made in the USA
Las Vegas, NV
29 October 2021